SUDDENLY BROKEN

BOOK 5 - THE DIRTY TEXAS SERIES

JA LOW

Copyright © 2019- 2021 by JA Low

All rights reserved. No part of this eBook or paperback book may be reproduced or transmitted in any form, including electronic or mechanical, without written permission from the publisher, except in the case of brief quotations embodied in critical articles or reviews.
This is a work of fiction. Names, characters, businesses, places, events, and incidents are either the products of the author's imagination or used in a fictitious manner. Any resemblance to actual persons, living or dead, or actual events is purely coincidental. JA low is in no way affiliated with any brands, songs, musicians, or artists mentioned in this book.
This eBook is licensed for your personal enjoyment only. This eBook may not be re-sold or given away to other people. If you would like to share this eBook with another person, please purchase an additional copy for each person you share it with. If you are reading this eBook and did not purchase it, or it was not purchased for your use only, then you should return it to the seller and purchase your own copy.
Thank you for respecting the author's work.

Reedited 2021 by Swish Editing
Cover by BookNerdFanGirl

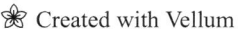 Created with Vellum

STACEY
PROLOGUE

"**B**abe, your phone's ringing." Oscar nudges me.

"It's four in the morning," I mumble, squinting at the bedside clock that's glowing right in front of me. "Who the hell is calling…"

"It's Amelia." That wakes me, quickly sitting up in my bed. Why is my niece calling at this time? I pick it up. "Amelia, is everything okay?" There's silence on the phone. "Amelia," I say again. Maybe she pocket-dialed me. Then I hear sniffling. "Amelia, I'm here. Is everything okay?"

"They're dead."

1
STACEY
THREE YEARS EARLIER

"You're engaged!" I stare at the glistening giant rock that sits on Sienna's left-hand ring finger through the computer screen, halfway on the other side of the world.

"He proposed atop of the Eiffel Tower," Derrick adds in the background.

"That's so romantic." I can see Sienna is glowing through the computer screen.

"I know. I wasn't expecting it. I thought we'd maybe start again for the sake of bean." Sienna has been traveling with Dirty Texas for the past couple of months through Europe after suffering an utterly humiliating divorce from her husband after he was caught with his mistress or his father's mistress. It's come out that the baby Sienna's ex, Beau, thought was his was actually his father's. I know, totally *Days of our Lives* storyline.

I worked for Sienna for years here in Sydney as her assistant, helping her organize her extremely hectic life. Everything changed on her thirtieth birthday when she found out about Beau and Diana's affair during her high-profile birthday party. *That wasn't a fun night.* Beau's family never liked Sienna, and they made sure she walked away with nothing when they broke up. They took her home and her business, everything she had worked for. Sienna is normally a happy-go-lucky girl, but this was the lowest point of her life.

Thankfully, Vanessa, her childhood friend, offered Sienna an escape from the media attention and asked her to join Dirty Texas' European tour, where Vanessa was their PR girl, as their stylist/wardrobe assistant. Sienna was the biggest Dirty Texas fan, especially of Evan Wyld, and who can blame her, the man is fine.

What she wasn't expecting was to fall for her celebrity crush and for him to fall right back. They had a rocky road to get to where they are today, if anyone deserves their happily ever after, it's Sienna. She may have been my boss, she was also one of my closest friends, giving me my first job and taking me under her wing as a naïve girl from the bush living in the big city for the first time.

"There's more." She claps excitedly.

"You're not having twins?" My eyes are widening.

"Oh, hell no. Please don't wish that on me." She chuckles. "No. It's about a job." Since Sienna's sudden departure from Australia, I've been looking after her affairs and tying them up for her in preparation for her to return, I'm judging that now she's pregnant and engaged to Evan, she'll be living in Hollywood with him. Not that she has anything left here. Beau's family took her thriving business when they separated—I guess that's what happens being married to a bunch of lawyers.

"You have been working so hard for me back in Australia, and I can't appreciate enough what you have done for me while I've been finding myself." I shrug because that's what friends do for each other. "I know that since I'm pregnant, now is not the right time to be starting a new business, I also know that I can't stay home and do nothing when I have this baby. I'm used to working that I... I can't stop. This break has been great traveling, I need to get back to what I love. Fashion."

"And you know the three of us make a great team," Derrick adds.

"The best team," Sienna agrees.

"I know. I miss you guys." For years I have spent every day with them both. It's like I'm missing a limb.

"Good. We miss you too." Sienna smiles. "And that's why I want to open another boutique, this time in LA."

"And we want you," Derrick adds, clapping his hands excitedly.

"Me?" Not quite believing what I'm hearing.

"Yes, you!" Sienna adds.

"In LA?" They both nod. "Doing what?"

"Everything, anything," Sienna tells me. "You're good at what you do, and I can't start this new adventure without you." My heart is racing. I love my life in Sydney, and I love my friends and family, it hasn't been the same without my closest friends. I miss the camaraderie we had every day. "What do you say?" Sienna presses.

"We can be roomies," Derrick adds. "Because let's be honest, this one here is knocked up and shacking up with a rock star, and she's not going to be a very good wing woman." I chuckle.

"That's the real reason you want me there, isn't it, D? To be your wing woman."

"You know me so well, my little possum." Derrick smiles.

"There are hot rock stars I can introduce you to," Sienna adds.

"And they are hot... smoking hot," Derrick adds.

"How can I say no to hot rock stars and being the ultimate wing woman while living in Hollywood?" Excitement bubbles through me.

"So, you're saying yes?" Sienna squeals.

"I'm saying hell, yes."

A month later

"You made it," Derrick squeals, pulling me into his arms and swinging me around at the airport. It's good to see him again. "Sisi couldn't make it. The paparazzi are hounding her." My stomach sinks. I feel bad for her—she's gone from being in the spotlight with Beau to now this. I guess marrying one of the biggest rock stars in the world will kind of amp up the attention.

"I have a fantastic rental right in the heart of everything."

"As long as it has a hot shower, that's all I'm worried about at the moment." Derrick wraps his arm around my shoulders and pulls me tight into his side.

"You're going to love it here." He winks at me.

We make our way into Los Angeles, along the long winding freeways and across the busy streets, where palm trees stick up out of concrete sidewalks. I can't believe I'm actually here. Derrick points out the sights as we drive through the streets. He gives me the Derrick Jones guided tour of LA, which includes a note of a glory hole he used once and got one of the best blow jobs of his life from. *That's probably one little bit of LA I didn't need to know.* Eventually, we arrive at a set of luxury apartments, where the electric parking gate opens for us, and we drive into the basement garage and park. Derrick grabs my bags, and we take the elevator up to his floor.

"Now, it's not very big, I'm saving up to buy my own home, this is only temporary. It's walking distance to the shop and Dirty

Texas Records and also has a gym and pool. What more could you want?" I'm excited.

Derrick unlocks the door and lets me in. A small hallway opens into the functional modern kitchen, and the living room is in front with one glass wall and opens out to a small balcony. The view is impressive, maybe not as impressive as my cute little bungalow at Coogee Beach in Sydney, where I had ocean views. This is a different kind of view, more urban, looking out over the flashing lights of West Hollywood.

"This is your room." Derrick points to the left. "It's a bigger bedroom, that's because I have a walk-in closet and en-suite in mine."

I walk into the cream-colored room with a queen-size bed and views. There's a large built-in closet which will fit all my things, and the bathroom is by the front door, it's not that far.

"This is perfect." Tears begin to well in my eyes.

"No, don't you dare start." His eyes are becoming glassy as well. I rush to him and pull him into a hug and cry, not sure why, though. I think I'm exhausted and overwhelmed a little bit. He hugs me tight. "Bitch, I'm happy you're here."

"Me too." I sniffle.

"We're going to have the time of our lives here. Sienna has already met her Prince Charming, maybe you're next." He wiggles his brows at me.

"I'm not looking for Prince Charming. I'd be happy with Prince Fuck Me Good." We both burst out laughing.

"Oh, how I've missed you. Go. Get freshened up because you know Sienna is dying to see you. She keeps messaging me telling me to hurry up and bring you to the store."

"Okay. Shower first, coffee second, and Sienna third."

"It really is within walking distance." Sipping on the biggest coffee cups I have ever seen, I'm probably going to be bouncing off the walls. We've walked maybe a block or two, and we're here. My mouth falls open when I read the sign.

"Wyld Jones." Derrick smiles.

"Pretty catchy, isn't it?" I nod. This is real. She's doing it. She's starting all over again. I remember the day Sienna opened her first store all those years ago, and now here we are standing in West Hollywood, a million miles from where she began. I feel nothing but pride for my girl. "Come on, put her out of her misery." Derrick pushes through the front doors. I can hear people inside and then silence as Sienna turns around and realizes who is here.

"Oh my God." She rushes over to me, and tears are already falling over her cheeks. I notice a larger belly on her petite frame as she crashes into me. "I've missed you so much." Her tears are hitting my shoulder as she hugs me tightly. "Thank you, thank you so much for coming." We embrace each other for what feels like hours until we eventually pull apart, both of us red-eyed from tears.

"You must be Stacey," a deep voice states from behind Sienna, and I'm struck by the gorgeous man behind her. Holy shit, it's Evan Wyld. He's holding out a tattooed hand to me, and I'm staring at him like some kind of star-struck groupie. I quickly snap myself out of it and take his hand. "I've heard so much about you, it feels like I know you already." My cheeks begin to burn as a blush forms across my face. *Get it together, Stacey.*

"And same about you." Evan steps away and places a tattooed arm across Sienna's shoulders. Her body molds against his as he kisses the top of her blonde hair. She sighs and looks happy. Her hand reaches down and touches her stomach.

"Look at you." My eyes land on her hand moving across her stomach.

"I know. He's really kicking up a storm at the moment." That's when I notice the slight tiredness in her eyes, she's still glowing.

"Well, you look happy." Sienna looks up at Evan, and their eyes meet. Love radiates between them. Holy smokes, it's getting hot in here. Evan leans down and kisses her ever so gently.

"I'm the luckiest man in the world," he declares, turning back to Derrick and me, looking as if he has won the best prize in the world. I guess he has—he's found his one. His forever.

"Yes, they are always this nauseatingly in love." Derrick rolls his eyes at them, making them chuckle.

"We make Derrick sick with our love." Sienna smiles.

"No. What makes me sick is walking in on you two all the time going like fucking rabbits. If you could get pregnant more than once at a time, Sienna would have a damn litter by now with the amount of banging they do." Evan shrugs, and Sienna's cheeks have gone bright red with embarrassment.

"Anyway, enough about us. Let's show you the space." Sienna moves away from Evan, hooks her arm with mine, and starts to tell me all about her plans for Wyld Jones.

2

STACEY

"Don't be nervous." Derrick elbows me as we travel back from the day spa. It's Sienna's birthday. Thankfully, this one won't be a disaster like last year's fiasco when she found out her husband was cheating on her. Tonight, I'm meeting the rest of Dirty Texas and the Sons of Brooklyn—two of the biggest rock bands in the world. It's kind of intimidating.

We slowly weave our way back up to the hills where Sienna now lives with Evan. Can you believe he surprised her with a house? A house! I can't even get a guy to buy me flowers or a drink, not that I'm looking for anything. I've been in LA for a month, and the dating scene is a little scary and intense. Eventually, the limousine comes to a stop in front of Sienna's house, and we all pile out of the car. The first thing we hear is shouting. Everyone looks at each other concerned. The shouting gets louder, everyone takes off through the front door.

"You can't stand the fact that your hot fiancée's lips were on mine. That her tongue was down my throat, her hot pussy grinding on my dick, that she wanted me before she ever wanted you."

"You fucker," someone roars. The sound of bone hitting bone echoes through the home.

"Fuck you!" a man yells.

"Evan!" Sienna screams at them. The two men look up from the ground, their tuxedos all tousled, their hair disheveled, and they both look equally as guilty.

"Evan, what the hell are you doing? Charlotte looks like she's on the verge of tears. Evan and the other guy jump up at the sound of her voice.

"Are you okay?" Charlotte asks the guy with the amazing aqua eyes.

"Yeah, we're all good," he says through gritted teeth.

"What the hell were you doing, Evan?" Charlotte yells at her brother. I'm kind of confused about what's going on too. Are all LA parties like this?

"Seriously, what the hell happened here?" Sienna questions with her no-nonsense pissed-off voice.

"Evan punched Blake because he brought up that you two had hooked up before." Christian fills everyone in. What the hell? Sienna and Blake from Sons of Brooklyn hooked up? She never told me any of this.

"What did you say?" Charlotte looks as confused as me by what's happened. Hang on, are Charlotte and this guy dating? Did Blake cheat on her with Sienna? So many questions. "Evan, what's he talking about? Blake and Sienna?" You can hear the hurt in her voice.

"Charlotte." Sienna moves closer to her. "When I arrived in LA, Vanessa threw me a welcome party, and things got a little crazy. I had seen Evan getting a blow job in the bushes." What the... I look over at Evan, whose face is bright red with embarrassment.

"What?" Charlotte looks at her brother with disappointment.

"Seriously?" Christian questions his friend.

"I was drunk, we kissed, that was all," Sienna adds. Charlotte looks taken aback by this news.

"I'm sorry. I need a moment." She turns on her heel and dashes away. These Hollywood parties are awfully dramatic. So much for Sienna having a drama-free birthday this year.

After the dramatic start to Sienna's birthday, all parties kissed and made up. Okay, that was a poor choice of words, you get what I mean. The night has been great, everyone getting on really well, the Dirty Texas boys telling the Sons of Brooklyn guys crazy stories from their touring days. I still can't believe I'm sitting here with these two bands. My nieces would be jealous. Would it be totally weird of me to ask for a photo of the Sons of Brooklyn boys? Is that creepy at a private party? Probably. I'm sure there will be a more appropriate time to get one.

"I bet the view is a little different than home," a deep voice rattles my bones. Turning around, Oscar Eriksen is walking toward me. He's hot. The man has to be seven feet tall. Okay, that's probably not right, he's huge. He looks as wide as a bus. He has to be wearing a custom tuxedo because there's no way a man of that size can fit into a standard tux. His arms are massive, I could swing off them. I bet he could throw you around the bedroom, he'd be strong enough. *Go away, dirty thoughts.* You have to be able to have a conversation with the hot Viking, and you can't if you're picturing him doing dirty things to you.

"Yeah, it is. So many lights." Good start, Stacey, even though you sound like a moron. At least you didn't blurt out how you wouldn't mind viewing him—naked. Take a sip of your beer, you dirty bitch.

"You're drinking beer?" He seems shocked by this.

"Umm, yeah. Sorry, was I not supposed to take one? Did someone bring them? Shit," I say, turning the glass in my hand.

First social event with celebrities, and I've already caused a major faux pas.

"No." He chuckles, the throaty laugh vibrating through my body, especially between my legs. "No, you don't notice many women in LA drinking it, that's all." I look down at the green bottle.

"Oh... the carbs," I mumble, realizing what he means.

"Yeah. Most women in LA are pretty self-conscious about those kinds of things." Is he inferring I'm fat? "It's refreshing," he adds, resting his elbows on the fence.

"I'm finding LA is pretty full-on." I rest my arms back on the fence too.

"Yeah, it is, you'll get used to it, eventually." His attention is focused on the twinkling lights.

"You know what I won't get used to is the coffee. I'm already missing my favorite brew from my local café." This makes him chuckle.

"Ness, D, and Sienna say the exact same thing. Seriously, is it really that bad? I moved here before I drank coffee, I grew up on the American stuff."

"I feel for you. When you taste good coffee, you'll understand. I need to find an Aussie café somewhere, I can grab some smashed avo and a good coffee, which basically is what I lived on back home."

"Smashed avo?" He gives me a confused look.

"Avocado." He smiles, shaking his head. We stand there in silence, nothing awkward, happy in each other's company.

"Oh, hope I'm not interrupting anything? If I am, I'll watch from behind this bush," Derrick calls out. Oscar and I look at each other and laugh at Derrick's not-so-subtle comment.

"My virtue is still intact, Derrick."

"Dammit. How boring. Are you losing your skills, Oscar, since retiring from being a rock star?" Oscar shakes his head.

"What, I can't have a conversation with a pretty girl?" He

thinks I'm pretty. *Hold it in. Hold it in, Stace.*

"Stacey is a helluva lot smarter than your usual type, she probably wouldn't fall for any of your normal lines." Yes, I would. I'm not that smart. Not when it comes to a real-life Thor standing in front of me.

"Well, then, I best be getting back to the party. See y'all around."

"Yeah, sure." Act cool. Derrick and I watch him walk back into the party.

"I'd climb that Viking dick as quick as look at you," Derrick comments.

"He could throw me around any day of the week." Derrick gives me a high five, and we burst out laughing.

"So..." Eric is fishing for some gossip.

"Nothing. Nothing happened. We chatted and looked out over the city."

"Boring. My vagina shriveled up over that story." I shake my head. "It's interesting that the Viking tracked you down when you were by yourself."

"Don't," I warn him.

"What?" He flutters his eyelashes at me.

"Don't try to matchmake. Nothing is going on between Oscar and me, and nothing will." Derrick sticks out his tongue at me, so childish.

"I thought you wouldn't be boring coming over here. Where's my little whore that I know lives deep inside her?" He pokes me in my chest.

"Your little whore is exhausted after working really long hours for a tyrant boss."

"It's Sienna's hormones. She can be such a bitch some days." I playfully slap him. We burst out laughing again. "I'm happy you're here." He wraps his arms around me, pulling me in close to him.

"Me, too, D."

3

STACEY

"Hi, I have a delivery for a Stacey Ferguson," a courier states, placing a large brown paper bag onto the front counter with a drinks tray.

"I'm Stacey. I didn't order this," I say, pointing to the food.

"Yeah, I know. Someone called Oscar did. He said to say hope it tastes as good as home." Then the courier is gone. I open the brown paper bag and inside is a plastic container. I take the lid off, and there's a smashed avocado on toast. My stomach does a little flip-flop, thinking that Oscar ordered this after our conversation the other night.

"I smell coffee." Derrick walks out. "Like real coffee."

"Um, yeah, Oscar sent it over." Derrick's eyes widen. "To all of us." Noting the three cups with each of our names on them.

"Interesting. Flowers would've been better." He takes his cup and sips the piping hot liquid. "Oh my God, this is like home. Shit. Did he fly this directly in from Australia?" I take a sip of mine and almost orgasm. Oh, coffee, how I have missed you. "Whatever was happening in the dark the other night, keep doing it. I need more coffee."

"D, honestly, nothing is happening. I told him how crap the

coffee was, and I guess he wanted to prove me wrong." Derrick doesn't look convinced, I honestly don't have stars in my eyes like he does over this. It's really a nice gesture.

"Do I smell coffee?" Sienna comes out, looking a little disheveled, and Evan is not far behind her.

"Seriously?" Derrick moans. Those two can't keep their hands off each other. Thankfully, today we couldn't hear them.

"There's a decaf one for you." Sienna takes an enthusiastic sip.

"Oh my God, it's like home." She sips again.

"Oscar sent it over." Sienna stops sipping.

"For who?" She looks between us.

"For Stacey," Derrick adds smugly.

"It's not like that. We had a conversion about crap coffee, and he sent me non-crap coffee. He was being nice." Evan chuckles.

"Oscar isn't known for being nice."

"Would you all stop it, please? Evan, could you thank Oscar for the coffee. It was lovely, and now I know where I can get good coffee." Evan smirks.

"You can thank him yourself. Here, let me give you his number."

"What? No, I don't want it." Evan hands me a piece of paper. He kisses his bride-to-be for way too long than is decent before rushing back to his office next door.

"Guys, I mean it. Stop it." Holding onto the paper.

"Not doing a thing," Derrick says smugly, sipping his coffee.

"Me, too," Sienna adds.

"He's being nice."

"Yeah, awfully nice," Derrick adds.

"Would you two fuck off? I have work to do." They both pull funny faces at me as they walk off laughing. Such assholes.

The piece of paper is burning a hole in my pocket. I really need to thank Oscar for the coffee, will he think I asked for his number? Should I tell him Evan gave it to me and that I didn't ask for it? Stop overthinking it, Stace. Say thank you and be done with it.

Stacey: *Thank you so much for the coffee this morning. What a wonderful surprise. Finally, good coffee in LA. This is going to be my new favorite place from now on. Stace. PS: Evan told me I should message you, so you didn't think it was weird or anything. But truly, thank you.*

And send. That wasn't so hard. My phone vibrates minutes later.

Oscar: *You were right. Once I had good coffee, I'd know the difference. It's delicious. And the smashed avo as you call it. Yeah. I see why you love it. Hope you're having a good day. O*

My heart is thundering in my chest. Oh my God. What the hell is going on? Oscar Eriksen is talking to me about avocados and coffee.

The next day, another three coffees arrived.
And the day after that.
And the day after that.

"Hey, do you mind dropping this over to Ness, please." Sienna points to the black cocktail dress. "I would, but my feet are swollen." Sienna shows me her feet. Yep. They were pretty bad.

"Of course." Taking the dress off the rack, I walk out the back door and down the street that connects the two buildings. As I walk into the Dirty Texas Records parking lot, a swarm of paparazzi converges around the back door, where I need to get in.

"Excuse me. Hey. Excuse me. I need to get through. I try to push my way through, but they push me back. "Hey," I say, getting an elbow to the stomach. "Fucker." Guess I'll walk around the front then. Off I go back around and down the little street, the next thing I know, I'm being knocked over and trampled on. I scream and scream, but people are still walking over me. Fuck. Fuck.

"Stacey?" A deep voice calls out my name. The next thing I know, I'm being pulled up to my feet. "Sammy, what the fuck."

"Sorry, boss," another voice calls out, then seconds later, there's distance around me. The black dress I was carrying is all crumbled and dirty. I brush the dirt all off of my pants, and my hands are stinging. I look down at them, and they are all cut up. And before I have a chance to look over anything else, I'm being bundled into the back of a car. Panic laces my body. What the hell is going on?

"Are you okay?" Turning, I notice Oscar getting in beside me. I'm utterly confused. "Drive," he yells at his driver, and we take off.

"What the hell happened?" I ask, feeling utterly disorientated.

"I'm sorry. That was all my fault. The paparazzi were out in force because of some bullshit story someone wrote."

"And that warrants them to mow down pedestrians?" Oscar looks over at me, catching the grimace of my hand.

"We have to stop at a CVS. Stacey's hurt," he tells his driver and security.

"No. I'll be fine. You can drop me back at work. There's a first-aid kit there." Oscar looks out the car where paparazzi on motorcycles are following us. Are they insane? "Never mind." Slumping back in the chair. "They ruined Vanessa's dress." Pointing at the dirt-covered material. "I'll get it cleaned."

"She needs it for tonight. They've ripped it." Oscar looks angry now.

"I'm sorry, Stace. I..." He rakes his hands through his hair. I reach out and touch his arm.

"Look, it's not your fault. It's their fault. I need to tell Sienna what happened, I don't have my phone on me."

"Sammy, can you call Evan and let him know what happened?" The big Samoan man in the front nods, and I hear him start to call Evan. I listen quietly as he relays what happened.

"Guess this isn't how you saw your Friday going, is it?" He smiles weakly at me.

"I've had better." He nods, and we both fall back into silence as I stare out the tinted glass windows, LA flashing by me.

"Where are we?" I ask as we pull into a driveaway.

"My place." Huh? What?

"Really?"

"Don't worry, Derrick is coming to pick you up, I thought you might like to get fixed up first." He points to my hands. Oh, yes, of course. Not that you would try and mend my broken vagina because I haven't had a decent shag since arriving. *Shut up, brain.* You're only acting like this because you're horny. I follow him inside.

"Here, take a seat." He places the bag full of first-aid supplies on the kitchen counter as I prop myself up on one of the bar stools. He pulls out the disinfectant and starts cleaning up the graze ever so gently. I can't help but look up at him. He smells good. Our eyes catch, and we have a small moment before he clears his throat and declares me clean.

"So... what was the story about?" He grabs himself a beer,

then hands one over to me. I gladly take it. I need a drink after all this craziness.

"It was about me and some actress." I look at him over the bottle, taking a long sip.

"Is it true?" He shakes his head.

"You won't see any of the girls I'm with in public," he adds, drinking his beer.

"You value your privacy, I get it." He gives me a look, I'm not too sure what it means.

"I'm very private," he adds. Of course, you're a megastar. I nod and enjoy my beer. "You have to be in this business." Sure, I get it.

"It must suck that people make up stories about you."

"Yeah, it does, especially when they are so vanilla." He rolls his eyes.

"Don't want your reputation tainted by being too 'vanilla.'" I use air quotes over the word.

"You could say that." He smirks at me. Is he flirting with me? Maybe I'm drunk? Did I hit my head? "Have you been enjoying your coffee?" he asks, suddenly changing the subject.

"Of course. It's amazing. I look forward to it every day, honestly, you don't have to keep buying us coffee."

"Look, I'm addicted. I order the office a round, I thought I might as well send a round to you guys too." Of course, he does. Did you think you were special, Stacey? This man is a rock star. He's interested in super models and non-vanilla women, which you're not.

"Well, thank you. Sienna appreciates it." Have another sip of that beer, Stacey. Fill in the awkward gaps. "Your house is nice." I internally groan at my assessment of his multi-million dollar, archaistically designed mansion.

"Thanks. Want a tour?"

"Sure." Because sitting here any longer means I'm going to embarrass the hell out of myself. He shows me around the first level, where we saw the movie theater, wine cellar, game room, bar, and then out to the pool. Now he's taking me upstairs to show me the guest bedrooms, which are all pretty impressive. Then we stop at the last room.

"This is my room." He points through the open door.

"Cool." Now I'm picturing him sleeping naked in his bed. These aren't the kind of thoughts I should be thinking about right now.

"You don't want to riffle through my underwear drawer?" I give him a strange look. "It happens more than you think."

"You mustn't be bringing home the right kind of girls, then." Oscar smiles.

"I think you'd be right there."

"You should have higher standards." Shut up. Stacey.

"Stacey. Where's my Stacey," Derrick bellows from below. He looks up and sees us walking from out of Oscar's room. His eyes narrow on the two of us, assessing what he thinks is going on.

"Oscar was giving me the cribs tour," I yell down to Derrick. "Thanks for today. It's been an adventure." I hand him my empty bottle of beer. I have a real buzz on now.

"Maybe we should do it again?" he suggests.

"Yeah, probably not." The words are out before I even realize how that sounds.

"Are you okay, princess?" Derrick pulls me into his arms and holds me tight. "You're safe now, Uncle Derrick is here." Nothing creepy about that at all, D. I'm ready to go.

"Thanks for the beer," I call back to Oscar. He gives me a small smile.

"I want all the details because what the fuck happened today?" Derrick questions.

"I have no idea, Derrick. No fucking idea."

4

STACEY
THREE MONTHS LATER

Australia

What an absolute whirlwind these past couple of months have been. As much as I love my new life in Los Angeles, coming home to Australia and soaking in that sunshine and clean air is what I needed to revitalize myself before going back again. I've been having so much fun with Derrick. We live in the best location, right in the heart of everything in West Hollywood. We never use the kitchen in our apartment because most nights we're out having dinner.

I've become good friends with Vanessa, Sienna's best friend, and Isla, Oscar's sister. She's also the band's assistant. It's nice having them around, especially Isla, as Sienna is in a different phase of her life compared to us single ladies who are still out partying until the early hours most weekends. Not that I'm looking for anything serious at the moment, maybe in a year when things have settled down with my job, I might be.

At the moment, I'm working eighteen-hour days and have little time for anything outside of work, it's not like I've been a nun while in LA. I've hooked up with a couple of different guys, they were one-nighters, the perfect stress relief, and that's all I'm looking for at the moment. I haven't heard from Oscar since I was attacked by the paparazzi, it's for the best. I have become close friends with his sister now, and she's told me all the horror stories about him and her friends. Plus, his best friend is marrying my best friend, and if anything happened and then it turned sour, it would ruin all the fun dinners and things we all do as a group.

We're currently in Byron Bay for Sienna and Evan's wedding. Her family owns a health retreat nestled in the hinterland of Byron Bay, which is basically paradise on earth. The lush green rainforests reach to the turquoise ocean. We've spent the day at Sienna's bridal and baby shower at a stunning private home that backs onto the world-famous beach. The boys had their own party on the beach not far from where we were.

Sienna was in her element with her tropical-themed party, and she looked like Boho Barbie, her beautiful bump on display. As the sun set, the party moved from a cute baby shower to a wild bachelorette party, especially when the strippers arrived. Derrick was the happiest of them all, of course. I'm pretty sure he organized them for him, Sienna's party giving him an excuse to do so.

The mood changed a little when Evan turned up and caught the strippers getting down and dirty with his baby mama. He didn't look happy, especially when he stomped upstairs hand in hand with her, whatever he did, Sienna came back smiling and very flushed before Evan whisked her back home. The parents joined them, leaving us singletons to enjoy the strippers and the unlimited bar. The champagne was replaced by tequila and vodka, and the boys eventually came up from the beach, joining us on the home's main floor.

"Body shots, body shots," Johnny from Sons of Brooklyn starts chanting. Everyone is pretty wasted. Derrick's disappeared with one of the strippers, Vanessa and Christian have gone somewhere, Isla said she needed to use the bathroom hasn't come back yet.

"I dare you." Camryn, the event planner and longtime friend of Vanessa's, nudges me.

"I'm pretty sure he's looking at you." Camryn's back straightens up at my comment.

"You think? He's a bit young." She focuses on the half-naked rock star in front of us.

"You're not looking for a husband, are you?" Camryn shakes her head. "Then why not have some fun? I bet he'd be fun. Worst case, he'd have stamina." Camryn turns and looks at me, and a wide smile crosses her face. She then grabs my face and gives me a quick kiss.

"That boy is going to have no idea what hit him." I watch in awe as she marches over to where Johnny is standing in nothing but a pair of low-slung board shorts, his impressive body covered in tattoos on display.

"I'm game." Camryn smirks at him. She's going to eat that boy alive, I don't think he cares because the look that comes over him tells me he'd happily be devoured by her.

"She's going to eat him alive, isn't she?" A deep voice startles me as a large shadow falls across me. I look to my side, and Oscar takes a seat beside me.

"It's like a car crash, you can't look away." My attention moves back to the craziness going on in front of us.

"You think we're going to get a show?" His blonde eyebrow arches up, a smirk forming across his face.

"I sure hope so," I say to shock Oscar. Instead, he stares at me intensely, those ice-blue eyes sending tiny prickles over my skin. He takes a sip of his beer, his intense stare is still there as if I'm a puzzle he's trying to work out.

"Do you like to watch?" Again, that blond eyebrow arches as if daring me to tell him my inner sexual thoughts. Is he flirting with me again? I can't tell. I will say he's looking mighty fine tonight. I take a sip of my drink and take him all in—his long blond hair is out, his beard is neatly trimmed, not too long and not too short, his bronze arms stretch the white sleeves of his tight t-shirt, and colorful ink peeks out from underneath the fabric, teasing me. I wish I was brave enough to take a closer peek at them, honestly, he scares me. Not in a serial killer kind of way maybe in a gee-I- wonder-if-this-man-is-big-all-over kind of intimidating away, and wonder if he breaks women when he sleeps with them. You know, the *normal* kind of thoughts.

"If someone is willing to put on a show, how can I say no?" I respond, arching my blonde brow back at him. Those blue eyes narrow, and a smile forms on his face. Have I ever seen Oscar smile this wide before? Does he do that before he kills his prey? Because it's making me super nervous.

"I don't think you're as prim and proper as I think you are." His comment catches me off guard.

"You think I'm prim and proper?" Looking down at the barely-there bikini I have on with the tiniest of sarongs tied around my waist, there isn't much left to the imagination. Oscar's eyes roam over me again, briefly landing on my chest, his look heating my skin with each scan. He nods and takes another sip of his beer. I watch as his pink, plush lips wrap around the bottle. I shouldn't be looking at him like that. My thighs shouldn't be rubbing together, I'm trying to stave off the heat that's throbbing between them. He's off-limits.

"Your shirt buttons are always done up." I frown at him. Why is he talking about my buttons? I look down at my chest, and there are none. "Every time I've seen you, the buttons on your work shirts are done one too many up." He's noticed my buttons? My cheeks begin to heat. This is weird flirting, I'll go along with it.

My attention is pulled back to what's happening in front of us. Holy Dooley, when did I tune back into the porn channel? Camryn is licking tequila from Johnny's body, and her tongue is running over his stomach muscles. She keeps moving further and further down his body until I watch in utter fascination as she cheekily sweeps a tongue along the band of his board shorts, supporting a rather large tent. Camryn looks up at him wickedly. Her tongue licks along her wet lips, and her body sways seductively in front of a mesmerized Johnny.

"I think I'm going to give them their privacy. I'm going to go back to the resort." I stand up from my seat.

"I'll come with you."

"You sure?"

"Unless they want a third, no point in me sticking around." Interesting. We make our way outside the private house into the waiting limousine for us. Oscar goes directly to the mini bar and rifles through it.

"They've got champagne, tequila, or vodka?"

"I'll take a couple of shots of tequila, please." He pours a couple of shots into the crystal tumblers, adds a couple of ice cubes to it, and then hands it to me.

"Cheers." We clink our glasses together. The smooth burn of the tequila flows down my throat.

"Question. Have you had many threesomes?" Oscar chokes on his drink at my overly personal question. "You mentioned you would stay if they wanted a third, I was curious?" Oscar recovers from the shock.

"Yes, of course."

"You say that like it's a normal thing? Is it? I've never had one, I have no idea." Is this tequila some kind of truth serum because he didn't need to know that?

"I guess with what I do, the opportunities are presented to me more often than to others." He sips his drink.

"Aren't you worried they will talk?" I lean back against the car's soft leather seat.

"Of course. Honestly, if a girl is selling her story about having a threesome with a rock star, you know that's going to make me look good."

"You're such a dick." I roll my eyes. "Unless she tells them you have a small dick or that you come too early." Oscar smiles hungrily at me.

"Look at me. You seriously think I'd have a small dick?" Oh, so cocky, yeah, I highly doubt it. He's probably packing Thor's hammer in those pants. He did say look at him, so I do. I lazily let myself take him in. When I'm finished, his hand moves to his crotch, and he adjusts himself. "You shouldn't look at me like that, Stacey," Oscar warns me.

"You told me to look at you." I take a sip of my drink.

"You're looking at me like you are imagining exactly how big my dick is and wondering if you can handle it."

"Cocky much?"

"Not cocky, you're easy to read." He's right. Sometimes I find it hard to hide my expressions.

"I was only curious because you brought it up, not my fault." I hold my hands up in the air.

"True, you were curious about how many threesomes I had. And to answer that question, many…"

"It doesn't impress me, you know." It intrigues me, though.

"Wasn't trying to." He smirks. We both fall into silence. A thread of sexual energy is weaving its way around.

"Would you want a threesome?"

"You offering?" I bite back.

"Yes." I still. This gets my attention, making me sit up

straight. "I think little Stacey Ferguson isn't as prim and proper as she appears."

"You assumed that by how many buttons I choose to do up? I thought I was being professional."

"I can see why you do. Your tits are magnificent." Huh. What? I look down at them. Really? He thinks they are magnificent, and I'm guessing he'd know. He seems like he'd be a boob expert.

"Thank you." I smile at him. Are we stepping over that line we're not meant to cross? Probably. I've had way too much drink to say no to my starving kitty downstairs.

5

OSCAR

I've been watching Stacey most of the night, which sounds creepy. *I promise I'm not a creep.* From the moment I met her months ago, there was something about her that intrigued me. Maybe it's the way she kind of flirts with me, it's casual I don't know if she is being nice or if she's attracted to me. She doesn't seem that fazed by my celebrity status. Actually, it seems like a turn-off for her, which is different from the women I usually meet. Maybe that's what has my dick interested —she's a challenge because she doesn't appear to be that into me, other than being a friendly acquaintance, especially now that she and Isla have become friends.

She's popped over to my house a couple of times for 'girl time,' which I have to make myself scarce for, I don't. I overhear their conversations about the guys they are meeting while out and the really bad sex she's been having. I don't understand how the guys can be selfish when they have someone as beautiful as Stacey in their bed. I'd make sure I worshiped her all night if she were in mine.

Something about Stacey Ferguson has me doing things I don't normally do, like the whole coffee thing. It started out as a nice welcoming present, the coffee was too good, so I continued. I realized I was maybe coming on a little strong the afternoon of the paparazzi incident when I took her home. I don't know why I did that. It was out of character for me, seeing her body crumbled on the ground and her frightened screams, I instantly became protective of her. I think I pushed her too far with the house tour because she couldn't get out of there fast enough when Derrick arrived. I subtly put feelers out that maybe we could catch up again, she squashed that, literally running out of my house. I felt a little weird after that, I've kept my distance from her until tonight.

Not when I saw her prancing around in that barely-there bikini. What the heck, I was shocked. The girl wears the buttons of her work shirts done up too high, and now, she's practically naked. Goddammit, her body is sinful. She has a great peachy ass that I want to bite and a nice pair of natural tits, which are the right amount for my large paws. She's all natural, especially compared to those Hollywood girls, who are all silicon, inch-thick makeup, and over-injected lips. I've noticed she barely wears makeup, a hint of gloss across her pink lips, and her hair is always pulled up in a messy ponytail, one that I wouldn't mind wrapping around my hand while she sucks my dick. See, this woman is driving me crazy. I can't touch, though, since she's friends with Isla, the girl is damn sexy. Now you understand why I'm sitting here watching her because otherwise, I'm going to want to touch.

I spot Camryn and Stacey together in a corner. She's giving Camryn a pep talk. Camryn stands up, grabs Stacey's face, and kisses her briefly enough for my dick to appreciate it. This wasn't the vision I needed to stay away. Someone up there is trying to kill me. Two beautiful blondes kissing in front of me.

They are testing me, really testing me. I could imagine it, all that bronze skin and blonde hair touching each other. Stop it, Oscar. Stop it. Tonight, isn't the night.

Camryn makes her way over to where Johnny and the Sons of Brooklyn boys are joking around. A look of determination is on her face. It looks like her sights are set on Johnny. Poor kid, he has no idea what's about to happen to him. Camryn is going to cougar the shit out of him. Hopefully, he doesn't fall for her because I think she's looking for someone to help scratch an itch. That leaves the seat beside Stacey vacant. Everyone else at the party is busy, and it wouldn't be right to leave her by herself like that. Honestly, I like chatting with her—it's easy. Everything about her is easy, not in that way, in that she's chilled, relaxed.

As I make my way over, I watch as Stacey is absorbed in what's happening in front of her. Her cheeks look a little flushed. I wonder if she's turned on by watching what's happening? I shake those thoughts from my mind. No, you can't take her to The Paradise Club. You can't try to corrupt her, no matter how much you want to. The longer I watch her watching the scene, the more I think that maybe I can.

"She's going to eat him alive, isn't she?" Taking a seat beside her, my voice makes her jump as my large frame tries to fit into one of the plastic chairs.

"It's like a car crash, you can't look away." That makes me smile.

"You think we're going to get a show?" I'm testing her, seeing how she reacts.

"I sure hope so." Her answer surprises me—not what I thought she'd say. I think most girls would say, "Eww... no, I hope not." She has my attention now as I look her over. I wonder if... no, don't even think it, Oscar.

"Do you like to watch?" I gently try to feel her out don't want to spook her.

"If someone is willing to put on a show, how can I say no?"

She arches a brow as if daring me. She leisurely takes a sip of her beer, and the starting of a smirk teases her lips. Who is this girl?

"I don't think you're as prim and proper as I assumed you are." Because Stacey Ferguson, you have my attention now.

"You think I'm prim and proper?" She looks offended by my comment.

"The shirt buttons are always done up." She looks down at her chest, and her nipples are hardening and pressing against the thin material. I wonder how she'd react if I sucked on them? Would she arch her back? Would she demand my teeth? Would she push me away?

"Every time I've seen you, the buttons on your work shirts are done up one too many." Stacey doesn't respond to my comment but turns and looks out back over the party, where things are getting a little hotter. I mean, Camryn is two seconds away from fucking Johnny on the table he's lying on, and he is already sporting some excitement over it. I look back over at Stacey, whose cheeks have turned a bright shade of pink, and her body seems a little tense. Miss Ferguson looks pretty turned on.

"I think I'm going to give them their privacy. I'm going to go back to the resort." Stacey makes a move to stand up.

"I'll come with you." There's not much point in my sticking around, plus I know we have a thirty-minute drive back to the resort. That's thirty minutes of alone time I could have with her, to test the water.

"You sure?"

"Unless they want a third, no point in me sticking around." Stacey stops and gives me a look before turning on her heels and making her way out to the car. I hold the door open for her as she jumps in, giving me a perfect look at her ass as she does. I close the door behind me and start looking through the mini bar.

"They've got champagne, tequila, or vodka?" Not much choice.

"I'll take a couple of shots of tequila, please." I pour them and hand them over.

"Cheers." We clink our glasses together.

"So, question. Have you had many threesomes?" I choke on my tequila. She came right out and asked. Curious little thing. "I mentioned it because you said you would stay if they wanted a third, so I was curious?"

"Yes, of course," I answer her question.

"You say that like it's a normal thing? Is it? I've never had one, so I have no idea." Interesting to know. Maybe I need to change that.

"I guess with what I do, the opportunities are presented to me more often than to others." I take a sip of my drink.

"Aren't you worried they will talk?" She leans back against the chair, the tequila relaxing her.

"Of course. Honestly, if a girl is selling her story about having a threesome with a rock star, you know that's going to make me look good."

"You're such a dick." She rolls her eyes at me. "Unless she tells them you have a small dick or that you come too early." Cheeky little thing.

"Look at me. You seriously think I'd have a small dick?" I'm a big guy, and that includes where it matters, right between my legs. Stacey's eyes hungrily scan me, making my dick twitch, and I try to subtly adjust myself. "You shouldn't look at me like that, Stacey." I warn her. Maybe it's the tequila, she's looking at me like she can't wait to rip my clothes off, and that makes my dick really happy.

"You told me to look at you."

"You're looking at me like you are imagining exactly how big my dick is and wondering if you can handle it." I stepped over that line. It's not my fault my dick is beginning to control things.

"Cocky much?"

"Not cocky, you're easy to read."

"I was only curious because you brought it up, not my fault." She holds her hands up in the air.

"True, you were curious about how many threesomes I had. And to answer that question, many…"

"It doesn't impress me, you know." She could fool me by all her questions.

"Wasn't trying to." I smirk. She turns and looks out the tinted windows, the car swirling with undeniable sexual tension. My mind is running away with the crazy thoughts going through it.

"Would you want a threesome?" Easy there, Oscar.

"You offering?" she challenges.

"Yes." If it means I get to taste her. My answer grabs her attention, and she sits up a little more in her seat. "I think little Stacey Ferguson isn't as prim and proper as she appears." I think Stacey might have a bit of a dormant kinky side, and I want to be the one to release it.

"You assume that by how many buttons I choose to do up? I thought I was being professional."

"I can see why you do. Your tits are magnificent." My comment flusters her.

"Thank you." She smiles. "No one has told me that before."

"Then you have been hanging around with the wrong men." I wink at her.

"You're happy to pick up the slack for all of them?" she teases.

"I usually do. Look at me." Stacey shakes her head, smiling.

"You're so used to women falling at your feet, aren't you?"

"Of course." I'm not being cocky, it's the truth. Women do.

"Well, let it be known, I'm not one of those women." She waggles her finger in my face. "A pretty face doesn't sway me."

"I was hoping for maybe handsome, rugged even, coming from you, I'll take pretty."

"Stop your flirting." Pointing that finger at me again. "You can't flirt with me."

"Why not?" I'm curious about her answer.

"Because you know why…"

"Not my fault I find you attractive." The tips of her ears go pink.

"You're only human." This makes me laugh.

"I like hanging out with you. It's easy," I confess. She's funny, smart, and beautiful. Usually, when I find that, all I can think about is banging them, maybe because I can't and sex is off the table, no matter how much we flirt, we both know nothing will happen between us.

"I guess you're not so bad, too… for a rock star." She smiles, rolling her eyes playfully.

"Not a fan of rock stars?" I wonder what her type is. She shrugs. If she's not impressed by people like me, what does impress her?

"So, who's your type, then?" Stacey turns and looks out the window.

"Not sure if I have a type."

"Everyone has a type."

"Someone who's up for no-strings-attached fun. Is that a type? It's what I go for." Is she serious? I study her reaction, waiting for her to burst out laughing, saying 'only joking,' she doesn't. She's serious. "Is that weird?"

I shake my head. "Hell, no. You're most men's fantasy."

"My girlfriends don't get it. I like sex. I like lots of it, honestly, I'm not looking for a relationship. My job takes up most of my waking hours. Plus, I live in LA, and the dating scene is pretty bad… full of douches. I understand the appeal of gigolos. No questions asked and dirty, hot sex." Stacey floored me. "I think I'd rather pay for good sex than free, crap sex." She shrugs, finishing off her tequila. I'm utterly speechless. "I wish there was a nightclub you could go to and basically pick up people who want sex, it would be safe."

Her last comment is like a little thought bubble in her head came out of her mouth. Where the hell did this girl come from? "Why are you so quiet?" She turns to me. "Did I freak you out? Do you think I'm a slut now?" Her face drops. "Tequila makes me chatty." I reach out and place my hand on her thigh, and a tiny gasp leaves her mouth as our skin touches. Her tongue subtly licks her lip.

"I'd never think you were a slut for enjoying sex. So many women pretend they do, in reality, they are telling you what you want to hear."

"My friends tell me I have a guy's mentality when it comes to sex." She gives me a sad smile. I think it bothers her that her friends don't understand how she's wired and that she can tell the difference between pure sexual release and making love.

"I think you're perfect exactly the way you are."

"Really?" Hope laces her voice. "I've had guys call me horrible names because I don't want to see them again, and they feel used, even though I made it clear at the start that I was there for one thing. I think they've given me a complex about it." My fingers dig into her thigh. Fuck me. What kind of idiots has she been hooking up with? I get why they would be pissed that Stacey doesn't want to see them again. The girl is amazing, acting like a little bitch isn't going to get you onto the booty call list. Idiots.

"Forget them. As far as I'm concerned, you and I have the same outlook on sex. I get it. I've had women throw vases and TVs at me because I have asked them to leave after a night together. They think that one night with them, and I'm going to give everything up and settle down and have the two-point-five kids, the white picket fence, the whole fairy tale. That isn't me."

"Fairy tales are overrated" Fuck me dead, she's perfect. My fingers dig further into her soft thigh as I try to control myself, I don't know if I can anymore. The air in the limousine crackles as we stare at each other, the sexual tension line is pulled tight, and its seconds away from snapping. Like a match to a flame, we both jump on each other. Stacey is straddling me. My lips are on her, and my fingers are lacing through her blonde hair. Her sweet little pussy is grinding on me, and tiny mews fall from her lips. I pull on her ponytail, unlocking our lips.

"One night, Stace. Just one night."

"No one can find out," she agrees. "I promise." I do too.

6

OSCAR

My fingers slip beneath the thin layer of her swimsuit. So wet. Stacey moans as my fingers find their place within her. God, she feels so good.

"So good," she whispers into my ear as my fingers find their rhythm. "More. Give me more," Stacey pleads. I like a woman who can tell me what she wants as I slip another finger into her. So full. "God, yes." Stacey's head falls back, exposing her magnificent tits to me. I nudge her bikini top across, exposing her blush nipple. I let my tongue tease it, not giving her exactly what she wants—my teeth. She bucks against my fingers, riding my hand like a rodeo star.

"Mm-hmm," she hums as I press my thumb against her clit, her body shaking as the sensations take over. I press a little harder, and she bucks wilder, grinding harder into me, taking everything, I'm giving her. My teeth bite down onto her puckered flesh, and the sounds she makes turn my dick to stone. My tongue circles her nipple, and I bite down on it again as my fingers turn, hitting those magic nerves deep inside her.

"Fuck, fuck, oh fuck," she yells as her body erupts into a series of volcanic explosions. Her body is shaking as she continues to ride my hand right through her intense orgasm. Tiny sparks convulse over her body, and her head falls to my shoulder, her breaths labored. My hand is still nestled tightly inside her. Stacey lifts her head, and her face is a beautiful flushed pink. Her tongue swipes over her plump lips. "That's a good start." Cheeky little wench.

"Told you I'd pick up the slack for the other men."

"I said it was a good start. Don't get a head of yourself."

"You're really saying it's good while my hand is still stuck up your cunt." Moving my fingers inside her again, reminding her, she shivers.

"I want more. I want to see what else you got. This right here…" she waves her hands between us, "… that was to take the edge off 'cause we've been flirting with each other all night." She has a point as I continue to slowly play with her again. "Plus, there's not much room in here. I was hoping you might throw me around a bit, Viking style."

"You want a little role play, do you?" Her teeth sink into her bottom lip.

"I haven't done that before." For how confident she is with sex, I'm surprised.

"You have no idea the fantasies I can make come true." I continue curling my fingers inside her, making her moan.

"Tonight?" she asks. Because we did agree it was one night.

"Maybe or…" letting the words hang between us.

"Or what?" Sounding intrigued.

"I can open a new world to you, Stace. You have no idea the things I can show you there." She stills.

"What do you mean?" My hand stills inside her. Have I pushed her too far? Did I read her curiosity wrong?

"Tell me a fantasy." Maybe I should start there.

"Umm… I…"

"You were curious about a threesome before." She nods. "I could give you that, depending on if you would like male or female." Stacey is silent for a couple of beats. Maybe I'm pushing her too far. I pull my fingers from her and slowly lick them. Humming over her delicious taste, Stacey gives me a satisfied smile.

"What happens if I can't choose?" My body stills. This is an interesting development.

"Do you like women?" Stacey gives me a shrug.

"I don't know… I haven't… but …" She looks nervous.

"But what? Don't be shy, not after I made you come."

"Fine. I find women attractive. Very attractive."

"Of course, women are lovely." I smile up at her. "You want to see if that attraction is something more." She nods in agreement. "You with another woman would be hot. Nothing sexier than watching two women enjoy each other." My hands grip her hip, pulling her closer to me. "I can make it happen for you, Stace."

"What with one of your groupies?" Her tone is more on the sarcastic side than the seductive side.

"No. I'm not that much of a dick." My fingers dig into the flesh of her ass. "There's a place that I go to that helps deliver fantasies, that's all I can say. Until …"

"Until what?" Her eyes widen.

"Until I can trust you. I've signed things that say I can't talk about it." A tiny frown crosses her brow.

"This place can deliver anything that I desire?" I nod. "Anything?" What does she have in mind?

"Within reason, of course."

"What happens if I want to be kidnapped, blindfolded, and fucked by many different people? They can make this happen?" Thought so, Stacey Ferguson is a dirty little girl.

"That's like a pretty specific request there." A sly smile crosses her face.

"Maybe. Could you deliver that?"

"Yes." Stacey's eyes widen. "We'd work our way up to that. Baby steps first."

"Do you think any less of me because of my fantasy?" The vulnerability is written all over her face. My hand comes out and reassuringly caresses her face.

"I love it. My mind is racing with ideas."

"Really?" Nodding yes to her, she leans down and kisses me, hunger seeping through her lips. Round two feels like it's about to start when we feel the car start to slow down. Shit. We're here. I don't want to leave this little bubble we have placed ourselves in. I'm worried that once those doors open, Stacey is going to realize she's a little drunk and that it was the tequila talking.

"Looks like we're here." Stacey moves off of me, fixing herself up. A door opens, and we both hop out. We both stare at each other in silence. The limousine pulls away from us, bathing us in darkness, and the song of the rainforest echoes all around us. Maybe I should walk her to her cabin. I mean, it's pitch black, and even though we're at a resort, I don't want anything to happen to her.

"So…" Stacey lets the words hang in the summer night's air.

"Let me walk you back to your cabin."

"Oh, thank you. That would be nice." Guess it's time for polite conversation then. No more sexy talk.

We set off in silence over the gravel road that winds its way into the dense forest. I keep looking over at her, wondering what's going through her mind. She probably thinks I'm a pervert. Good one, Oscar.

"So…" Stacey starts before turning around and walking backward, so she can talk to me, those green eyes staring at me. "I think we've gotten to know each other a little better tonight, don't you think?" She gives me a cheeky smile.

"You could say that." Tread carefully, Oscar.

"And we both agree that what happens here is a bit of fun." Is this going where I think it is?

"It will be fun, I can guarantee that."

"And it's going to be sex, right? No wanting anything more?"

"Just sex, mind-blowing sex." Stacey giggles as she weaves her way along the rainforest track.

"And if you like it, you might… I don't know, maybe you might want to take me to your secret place." My feet stop walking as does Stacey's.

"You would want to go?" She nods quickly. "You do realize that if I took you, you might have to watch me fucking other women."

"And I hope that I'd be getting to fuck other men too? Or maybe even join in with you and the women." I'm sorry, this can't possibly be happening to me at this moment. Where the hell did Stacey Ferguson come from? I rush toward her, grabbing her face in mine and kissing her hungrily.

"Where the hell have you been hiding all my life?" I kiss her thoroughly.

"I could say the same thing about you. I've had these thoughts and desires, and whenever I have voiced them to a guy before, they have called me a pervert and a freak. They have made me feel utterly self-conscious for wanting something different than… you know, traditional sex."

"Stick with me, babe. I can show you a whole new world of fantasy and desire that you never dreamed of."

7

STACEY

Oscar Eriksen isn't at all what I was expecting. Of course, he's cocky, a pretty standard attribute for a rock star, I wasn't expecting to see his softer side. He's funny and quick-witted. We have great banter together. It's easy hanging out with him. Of course, the man is good with his hands—he plucks strings for a living—they are quick and strong and know exactly what rhythm to play to get you off. I'm not stupid enough to sing his praises directly to him because his ego is as big as his… well, I haven't seen it yet, but I damn well felt it in the back of the limousine, and holy moly, Thor's hammer doesn't have shit on Oscar's. I can't wait to take it for a test drive.

Oscar practically whisks me off my feet and carries me the last sixty meters with my legs wrapped around him like a koala. I swipe my key across the lock, the click of the door opens, and he carries me inside. Untangling myself from his large frame, I slowly slide down his hard chest. His hands cup my face.

"Do you have an outside shower?" he asks. That's a strange request.

"Yes, out on the back deck." He kisses me slowly, and my insides explode with butterflies.

"Then go. I want you naked and lathered up by the time I get there." This is a new tone I have never heard from Oscar before. It does strange things to my lady bits. It's like a dog whistle—the frequency is so low that only vaginas can register it. I strip off quickly as I make my way through my villa, kicking off my flip-flops, then my sarong, my bikini top comes off next, and with a couple of wobbly hops, my bikini bottoms are on the floor. Thankfully, it's a warm night.

As I turn the cold water on, I tentatively put my hand under it, waiting for it to warm up from glacial to something tolerable. Once the temperature is right, I jump under it. When I turn around, Oscar is slowly undressing too. His t-shirt is gone by the time I turn around, exposing his spectacular body—the colorful tattoos up his arms, the six-pack on his stomach, and the muscle upon muscle encased in bronzed skin. Next is his board shorts. The man had been commando underneath them. Oh my! That's when I see Thor's hammer. Now I get the cockiness. It's pointing straight out. You could use it as a ring-toss game, it's so long and girthy. My lady bits do a little dance, the closer he gets, the more she doesn't feel so confident. *Don't worry, girl, you can do it. I have faith in you.*

"Like what you see?" Does he really need me to answer that? Cocky bastard. He eventually joins me in the shower. He grabs the shower gel and squirts me all over. His hands run up and down my body. Haven't we had enough foreplay tonight? Not to sound utterly ungrateful because there are many men who don't put this much time and effort into getting a lady ready, I'm really ready to test out Thor's hammer. After about five minutes of us soaping each other up, we rinse off, and Oscar turns the shower off.

"Move to the daybed and kneel on all fours. Do not turn around." His voice is controlled and commanding. I feel a little self-conscious about it, I do it. "Good girl." His rough palms graze my skin. "Have you ever been spanked?" My heart beats a little quicker.

"No," I squeak, the adrenaline kicking in.

"Oh, kitten. You have so much to experience." Then a hard hand connects with my skin, pushing me forward.

"Ow!" Is the first word that comes out of my mouth because it bloody well hurts.

"The only thing I want to hear out of your mouth is you telling me you want more." Shit, kinky Oscar is hot. "Do you understand?" I nod my head because he said I couldn't speak. "Good girl, you catch on quick."

I brace myself again as his hand collides with my wet skin, the sound echoing into the night. Once the initial shock is over, it's not so bad. He gives it to me over and over again. I'm so far in my head that I almost collapse when I feel his fingers inside me. "Thought you'd like that. You're so fucking wet." His fingers are sliding in and out of me easily. I should be embarrassed at how wet he's got me, it feels too good to care. His thumb circles my puckered hole, making me bite my lip. "Has anyone?" He pushes his fingers against my back entrance.

"No."

"Mm-hmm," he hums. "Is that something that might interest you?" His thumb slowly massages the entrance, relaxing me, so he can slowly push a little more as a finger grazes my throbbing clit.

"Oh my ..." The sensation is overwhelming.

"Relax, kitten." His voice is soothing as he continues doing magical things between my legs. "We can work up to this if you like." I nod as my body begins to quake with the teasing melody he's playing with my body. "Relax a little more for me. I need you good and ready for me."Closing my eyes, I let all my insecurities melt away and focus on the enjoyment he's giving me. I focus on the steady cadence of my heart, my increased breathing, and the shivers that prickle my skin from the dried water droplets. I tune myself into my body. *Enjoy this moment, Stacey.* Then out of nowhere, my body shatters into a million microscopic orgasms, my arms become weak as my body quakes, my legs shake, and my head falls forward. Slowly, my bones feel like they are turning to jelly. "Good girl, so, so good." Oscar's deep vibrating voice penetrates through and warms me.

Then next thing I know, he's entering me from behind, setting off secondary shudders. His hand wraps around my ponytail and pulls my head back, making my back arch. "You feel... so fucking... good." His words are stilted as he slowly moves within me. "So tight. So wet. Delicious," he whispers.

Yes, to the dirty talk. Usually, I can't do dirty talk, I guess all I needed was a Viking to tell me what a dirty girl I am to get going. Oscar pulls hard on my hair, pulling me back, so we're back to front, his left hand grabbing my breast. Rough fingertips roll the sensitive bud around. My body doesn't know what's going on, so many sensations. It's almost overloading.

"Fuck me, Stacey," Oscar demands. "Push back, and show me how much you want to be fucked." I do as I'm told and push back, pressing myself hard against him. "That's it. Yes. Yes." He still has my ponytail wrapped around his palm. It's primal and possessive, and I like it. No one has ever fucked me this way before. I've had guys think they know how to fuck, and I've been sorely mistaken. Oscar, I'll happily pray at the altar of Thor's hammer, especially as he has given me two orgasms tonight. Usually, I'm lucky if I get one.

Speaking of orgasm. No. How? Seriously? Does he have a magic dick? No man has ever been able to make me come through intercourse, he's doing it. He is reaching deep inside me and touching places this little lady has never been touched before. Yes. Oscar. Yes. Yes. Yes.

As his rhythmic thrusts continue, he takes me higher and higher. Yes. Fuck me. Fuck. Holy shit. This is intense. Oh my

Suddenly Broken　　　　　　　　　　　　　　47

God. I think, oh shit, I'm coming again. Moments later, Oscar joins me, roaring into the night.

When Oscar has finished, he lets go of my hair, I fall forward, and he pulls himself from me. I'm a pile of liquid on the daybed. He disposes of the condom, then scoops me up from the bed and carries me into the villa. He places me on another bed, and I snuggle into the soft duvet. The space beside me remains empty. I force my eyes open and see him walking toward his clothing.

"Oscar." He turns around quickly, the soft light illuminating his impressive body. "I know you're not into staying." Slight panic flies across his face. He probably thinks I lied about my sex is sex chat. "Stop freaking out, I can see it on your face." He schools his expression. "If you want to wake up to a blow job, stay. If you don't and want to go back to your villa and wake up to your hand in the morning, go." He smirks at me.

"Better be a fucking good blow job." He drops his clothes and stalks toward the bed.

"I promise it will be the best I have ever given." The bed dips as he jumps in.

"Get some rest, little one." He kisses my forehead. "Because I'm going to make you work for it in the morning." I snuggle into him, he wraps his large arms around me, and we fall asleep.

The sun is streaming through the window. I rub my eyes. What's that? I realize there's a tanned arm wrapped around me. Shit, that's right. Last night comes flooding back, and the throbbing between my legs is there again. I look over at Oscar and take him all in—the intricate tattoos, every line of muscle on his body, till I get to Thor's hammer standing at attention, looking awfully lonely.

I did promise him I'd wake him up with a blow job, and I'm

a woman of my word. I ease his arm off me and slide down. He is spread out in a star shape, almost as if he's subconsciously ready for me. I slip between his thick thighs and stretch my mouth out a little, warm her up because I think she's about to get the workout of her life. Once my lips are good and wet, I slip them over the tip. Slowly. Ever so slowly, I sink my lips lower over him. A grunt comes from the sleeping giant. His dick twitches. I suck harder and push further down until I'm almost to the base of his cock. Strong hands hold me there.

"Take it all, kitten. You promised me," Oscar's gravelly voice commands me. Relaxing, I take the last inch until he's almost down the back of my throat. Those strong fingers lace through my hair as he starts to control me. I suck him harder, and he rewards me with a sweet groan. "Good girl. You're so good at sucking my cock." Hell, yeah, I am. "Spin around, Stacey." I still. "I want you on my face." He pulls my face up, those ice-blue eyes staring hungrily at me. I do as I'm told and swing my body around and nestle myself over his face.

8

STACEY

We've been back from Australia for a couple of weeks. Before we left for Australia, Derrick closed on a gorgeous bungalow. It's not far and was a good price, so how could he not take it? Although I'm a little bummed coming home to an empty home most nights, it's nice having time to myself. I love Derrick, he's a little full-on. Working with him and then living with him, my quota of Derrick was filling up fast.

While in Australia, Oscar and I hooked up a couple more times. It was amazing. I have enough spank bank material to last me a lifetime. We both agreed that whatever happened between us was fun and nothing more. He did mention that he would sort out one night where he'd take me to his favorite place, the one which brings fantasies to life. I'm not turning down that offer for anything. I'm utterly curious, especially the strict rules about it. Intriguing.

Tonight is Oscar's thirtieth birthday. Apparently, he's hosting a huge Hollywood party at a friend's house. Isla tells me there will be at least a hundred people there and heaps of eligible bachelors, meaning the party is probably full of immature douchebags, who can turn down free food and drinks? Not this little bird. Derrick, Vanessa, Isla, and I arrived together. Sienna is on bed rest after all that international travel while heavily pregnant.

"I'm not looking forward to this," Vanessa moans, clutching Derrick tightly.

"You'll be fine," he whispers to her. Isla and I look at each other. Something happened between Vanessa and Christian while in Australia, she won't talk about it. When we got back to LA, it was like World War III between the two of them. She's even contemplating moving out and staying with Derrick for a little while. It must be something really bad because these guys have been friends forever. I guess when Vanessa is ready to talk, she will. Our names are checked at the door, and we're allowed in. I haven't been to too many of these Hollywood parties, so the opulence still astounds me. The music is pumping, and people are everywhere. As you enter, there's a pool to the right in the middle of the house. A pool!

"Let's find the bar," Derrick shouts over the music. We follow him through the throngs of people. It's overwhelming when people I know from television or movies are standing around you. Derrick hands over four tequila shots to us all, and we throw them back.

"Oh, for fuck's sake," Vanessa groans. "Look up there." She points to a mezzanine level, and there sits Dirty Texas minus Evan, and they are surrounded by a bevy of beautiful women. Derrick hands us a cocktail. My eyes bounce between the famous rock stars, each with a beauty on their lap until I get to the birthday boy. There he is with a beautiful brunette who is trapped all over him. He appears somewhat interested, she's most definitely trying hard to keep his attention by thrusting her enormous fake tits in his face. He told me he's a boob guy, he's not too into fake boobs. Alas, the girl doesn't realize.

Oscar looks down at that moment and catches me staring at him. Great, now he probably thinks I'm being weird. I hold up my cocktail in his direction and mouth happy birthday to him. He smiles back and raises his glass back in my direction. The brunette notices the exchange and doesn't look happy, the daggers she's throwing my way indicating so.

"Fuck, I'm over this." Vanessa turns on her heel when Christian starts kissing the blonde on his lap. Derrick follows after her.

"Men suck," Isla adds when we're alone. Finn is preoccupied too with a groupie.

"They do. You know what, screw them. They're all having a great time, so why are we sitting here feeling shit about ourselves?"

"You jealous about Oscar?" I choke on my drink at Isla's question. How the hell does she know? "Derrick tricked the boys and got it out of him that way. Lucky you only kissed." She thinks we only kissed, so I'm guessing that's all Oscar let slip. Thankfully.

"I'm sorry I didn't tell you. It was a drunken kiss."

"Look, I'm not blind. Oscar is attracted to you, and there's some chemistry between you both. Don't get your hopes up. Because up there…" she points to the group of girls, "… is what he loves. He's addicted to groupies… they all are. I mean, they have sex laid out on a platter for them. Why the hell would they have to work for it?" She's right. I see what she means.

"Issy. I'm fine, honestly. I can tell the difference between a quickie and long-term potential." She throws her arm around my shoulder.

"I wish I could be more like you because seeing Finn up there is killing me." One drunken night at my place, Isla sort of filled me on her secret relationship with Finn. I feel for her.

"You and Finn have a long history together. Oscar and I have met a handful of times." She shrugs. "Come on. Forget about those rock stars. Let's circle this party and see what fresh meat is out there.

"I like your thinking."

.

We found some fun in the shape of hot nerds—tech guys from Silicon Valley for a meeting and got wrangled into coming to this party before they headed back up north. They are charming, witty, funny, and extremely intelligent. They were surprised we were interested in talking to them because most of the women at the party were more interested in the actors and rock stars dotted throughout.

Well, the gold diggers at this party are doing a bad job—they have latched onto the wrong guys. Always go for the hot nerds. They make billions. Rock stars and actors only make millions. Not that I care about money. It doesn't impress me at all. Most of the night, I've been talking to an Aussie guy named Adam. He creates video games. Ones I haven't heard of, I'm sure are popular. It was nice chatting about how different America is to back home.

"Do you mind excusing me? I need to nip to the toilets," I tell Adam.

"Need me to come with you?" Is he propositioning me? "Shit, not like that. Just as you…" Adam gets flustered trying to make it right.

"It's okay. I won't be long." He nods and sips his beer nervously.

"Hey, I'm popping to the loo," I tell Isla, who tells me she's happy to stay with the boys. She's clicking with one of them. Slowly, I make my way through the crowd no bathrooms. I spot the staircase. There has to be one upstairs.

"Hey." The deep voice makes me turn around. I'm shocked to see Oscar.

"Hey, happy birthday." I hug him.

"Thanks. What are you doing upstairs?"

"Trying to find the toilets." He tells me to follow him, taking me into a bedroom off the hallway.

"Just in there." He points. The room is empty. I quickly do my business and make my way out.

"The party is crazy. Are you having fun?" He shrugs.

"I don't really know anyone." Huh, it's his birthday. That's incredibly sad.

"Then why on earth are you having this party?"

"It's what you do. Network. Have fun. Meet people." Guess that makes sense.

"Well, I hope your night is a success. I better get back downstairs." He takes a step closer to me, those ice-blue eyes staring down at me.

"It will be."

"Oh, yeah, have fun with that brunette. She's hot." Oscar's eyes narrow on me.

"Are you jealous?"

"No. I told you that in Australia. It's your birthday, so I hope you have fun." I give him a reassuring smile, and he frowns at me. "Seriously, Oscar. You don't believe me?" He shakes his head. "Fine, come with me." I grab his hand and pull him out of the bedroom. "Hey, girls." I point to the blonde and redhead talking in the corridor. Their eyes light up when they see Oscar tailing behind me. "Do you ladies know who this is?" They both nod enthusiastically. "Do you mind coming with me for a moment? I promise you it's nothing bad. Actually, I think it might be fun." They both agree. Oscar looks a little shellshocked. I pull him back into the room we vacated.

"Hi. I'm Stacey. This is Oscar. I need you ladies to prove a point for me. Do you girls mind kissing him for me?" They both look at each other and giggle. "One at a time or together, whatever works." They both toddle up to Oscar and take turns kissing him. His eyes are on me the entire time. I give him a thumbs-up, which he doesn't appreciate, pulling himself from the girls.

"Ladies, I need you both to do me a favor now. I promise you I'll finish what we started. Stacey has given me two perfect presents for my birthday."

"That's because I'm a good friend," I say, crossing my arms.

"Yes, yes you are." The girls' heads turn between the both of us. "Now, I want to be a good friend to you." What does he have planned? "My friend here has never kissed a woman, and I want her to kiss one for my birthday." My eyes widen. He thinks I won't do it.

"Me. Can I do it? She's super cute," the blonde pipes up.

"Aww… really?" I say to her, a little shocked.

"Oh my God, yes. And that accent. You're a total babe." Oscar chuckles behind us. His arm lazily rests over the redhead's shoulders. The blonde moves closer to me. "I promise, I'll make it good." Then the next thing I know, her lips are on mine. They are soft, so very soft, and she tastes like caramel—it must be her lipstick. Her hand is soft against my face. It feels the same yet different. She pulls away and turns to Oscar proudly.

"That was the perfect birthday present." He smirks at me. I'm a little shell-shocked, it was nice.

"Well, thanks for that. It was lovely. I'll leave you guys to it, have fun." I give them all a wave. Stepping back out into the corridor, I make my way back downstairs.

"Hey, there you are." Adam runs into me. "I was worried. Isla told me to come find you."

"This place is like a maze." Why do I feel like I cheated? "Thanks for looking for me."

"No worries at all." He gives me a lazy smile. God, he's cute. The next thing I do is kiss him to see how I feel about that kiss. He pushes me up against the wall. I wasn't expecting him to be so forceful. He presses himself into me, and I can feel underneath his clothes is a man who looks after himself. A throat clears, and I turn to see Oscar and his two friends staring at me. The girls are giving me thumbs up, the look Oscar is giving me feels mixed. Did he seriously think he'd be the only one picking up tonight?

"Do you know him?" Adam asks, looking over at the striking Viking.

"He's the birthday boy."

"Have a great night, Oscar." I throw him a salute. He grunts, then turns on his heel, the two girls following him. The door shuts with a bang.

"Is he?" Adam asks, noticing three people entered the room.

"Sure is." He looks a little impressed. Poor little nerd.

"So, umm…. Isla wanted me to tell you that she and Seth were going to leave and wondered if we were interested in leaving too." Adam nervously rubs his neck.

"Where are we going?" My hands are resting on his hips.

"Umm…" His cheeks flush. "To a hotel." He bites his lip.

"Are you asking for a sleepover?" I tease. This makes him smile. "If you're interested, yes."

"I'm very interested." I pull him closer to me and kiss him.

9

STACEY

I pop my head into Isla's office, she's not there.
"You looking for Issy?" I clutch my chest at the voice behind me.

"You scared me." Oscar grins down at me, amused.

"Vanessa and Issy left early today. I think they headed to The California Bros. down in Venice. They mumbled something about men are dicks. I didn't think it was my place to butt in."

"Thanks. I might skip heading down there at this time of night. The traffic will be crazy." Oscar nods his head in agreement. "I think it's a night on the couch with some takeout for me." There's a crash in the distance from one of the offices, and we both look at each other.

"Ignore Christian. Things haven't been great since Ness moved out."

"Shit. I knew it was bad didn't realize it was like this." You could feel the tension radiate through the office. "Guess I'll let you go deal with that." I turn on my heel.

"Wait," Oscar calls out. "I was about to leave… did you want to grab something to eat?" I'm a little shocked by his request, I am hungry.

"Sure. It beats eating alone." Taking a couple of steps forward, I quickly turn around, running right into the Viking. Damn him for being a wall. "Hang on. You can't go out and eat like a normal person. Don't you need security or a motorcade or something?"

"Well... I was kind of hoping for takeout on your couch if it's on offer." Really? I place my hands on my hips. "I haven't seen your place before. I'm intrigued" My eyes narrow on him. "Plus, I can order from any restaurant you like and have it delivered."

"Any?" He gives me a crooked smile.

"Yeah, any. You know who I am, don't you?" I roll my eyes while shaking my head at him.

"Wow, never thought I'd hear that line in person. Mighty big ego there, Mr. Eriksen." He moves closer to me.

"Matches everything else that's big," he says with such a straight face, I burst out laughing. We're talking, bent over, full bellyache laughing. Oscar stares at me in bewilderment.

"Oh, you're serious. Was that supposed to be a pick-up line?"

"I'm guessing it didn't work." He folds his large arms across his chest.

"Yeah. Nah. Totally didn't, I'm too starved to say no to a free feed, though." This makes him smile.

"Least I can do for subjecting you to such bad pick-up lines."

"Oh no. Those lines deserve alcohol. Your shout for dinner is because I'm gracing you with my presence." I get a hard swat across my ass.

"I guess you're worth it." He gives me a heated look. Tonight might get interesting.

We arrive at my apartment easily enough without anyone spotting him. He orders from his favorite restaurant and gets them to add in a couple of bottles of wine.

"This is nice." He looks around my apartment. I always thought it was spacious, it feels rather small now with a hulking Viking in my living room. Oscar takes a seat on my sofa, his body taking up most of the two-seater. I take an armchair to give us some distance.

"How are things going with the shop?"

"Since Sienna had Ryder, who's adorable, isn't he?" I don't wait for Oscar to answer. "It's been pretty busy, especially with Derrick getting so much publicity after styling all those actresses for awards season." Most of that went over Oscar's head. "Tonight is actually the first early night I have had."

"That's good. And you're enjoying living by yourself?"

"I love Derrick, but it's Derrick." This makes him laugh.

"He's an interesting character." That he is. "So, did you do anything for Valentine's Day?" I sit back in my chair and look over at him.

"Is that your way of fishing for gossip?" I raise a brow at him.

"I'm making polite conversation," he tells me.

"Yes. I had a great Valentine's Day. I caught up with Adam, the guy I met at your birthday party. He was down from San Fran for business, so we caught up."

"So, you're dating?" I shake my head.

"No. He works mainly in Silicon Valley. We agreed we'd catch up when in town." Oscar nods, his mind looks like it's elsewhere.

"I have to ask." This sounds serious. "You really didn't mind that I took those two girls to bed on my birthday?"

"Did you mind that I took Adam home?"

"No," he states firmly.

"Exactly. I was the same. I hope you had fun. They looked

like they would've been fun." Oscar stares at me. "You still don't believe me, do you?"

"It's just..." He lets out a heavy sigh. "I have never met a woman like you before, and I guess, no... I hope that it was the truth. Because I have fun with you, Stace, I also enjoy my freedom."

"I do too."

"And if I said I wanted to fuck you tonight?"

"I'd tell you that you're pretty transparent. That asking to come over for dinner to 'catch up' was a code word for booty call." This makes him burst out laughing.

"Then, I guess I'm pretty transparent."

"Can we eat first? I skipped lunch today, and I'm starving."

"Of course. You're going to need your strength."

Dinner was perfect—a steak and salad with a bottle of good red wine, which I'm slowly sipping on. Oscar clears away the plates as I move to the sofa, kicking up my feet onto the coffee table, admiring my view of the city. Oscar takes a seat beside me, a glass of red in his hand.

"I've noticed your buttons." Such a weird statement, then I remember our conversation in Australia.

"I guess a wise man once told me that he thought I was too prim and proper because my buttons were done up too high. Didn't want people to get the wrong idea." Knocking my shoulder against his makes him smile.

"Wish I never said anything now because every man and his dog can now see what an amazing rack you have. Not sure if I like that."

"Why, thank you, sir. You have such a way with words." He grumbles beside me. "Lucky, you don't have a say in who sees my cleavage, either." Another grumble. "Want me to do my buttons up. I mean, my magnificent cleavage might distract you."

"Can't you just accept a compliment without busting my balls?"

"I can, but where's the fun in that?" I smile over my glass at him, and he rolls his eyes.

A couple of hours later after two more bottles of wine have been consumed, we watch some Netflix, we haven't quite got to the chill bit of the night, and I'm becoming sleepy. I must doze off at some point because I wake up to a loud explosion and realize it's the television.

"I'm so sorry." Wiping my mouth, since I probably drooled all over him.

"I guess I'm a boring dinner guest." He chuckles.

"No. No. Sorry, it's me. I've been a bad host. This wine is so good, it relaxed me into a coma."

"Note to self... next time bring crap wine so Stacey doesn't fall asleep." I give him a playful shove, making him chuckle.

"But now you're awake... you're awake, aren't you?" I nod, trying to stifle a yawn. "I actually wanted to talk to you about something." His tone turns serious. He has my attention. "I was wondering if you were free Saturday night?" Is he asking me out on a date?

"I don't have any plans." He rubs his hands along his thighs. Is he nervous?

"I wanted to take you somewhere, I can't tell you about it until you get there. All I can say is, I've been granted permission to invite you along to the place that delivers fantasies." Butterflies flutter in my stomach. "Is that something that might interest you?"

"Would you be there with me?"

"Of course. I won't leave you alone unless you ask me to." I nod.

"What do you think they will do to me?" Not going to lie, I'm a little nervous.

"Do you really want to know?"

"Maybe for the first time. Just so it gives me a couple of days for it to sink in." Oscar reaches out and touches my face.

"You don't have to do it. You don't have to do anything."

"I'm curious now." His thumb brushes over my lips.

"I promise you'll like it very, very much." My body shivers at the seductive promise.

"Do I need to wear anything special?"

"Something easy to remove might be a start." My heart is definitely beating a hundred miles an hour now. "I'm sure you'll look hot in anything you wear." That doesn't really ease my nerves. "I better go." He leans in and kisses me, softly, then slowly, before pulling away. "See 'ya Saturday, kitten. Sleep tight."

10

OSCAR

I'm a little nervous about tonight. This is the first night I'm bringing Stacey to The Paradise Club.

"Relax." Axel pats me on the back. "I've never seen you nervous before about a chick. Stacey must have done a number on you." I give him a skeptical look.

"Please. I'm not pussy whipped like Evan is." Axel gives me a smirk. "You know how hard it is to find someone who likes things the way we do?" Axel nods in understanding. I've confided in Axel about what has been happening between Stacey and me, that we catch up, we fuck, we see other people, and she isn't the least bit jealous. I know for a fact she's going out too, thanks to the chatty conversations my sister likes to have about it. Tonight will be a real test to see if she really is wired the same way as Axel and I are. Because if she's...

"Mr. Ericksen, your guest has arrived." The receptionist calls me over. I take a deep breath as I stride across the bar area toward the main door. The receptionist holds it open for me, and I step through to the entry foyer. Stacey is standing there looking nervous but beautiful. She's dressed in a short black cocktail dress, pointy heels, her blonde hair swept up to one side, exposing one-half of her neck. At the sound of movement, she looks up at me, her green eyes sparkling when she sees me, her cheeks turning the faintest pink color. I stride over to her.

"You look beautiful," I say as I kiss her cheeks.

"Thank you. I didn't know what to wear." She gives herself a little shrug.

"It's perfect." Because it is. I'm thinking about the things I want to do with her without even having to get her undressed. The hem of her dress is the perfect height to have some fun in. We make our way through the door again and into the club. Stacey is silent as she takes it all in.

"This isn't at all what I was thinking." She looks around at the luxurious surroundings.

"Did you seriously think I was taking you to some kind of dirty sex den?" She pauses in her steps and looks up at me.

"No. I trust you, Oscar." Her words hit like an arrow through my heart. "I wasn't expecting something this gorgeous." She smiles. I wrap my arm around her shoulders and pull her into my side. I kiss her head and usher her toward the bar where Axel is sitting.

"Oh." She stares when she sees Axel here.

"Stacey, you look gorgeous," Axel greets her, kissing her cheeks. She has no idea what I have in mind with her and him tonight. Stacey's cheeks flush at Axel's compliment. Good, I want her to be attracted to him. There's a glass of champagne waiting for her at the bar. She takes it and quickly drinks it, nerves obviously getting the better of her.

"Would you like another? I ask. She nods, and the bartender gives her another glass, this time, she sips it slowly. "You don't have to be nervous, little one."

"I know. It's the anticipation is getting to me. You know, the images I have probably thought up in my mind are worse than what's happening in reality."

"Depends on what you're into," Axel adds playfully. I hit

him. She's nervous enough as it is, so he doesn't need to scare her anymore.

"On this level, there's no play allowed. It's for drinking, talking, and dancing like a normal nightclub," I explain.

"Shall we go upstairs to where the fun happens?" Axel asks. We both look over to Stacey, and she nods. I take her hand as we follow Axel up to the next level. We start to ascend the grand staircase, and I explain the different levels.

"This is Level One. It's where beginners or people who want to take things slow hang out. Nothing hard core, good old-fashion play." Of course, the glass cube is the first thing she sees when she reaches the top of the stairs. It's a great introduction to the club, especially when it's occupied for everyone to watch. We move through the crowd to find a spot that isn't so crowded. Her steps slow as she realizes what's happening before us.

"Anyone can join them," Axel adds.

"Is that what…" She doesn't finish her question.

"Little one, you're not ready for that… yet." She nods, her eyes are glued to the show currently playing out in the box. Axel and I look over the top of her, and he nods with a smile. Okay, he's still in. Stacey's cheeks are flushed pink.

"Have you ever gone in there?"

"A couple of times, I'm not really that much of an exhibitionist. I'm more of a voyeur." She nods, taking it all in. "Is that something that might interest you?" She frowns a little.

"I'm not sure. I mean… it's all so… you know… overwhelming." She then looks around us for the first time and notices the people in various states of arousal. Her eyes widen when she recognizes people, she doesn't say a word. She hasn't run away screaming yet, so I think it might be a win. Let's hope she will still be okay when we take this to a private room.

"Do people … you know… do it while watching?" I whisper yes to her. Stacey's eyes widen as she takes another tentative look around the club.

"Are you ready to see more?"

"Yes, please." There's a slight tone of eagerness to her voice. We head toward the corridor which leads to private rooms.

"The rooms with a red light on are occupied. Some have sound on, so people can listen, some have the blinds open so you can see in, and some have everything open for you to enjoy," Axel advises her, pointing at the different rooms. "Here, press this," Axel tells her. She presses the button, and the sound of sex comes through in stereo. Her eyes widen, and a grin falls across her face.

"They sound like they are having fun." She giggles.

"The rooms also allow for total privacy too. Not everyone likes to share what's happening behind the curtains."

"Would you like to see your room?" Axel asks.

"I have a room?" Stacey turns to me.

"Yes. You have a room."

"Can I see it?" she asks eagerly. Axel smiles and takes her hand, pulling her back down the corridor to the green light.

"After you." Axel holds open the door for her. Stacey rushes in, and I step in after her. I have chosen a simple room. It looks more like a luxury hotel room.

"I wasn't expecting this." The door closes behind us with a click.

"Don't you like it?" Did I choose wrong?

"No. I like it. It doesn't feel as terrifying as the other rooms."

"Tonight is to test to see whether or not you like certain things. If you do, we can explore more, and if you don't, then you have a fun story in your spank bank," I explain to her.

"I had no idea something like this existed."

"That's the point. No one is meant to know," Axel advises her.

"I get it now. There's no way I'd be telling anyone about this place. It's... magical." That's a good sign. Magical is a good word. Stacey is becoming more relaxed as she moves around the room.

"Would you like more champagne? Strawberries and cream?" I ask.

"Or only cream?" Axel adds. Stacey pauses and looks over at the two of us. Those green eyes narrow.

"I'd like some more champagne, please, chocolate-dipped strawberries and whipped cream." Axel turns to me, giving me a devilish smile. I think Stacey's caught on with what's happening tonight.

"What's this for?" she asks, running her hand over the curved chair.

"It's a sex chair," I tell her. She tilts her head, eyeing it. Is she imagining all the things that could happen on it?

"How do you use it?"

"Let me show you," Axel interrupts, walking over to where the chair is. "You place your hands here." He points to the lower end, which makes Stacey have to bend over. Her dress is short enough that it exposes her G-string-clad ass. Fuck, it looks delicious. Axel's eyes are firming on her peachy bottom. "You might have to open your legs a little." Axel walks behind Stacey, placing his hands on her hips and moving her legs wider. He presses himself against her. "Is this okay?" Axel asks before he touches her more.

"Yep," she says, the 'P' making a pop sound. Axel turns back to me, nodding. He's going to test the waters. So far, so good. His hand moves down and over her ass a couple of times.

"Want to try another position?"

"Yes, please."

"Lay down." Stacey lays down against the chair. "Open your legs." She follows Axel's instructions, and he falls to his knees in front of her. "It's the position I like to start the night in." Stacey bites her bottom lip as she studies Axel before her.

"Your requests have arrived," I tell Stacey. They were slipped through the secret compartment. "Walking over to her with the tray of goodies, there's a bottle of champagne in an ice bucket, a bowl of chocolate-dipped strawberries, and a can of whipped cream beside it. Stacey's eyes light up. She goes to sit up, I tell her not to move, that I'd like to serve her. I hold a strawberry up to her mouth, and she bites it all the way to my finger. As she sucks the berry into her mouth, she takes my finger with it. I think someone is getting into the mood. She hums against the berry. Axel walks around and grabs the can of whipped cream, a hungry glint in his eye. He sprays a bit on his finger and holds it out for Stacey to suck off, which she does. I pop the champagne and pour her a glass, she takes a nervous sip, then finishes the glass quickly. I pour her another, and she does the same. This concerns me.

"Are you okay?"

"Oh yes, most definitely. I have a question, though." Axel and I wait. "Do you two..." she moves her fingers between us. We both shake our heads no, we don't swing the other way. "Such a shame. It would've been hot." She gives us both a wicked smile.

"We will happily find you someone to watch another night."

"Okay. I have another question." I tilt my head to indicate for her to continue. "Are you both playing tonight?"

"Yes. If you would like me to."

"The question is, do you want to?"

"Very much so." Axel grins. Stacey looks over at me.

"You're giving me a threesome, aren't you?" She smiles.

"Yes. I trust Axel, and I thought you might be comfortable with him."

"And tonight is my night. My fantasy?" Axel and I nod. "So if I ask you both to strip for me, you would?" We both nod. "Then strip," she commands. A thrill laces my body at how commanding she sounds and how confident she's feeling, laying back against the sex chair like a queen. Tonight we're going to treat her like one. We're going to give her exactly what she has always desired.

11

STACEY

I want to pinch myself because I have seriously woken up into one of my ultimate fantasies. Two hot men, under my command, catering to my every desire. This place is insane. This place is like Neverland for adults—dirty, kinky adults.

My attention is split between Oscar and Axel. On the one hand, I can't wait to see Thor's hammer again, and on the other, I'm curious to see what Axel looks like naked. Yep. Axel is as gorgeous in the flesh as he is fully clothed. He's leaner than Oscar, that's most people. He has blue, Japanese tattoos all over his arms, which is a stark contrast to Oscar's colorful patterns. His body is cut, not too much, enough to know he looks after himself. Then, there's Oscar, who looks like he's spent all his time cutting logs and fighting bears in the wilderness. I bite my bottom lip.

"I'd like a strawberry, please." Oscar reaches out and places the sweet berry on my tongue. It bursts in my mouth. These chocolate-dipped strawberries are delicious. I reach out and wrap my hand around his enlarging dick, shocking him. I give him a couple of pumps to tease him. "My shoes, please," I say, pointing to my heels. Axel steps up and takes my heels off, placing them to the side. "Axel, would you mind showing me some more of your favorite positions on this chair?"

"Of course." Holding out his hand to me, I take it, and he pulls me up into him. He leans down and kisses me. For a split second, I hesitate because Oscar is in the room, then I realize this is something they are used to, so I go for it. *I mean, it's only for one night, so throw caution to the wind, Stacey, and go with it.* He moves me around the chair until his back is to it. He lets go of me and lays down, his dick sky high. I look over at Oscar for a second, and the heated look he's giving me is intense.

"Place a foot on either side of my face," Axel instructs. I'm still fully clothed, I'm not wearing much—a black slip dress and barely-there underwear. I do as I'm told. Not going to lie, I'm extremely nervous. Oscar moves around to the higher side of the plush leather sex chair. He grabs the can of whipped cream and sprays it along his dick. He looks up, smirking at me. Axel's fingers dig into my thigh as he positions me over him. Then I feel it.

The first swipe across the lace of my underwear makes me groan. I lean forward and lick the cream right off him. Axel nudges my underwear to the side. Then he swipes directly across my wetness, letting out a guttural moan as he tastes me. My back arches as I sink over his mouth. Oscar smiles down at me as I fall forward. I grab onto his dick and take it in my mouth, all the while riding Axel's face. The closer Axel pulls me to the edge, the harder I suck Oscar into my mouth. It doesn't take Axel long, as I'm incredibly turned on. He takes me closer and closer to the edge until he pushes me right over. My chest is heaving as I fall against the chair. Axle pulls me down to his chest, so I don't suffocate him.

"You were delicious." Axel grins. I grab a chocolate-dipped strawberry from beside me and place it against his lips. He takes it whole from my fingers. Oscar moves around me and unzips the back of my dress, pulling it up and over my head, throwing it to the concrete floor. Thankfully, I'm not wearing a bra. Axel grabs the cream and sprays it against my nipple, licking it off. It tickles. Oscar goes to a drawer, pulls out some condoms, and places them beside the chair.

"Turn around, Stacey. On your knees," Oscar commands. I do as I'm told. Axel moves from his position under me and sheaths himself. I place my hands on the edge of the chair and my knees in the middle. I'm now facing Oscar. He taps my chin, asking for me to open wide for him. Axel moves into position behind me. My mouth wraps around Oscar as Axel gently slides into me. The way the chair is designed, it puts me at the right angle for each man. Axel's fingers dig into my hip as he slowly moves inside me. Oscar holds my chin up, making sure I look at him at all times. He reaches out every so often to pull my nipple while Axel lets a finger slip over my clit, making me hum around Oscar's dick.

"You're doing so well, little one," Oscar praises me. Even though I probably look a fright, and my mascara is probably running, I can feel the saliva falling down my chin as Axel pushes Oscar's dick further and further down my throat, and I'm choking on it. The sensations are too amazing that my mind takes me somewhere else, and I take it. I take it all as male grunts fill the room. The guttural sound of two men giving me exactly what I desired. What I fantasized about. Who knew threesomes were this good? Probably many people, for me, it's all new. Then moments later, Axel moans as he climaxes. Oscar isn't far behind him as he comes down my throat.

We're all lying naked in the bed. I'm sandwiched between Oscar to my back and Axel to my front, both of them lazily touching me.

"Was everything okay?" Oscar asks. I can hear the concern in his voice.

"Everything was perfect." My hand finds him hard and ready behind me. I'm feeling a lot more confident now. Turning my attention to Axel, I say, "Thank you."

"The night isn't over yet," Axel reminds me, taking a nipple into his mouth.

"We have all night, little one," Oscar whispers into my ear. His hand dips between my legs. "And it looks like you might be ready for round two?" His fingers curl inside me. My nerves are sensitive from the first round, and he finds them easily receptive.

"Axel," I call out. "I need you in my mouth."

"Your wish is my command." Axel moves to the head of the bed, where I move to my back, and Axel stands above me. I reach out for him and position him at my lips. Oscar has sheathed himself and enters me. My body feels like jelly as the boys take me. Oscar ravages me, thrusting quickly into me, pushing Axel further down my throat. Then Oscar places his thumb over my clit, and that's it. My body explodes. My body shatters into a million pieces. How am I ever going to go back to normal sex after this?

Oscar dresses me as I'm too exhausted to do it.

"Thank you for a beautiful night, Stacey." Axel kisses me. "I look forward to more fun-filled evenings. My head flips side to side in agreement. He chuckles, shakes Oscar's hand, and leaves.

"Let's get you home, little one." Oscar picks me up, I close my eyes, and I don't open them again until Oscar is placing me in my own bed.

"Hey." I open my eyes.

"Shh. Go back to sleep. We'll catch up another day." I reach out to him.

"You can stay. I know that's not our thing, we can have

breakfast here and talk about tonight." He kisses my forehead, and I fall asleep again.

The smell of bacon wakes me up. Where the hell am I? Rubbing my eyes, I glare at the sun coming in through my blinds. I go to stand up, and my entire body aches. What the hell did I do last night? Then I remember. Wow. That was. Wow. A humming male voice grabs my attention. Kicking back the covers, I'm still dressed in the same dress I was in last night. I quickly throw it off and grab a t-shirt from my drawer. I step out into the living space, and there's Oscar moving around my kitchen with such ease it's as if he lives here.

"Morning," I call out, surprising him.

"Morning." He smiles, walks over, and kisses me, surprising me.

"I've made bacon and eggs this morning," he announces as he plates the delicious-smelling food.

"Thanks so much." I dig into the gourmet feast. This is the first time a guy has ever cooked for me, and it feels pretty good. We eat in relative silence until the first wave of hunger has subsided.

"So, last night, huh…" I start the conversation because I don't want it to be awkward this morning.

"Last night was…" Oscar lets the words hang.

"Fun. Dirty. Amazing. Liberating." This makes him chuckle.

"I'm glad you enjoyed it."

"Did you? I mean, 'cause you know, Axel was there."

"Watching you lose control before my very eyes was the biggest turn-on."

"And you weren't jealous?" I ask the question I know he'd ask if the roles were reversed.

"No. I trust him." Good enough answer. We continue eating

our breakfast. "So, do you think it's something you would like to do again?"

"Yeah. It is, actually. I'm a little worried you have ruined me for all other guys not in a white-picket-fence way." I see Oscar's face pale. "But in a... how can I go back to missionary after that?" Oscar reaches out and links his fingers with mine.

"I'd love to show you more."

"I'd love to see more."

"So you want to do this?"

"If by this, you mean we can go back to that magic sex club, then yes." He smiles while his fingers lazily trace mine.

"And you're okay with sharing me? Next time, it could be with a woman." My eyes widen.

"That would be a new experience, something I'm not adverse to."

12

STACEY

Oscar and I have been spending more and more time together at The Paradise Club. I've been able to experience things that I have only ever fantasized about. Never in my wildest dreams did I ever think I'd get to do them, Oscar has opened a whole new world to me. We still agree that we can see other people. I caught up with Adam the other day when he was in town, and I know Oscar is hooking up with girls because Isla has found a couple that have wandered into her room lost. She wasn't happy.

We both agreed not to tell anyone in the group about us, even though there isn't an us. Of course, Axel knows the extent of what's happening between us, because well, he's been included in it. I don't think the others would understand, especially not watching the person you are, I guess kind of dating, fuck another girl in front of you. They wouldn't get it. Most people probably don't understand it, they don't need to because it doesn't affect them. So, it remains our dirty little secret. Tonight it might all come crashing down.

. . .

Derrick has been accepted as The Paradise Club's latest member, and on his first night at the club, he's allowed to bring some guests to experience it. I tried everything to get out of it, all the girls were eager to go because they know the Dirty Texas guys go there, and they are keen to check it out. Vanessa and Christian have semi-made up after Ryder's christening. So the group is at ease again.

The limousine pulls up in front of what looks like an abandoned building. Nerves tickle my stomach as I walk the familiar path toward the concealed entry. None of the girls know I have been coming here with Oscar. I'm not ashamed about the sexual awakening Oscar has given me, I still don't think they would understand because I see how jealous they get over the guys. Maybe there's something wrong with me that I don't get jealous even when I've been in the same room watching Oscar screw another woman. All I thought was it was hot. Isla links her arms with me nervously as we walk toward the building.

"Where's the door?" Vanessa stares at the solid brick wall. Derrick pulls up his phone and checks the details.

"There should be a pin-code box somewhere." I know exactly where it is, I stay quiet. "Here." Derrick points to the red flashing light. He punches in his personal code, the door slides open, and we walk in.

"Welcome, Mr. Jones," a tuxedo-dressed doorman greets us. "Congratulations on becoming the newest member of The Paradise Club. Here is your card." He hands over what looks like a gold credit card. "Swipe this when you want to move through the different floors. Each level has a security door, and you'll need this to get to the next level. Miss Roberts, Miss Ferguson, Miss Eriksen, here are your temporary cards. It has the same access as Mr. Jones' only for one night."

Thankfully, Luke, the doorman, is going along with my ruse

as if it's the first time I've been there. He hands out the multi-colored bands for our wrists and explains how the colors work for play inside. I look over at my friends, who all look a little freaked out. Luke then explains the club rules as Lucy joins us, our guide for the evening.

Walking through the golden doors to the club is still as impressive as the first time I came here. It has a cool 1920's vibe, very Gatsby-esque, old Hollywood style. We're standing in a large room, where many people are milling around. Black leather booths line the room's walls, large ornate gold chandeliers hang from the ceilings, the walls are painted black with gold art deco designs swirling across them, and soft jazz music is playing. Lucy guides us toward the studded leather bar. The beautiful bar staff hands over a couple of glasses of champagne to us. Lucy explains how the club works, and my friends silently listen. Isla squeezes my hand as we follow Lucy up to the first level.

"This is exciting," I whisper to Isla because she looks really nervous.

"This level is for voyeurs and exhibitionists." Lucy points to a large glass cube room in the middle of the area. Inside it are two women and a man. He's lying on his back with one girl riding him, and the other girl is riding his face, the two girls kissing. I turn to see how my friends are faring with what they are seeing. Derrick isn't that interested, he's busy looking around at the people in the crowd, I can see Vanessa and Isla's cheeks have a faint pink color to them. They are both absorbed in what's happening.

"That's hot," I mumble. Isla and Vanessa nod in agreement.

"I'll be leaving you on this level, you have your map," Lucy tells us. "Please know that at any time, you can use the club's safe word, *Paradise*. When it's used, everything stops, and if it doesn't, then one of the bouncers will make sure it does." Lucy points to the many men dressed in black scattered around the club, then she leaves us to our own devices.

"Okay, I'm trying not to freak out, we watched people have sex." Isla giggles.

"I know, it's kind of hot." The group laughs nervously at my comment.

"Maybe we should go back down to the safe room, have some drinks, and then work up the courage to continue our journey," Derrick suggests. We follow his lead and head back downstairs and straight toward the bar. "Tequila shots, kind sir," Derrick flirtatiously asks the handsome bartender.

"Coming right up, sir." He flirts back at him.

"Not yet, maybe later I'll be," Derrick fires right back.

"Sounds like something I'd like to be a part of," the bartender states, showing off his multi-colored bands on his wrist. Derrick is in luck as he sees the blue bracelet dangling from the bartender's wrist. Our tequila shots arrive, and we all slam them down quickly, nerves getting the better of us. "Is it going to be weird if... you know, we see each other doing something?" Isla asks.

"Maybe, I don't know. As long as you don't ask to join me, we should be fine." The words came out like a lie because if I were normal, it's what I should say.

"Well, I wouldn't mind watching Derrick and the hot bartender later on." Vanessa elbows D in the ribs.

"I know you want all up on this, Miss V, check the bands, girl, no pink on this wrist." He shakes his bands in front of my face.

"Ew, I don't want to join in, I wouldn't mind watching." Ness giggles.

"You're only human." Derrick grins at Ness, they turn and whisper something between each other.

"I'm so nervous," Isla confesses to me.

"Me too. I've never been somewhere so... sexual." I hate that I'm lying to my friend. I take another shot of tequila.

"Oh shit," Derrick curses under his breath. We follow his line of sight and see Axel, Christian, Oscar, and Finn walk into the club. Shit, Oscar got my text message.

"What the hell are you doing here?" Oscar doesn't look happy at all. His ice-blue eyes fall on me for a couple of beats, then back to his sister.

"I'm here having fun." Isla straightens, the couple of tequilas giving her strength to fight back.

"I don't want you here," Oscar tells her. I stiffen beside her. He's being a dick. I shoot daggers at him from behind Isla's back.

"Too fucking bad. Derrick invited me, and I'm determined to have fun, so you can fuck off." Isla crosses her arms in defiance. Silence falls all around us as we watch Oscar and Isla stare each other down.

"Sorry, Ragnar," Derrick interrupts, using his nickname for Oscar. "Little sis is here to have fun. You need to let the leash go, or maybe not, depends on if we make it to the BDSM level." Derrick bursts out laughing at his joke, which Oscar doesn't find funny at all.

"Isla, it's a little awkward for us to be in a sex club with you." What the hell is Finn doing? Dick.

"Then you can leave, you're a member, and you both can come anytime you want. For me, this is my one and only night. So, you either stay and see something you might not like or you can both fuck off." I mentally high-five my girl because the boys are being jerks. I knew Oscar wouldn't be happy, I really underestimated his protectiveness. Oscar looks over at me, I nod, and let him know that he's not going to win this round. He lets out a heavy sigh.

"Fine, I'll go," Oscar tells his sister. Then he turns to his friend. "Finn, stay, keep an eye on her. Make sure no fuckers mess with her, okay?" I shake my head, he couldn't do it. Of course, Finn is going to look after his little sister and make sure Isla doesn't get lucky at all. I watch as Oscar leaves the club with slumped shoulders, looking deflated.

"Okay, now that matter is over with, let's get our freak on," Derrick cheers. I pull out my phone and text Oscar.

Stacey: *Wait for me. I'll be out in 10.*
Oscar: *Fine.*

"Hey, you coming?" Isla asks as the group makes their way back up to the first level.

"I'll be up soon."

"I can't leave you here."

"I'm fine. My sister texted me about something going on at home, so I had better call her. Go. Finn is waiting." She turns and looks at Finn chatting with the bouncers.

"Nothing is going to happen. Tonight is about me."

"Good. Go have fun." Isla frowns at me. "I'd say I would come find you later, I don't really want to see you in a compromising position." This makes her laugh.

"Text me then. And if I'm not indisposed, we can catch up." I nod, and she reluctantly moves away. I wait until they disappear upstairs, then walk straight out the golden doors and into the cool night. Oscar's limousine is waiting out outside. I open the door and see he's brooding in the corner, angrily texting. He looks up at me, and his face softens a little. I get in and sit across from him.

"That didn't go as planned," Oscar states.

"Of course not. You came in with all guns blazing. You know how much that gets Isla's back up.

"I ..." He rakes his large hand through his hair. "I..." I move and sit beside him, taking his hand in mine.

"I get that she's your sister, and you're protective." His fingers link with mine. "She's not twelve anymore. She's a woman and can look after herself."

"I know. I know. I can't. I... you know why." He turns and looks over at me. I rest my head on his solid shoulder, snuggling into him.

"I know." Oscar told me early on about how he saved Isla from one of his friends who was a predator. All these years, and he still harbors so much guilt. We sit in silence for a couple of minutes.

"You didn't want to stay?" he asks.

"Nah, I don't think I'd relax with them being there." I feel his lips hit my scalp. "Plus, we kind of had a deal, remember?"

"Yeah, this was extenuating circumstances." I shrug. And silence falls between us again.

"I've been." My stomach sinks. Of course, he has. Why would I think the agreement we had between each other would extend to him? He doesn't want me to go to the club without him, especially now that I have been given membership due to how frequently Oscar takes me and from Axel vouching for me. Apparently, they are friends with the owner. "I'm sorry."

"You have nothing to apologize for." I look up at him.

"I'm the one who suggested it, and I'm the one who broke it."

"It is what it is."

"I've hurt you." I sit up straight.

"No, you haven't. Oscar, we aren't together. I know we've been spending a lot of time together, we both agreed we're not monogamous, that we don't date, and we're only having fun. I'm slightly disappointed only because we had an agreement."

"I should've texted. Like you did tonight. It was a last-minute thing, and I didn't think. I'm not used to thinking of other people."

"Oscar, seriously, you don't have to think of me. That's the point." He frowns, looking down at me.

"I do think about you. Much more than I ever thought I would." His confession surprises me. "For the first time, I feel guilty about my actions."

"I'm okay."

"I know all this." He rakes his hand through his hair again. "I like you, Stacey." Wow. Was not expecting that. "And not only in a sexual way either. You have become one of my closest female friends." Aw, that's so sweet. I like this side of him. "Actually, my only female friend. And I guess most of all, I don't want to lose that." I squeeze his hand.

"You won't lose me, Oscar. Communicate with me, that's all. I may not be monogamous, that doesn't mean I'm not loyal." He leans down and kisses my lips ever so softly.

"Thank you. So, we're non-monogamously loyal." That perfectly sums us up.

My phone vibrates with a text, and looking down, I see Isla's name. I pick up my phone.

Isla: *OMG. You need to get up here, it's insane.*

Oscar stiffens beside me as he reads over my shoulder. I push him away.

Stacey: *I've met someone at the bar.*

I'm such a bad friend. So much lying.

. . .

Isla: *Go, girl. Okay. Have fun. Text me if you leave with them.*
Stacey: *Okay. Have fun. Don't behave.*
Isla: *I'm planning on it.*

I can feel Oscar fuming beside me. "Calm down." I turn to him, throwing my phone back onto the seat. Tension is radiating off of him, thinking about his little sister in such a debaucherous place. He needs a distraction, and I have the perfect cure. Straddling him. This grabs his attention. "You don't have to worry about her tonight. Finn is there totally cockblocking her, or is that pussy blocking?" He doesn't need to know the real reason Finn doesn't want to see Isla with anyone else. Oscar grunts and grumbles some bullshit that I ignore.

"You look awfully tense, Mr. Eriksen," I say, raising a brow at him. "Can I help you with anything?" My flirting brings him back around.

"Yes. I want you on your knees with my cock in your mouth."

"I'm at your service, sir." I give him a seductive wink.

13

STACEY

We've arrived in Vegas for Christian and Axel's thirtieth birthday. Everyone is looking forward to this weekend away, especially Vanessa, who is finally healed enough from her double mastectomy to party. The past couple of months the gang has rallied around Vanessa, who tested positive to the BRCA gene. She took the extreme measure of removing her breasts to give herself a fighting chance because her family has such a strong history of cancer. And through it all, Christian has been her rock. It took her diagnosis for them to put all their petty bullshit aside and decide that they would be together, and they have been happy ever since.

Oscar and I are still seeing each other, and we still frequent The Paradise Club, I have been dating as well, mostly to help Isla move on from Finn, also because, why not? Since we had our chat months ago about defining us as non-monogamously loyal, it has strengthened our friendship. We communicate more, he comes over, and we watch movies.

We've become a little more open with our friendship amongst the group. They might all assume something is going on, they don't actually know. Isla, of course, knows because she busted us coming home early one day. It was the only time we actually did anything at his place for that exact reason. Thankfully, we were making out in the kitchen and hadn't gone too far when she walked in. Oscar and I sat her down and explained that we're good friends who have fun at The Paradise Club together. At first, Isla was a little confused, a tiny bit pissed, in the end, she was fine. She confessed that Oscar is always happy when I'm around, and she thinks I'm good for him. I told her that my feelings for Oscar are only friendship and sex, she rolls her eyes as if she doesn't believe me. I knew she wouldn't understand, so I let her think what she liked to save an argument.

"Spa day," Sienna says excitedly as we meet at the hotel's luxurious spa. The boys have gone out on some ultimate guy day thing Derrick has planned for them, which should be interesting. I'm looking forward to getting pampered and catching up with the girls. "I have been looking forward to this day for so long." Sienna sounds almost giddy, which makes us laugh. "Don't look at me like that. Wait until you have kids one day, ladies. You have no idea how much you crave your personal time and space. Having a kid is so claustrophobic, and Ryder is always on me."

"Lucky he's cute," Charlotte adds.

"Yeah, he is," Sienna practically glows talking about Ryder. He's cute, kids aren't in the cards for me. I have no interest in having any. The spa director comes out and greets us all and directs us to the VIP spa area. We're welcomed into our own room, where there's a heated spa, a bottle of champagne, and a tray of chocolate-dipped strawberries waiting for us. We strip off our robes and lay down on the beds beside the pool. We're each given a glass of champagne by the spa director.

"Please press the buzzer when you're ready for your treatments." The spa director points to the button on the wall, then disappears.

"If I fall asleep, ladies, I apologize now because this is so relaxing, and I'm so tired," Sienna moans as she sinks her teeth into a chocolate strawberry.

"So, you and Christian seem to be going well?" Isla asks, sipping on her champagne.

"Yeah, we are. He's been brilliant, especially with the whole boob and cancer thing."

"That's because he loves you, Ness," Sienna states.

"Yeah, he does. It took me a long time to realize I felt the same way, I'm finally there. I'm one lucky woman." We all cheer her over it.

"Thank fuck because having you two at war sucked," Isla moans.

"Yeah, sorry about that," Vanessa apologizes. Isla smiles and waves her away.

"So, when are you two going to get married?" Charlotte asks, making Vanessa choke on her champagne.

"Umm..." Vanessa stutters.

"Please, you two will be married by the end of the year. That boy is so desperate to lock you down," Sienna adds.

"I think you'll be pregnant again before Christian and I walk down that aisle," Vanessa fires back.

"Oh, fuck off. Evan is hounding me for more babies. I'm like no way, our life has started to slowly settle down. Ryder is crawling, and that creates so many hazards, throw in a baby and fuck me dead," she groans, and we all laugh because she's so going to be knocked up by the end of the year. There's no way in hell Evan will let her get her way. He wants babies and lots of them.

"And what about you and Blake?" Sienna asks her sister-in-law.

"Being on tour with them sucks," Charlotte groans. "We are both so busy. He's got shit going on in his home life, and we're both young. I don't want to lock myself down yet."

"Sowing your wild oats, are you?" Vanessa asks.

"Yeah, something like that. We're friends, and that's kind of how I want to keep it. My career comes first." Charlotte's photos of the band on tour have been selling out. Magazines and collectors have been contacting her about them. She's super talented.

"And what about you and Finn?" Vanessa asks Isla.

"Nothing's going on there. In fact, my crush is one hundred percent done and dusted." The room erupts in laughter, not because we're mean because we have heard this a thousand times before. "What happened to Wes?" Vanessa pushes. Wes owns The California Bros. Brewery down in Venice Beach, and we go there a lot. He and his brothers, who run the tattoo parlor and barber shop next door, are really close friends with the Dirty Texas guys.

"We're friends. He's a nice guy, you know…" She twists her glass in her hand.

"He's not Finn," Vanessa says quietly.

"I hate it. I hate that he has this hold over me, and I can't get over him. Why the hell can't I get over a man who isn't interested in me?" Isla's eyes fill with tears.

"Hey, hey, don't cry over him," I console, sitting beside Isla on the couch. I know how much this whole Finn thing gets to her. "He's a boy, and boys suck. They are so blind when it comes to a good woman," I reassure her because you can see Finn likes her, he's still too involved in the rock-star life. He's not ready to give that all up yet, what he doesn't know is if Isla will still be waiting for him.

"Is that what you think of my brother?"

The room goes silent. All eyes are on me. I think Isla forgot we weren't alone at that moment.

"Your brother is cute, but…"

"Back this train up, you and Oscar?" Sienna looks a little confused.

"I didn't tell you because it was nothing. Oscar and I hooked up at your wedding." Everyone looks at me, and I can see they have so many questions.

"So, it was like a one-time thing?" Vanessa asks.

"No, I've done it a couple of times since being back in LA but nothing serious. Sorry, Issy, close your ears." Because I know she doesn't like hearing about the two of us. "Your brother is kind of kinky." She rolls her eyes. "We have an understanding."

"So, you're saying you're kinky as well?" Vanessa stares at me, trying to work me out.

"Maybe." I'm a little hesitant to say anymore. "Come on, don't leave us hanging." Sienna pushes. "There's nothing to tell. Just that I like to, you know, experiment with things, and I'm okay if it's either with a guy or a girl." The room goes quiet as I look at the shocked faces of my friends. My stomach sinks. I've said too much.

"You like girls?" Charlotte asks quietly.

"Yes." This was something Oscar helped me explore recently. It's been fun. "I'm not looking to date a woman, I'm heterosexual in that aspect, sexually, I like to play with both. Is that going to make things awkward?" Because I feel a little judged at the moment.

"Hell no, babe." Sienna gets up and sits beside me. She takes my hand into hers. "We still love you. We don't care who you're sleeping with as long as you are happy. And who hasn't kissed a girl and liked it?" Sienna giggles. There's a story there, and I think I need to know more.

"Thanks, guys." I feel like a weight has been lifted from me.

"Girls, forget about rock stars. We're in Vegas. I'm sure three sexy single ladies can find some hot men or two or three to play with." Vanessa raises her glass.

"Yes, give those boys a taste of their own medicine," Sienna adds.

"Take it from us. One thing those rock stars hate in the world is sharing their women." Vanessa has no idea how wrong she is with that statement, I cheer her anyway.

14

OSCAR

"Fuck, what are you doing here?" Christian looks a little scared. Totally pussy-whipped. Poor fucker. "This is my club," Nate states as we head toward the entry. Nate Lewis owns The Paradise Club and has clubs all around the world. "It opens next month. Thought I'd let my best customers check it out first." That doesn't ease Christian's tension, which is the complete opposite look than what Axel is wearing. They may be twins, they are complete opposites. We have come straight from experiencing Derrick's Bro Day, so after changing our clothes and freshening up, we follow Nate through the club to whatever Derrick has planned next. Nate leads us into a dark room, where there's a stage and a couple of stripper poles.

"Derrick, this better not be strippers?" Christian sounds pissed.

"Dude, we're in Vegas, and it's your birthday. Of course, you're getting strippers." Derrick must have a death wish.

"No, I don't want to be here, and I won't do that to Ness," Christian tells him.

"Fuck, I lost a twenty-dollar bet. Ness told me you would not be into this, I thought no way in hell. I honestly thought you would be up for strippers like the old days." The spotlights on the stage turn on and out walks Vanessa with two strippers, each carrying a chair. They place them back to front in the middle of the stage.

"Axel, Christian, your ladies are waiting," Vanessa calls down to them. Axel practically sprints to the stage, and Christian begrudgingly follows his brother. Vanessa whispers something into his ear, which calms him. Vanessa walks off the stage and behind the curtain, leaving the boys with the two blondes. The lights dim, the music begins, we all take a seat in the front row. Christian's face is hilarious. He's not enjoying any of this at all. Axel, on the other hand, has a Cheshire grin. At least someone is enjoying his birthday. The curtain pulls back again, and more women come out, this time, they head straight off the stage and into the audience. A stunning brunette stands in front of me and starts grinding on my dick.

"I'm out." Evan stands up and walks out of the club with his phone to his ear.

"You should be a bit more exclusive for all tastes, Nate," Derrick complains beside me.

"I didn't forget you."

As a man enters from the other side of the stage.

"Yippee. Daddy is going to have fun tonight."

"Follow me." The brunette who has been giving me an incredible lap dance takes my hand and escorts me to a private room. "Sit." She instructs me, then disappears. In comes Jackson, taking a seat beside me, then the birthday boy, Axel, who has lipstick all over his face.

"What are we doing in here?" Jackson asks.

"I have no clue. It's probably going to be good." Axel grins, rubbing his hands together. There's a black curtain in front of us, which has me intrigued. The lights dim, and slowly the curtain pulls back, exposing a glass wall. Whatever is behind it is bathed in darkness. We look at each other, wondering what's happening. Slowly, light begins to filter through the room, exposing what it is. A king-size mattress in the center of the room with white sheets and pillows scattered across it, it's made.

"I think we're getting a show," Axel states. I guess we are. I kind of wish Stacey was here to watch with us. We've been having some fun, the four of us lately. We introduced Jackson to the club not long after he started working with us. The first time Axel and I brought him there, Stacey asked if she could show him around. I had a millisecond of jealousy hit me when I watched them walk away, hand in hand to play. She made it up to me, sending Natalia over to me, so I wouldn't be lonely. This made me fall for Stacey that little bit more.

From that first night, Jackson plays with us regularly, and he gets on with Stacey. Who doesn't, she's an easy-going person. There's much to like about her and not because she's turned into this sexually confident woman, who knows exactly what she wants and goes after it—she's a good person inside and out. I've never really developed feelings for a woman before, beyond my own sexual need, Stacey Ferguson does something to me. She's embedded herself inside me. Once a week, we catch up at her place for a regular 'date,' I guess you would say. We get takeout, we watch television, and I stay the night. I even have my own key. It's as close to normal as we both want it to be.

The sound of high heels grabs our attention as it echoes through the room in stereo. It's the brunette that gave me the lap dance earlier. She kicks off her heels, then slowly and seductively slips out of her dress, and she's completely naked underneath. Her back is to us as she rubs her hands all over her tanned body. Another echo of heel's filters through the room. This time it's the blonde who was with Axel. She does the same thing as the other girl—undresses herself and makes her way over to the brunette, who pulls her into a kiss. We all groan in appreciation. They pull apart and move to a side of the bed and look to the back of their room, where another woman appears.

"No fucking way." Jackson groans.

"What's she doing in there?" Axel questions. Stacey slowly walks around the room and stands before us, a smile nestled on her face.

"Happy birthday, Axel." She blows him a kiss. "I hope you like my present." Axel's head is nodding enthusiastically, I'm not sure if she can see him or not. Stacey unzips the dress she's wearing, and it falls to the floor, standing there naked in front of us. Jackson bites his knuckles. Axel claps his hands with excitement. And I'm left staring at the most beautiful woman in the world.

Stacey turns and saunters back to the bed, her hand lazily caressing one of the girls as she passes them. She stands in the middle of the bed, where the two girls join her. Something begins to lower from the ceiling. We all lean forward a little closer to get a look. It's a swing. I grin. Stacey has started using the swing, and she loves it. The girls help her into it and move away when she's in place. Stacey rises higher, positioning her at not quite standing height for the other two girls. Her bottom is nestled inside the harness, her legs are bent into the foot holds, she's able to straighten them if she wants. The girls walk around her, touching her, teasing her until she's wriggling in her restraints. It doesn't take the blonde long until she positions herself between Stacey's thighs.

"Shit," Axel moans. Whatever audio equipment they have in that room is five-star because we can hear every mew, gasp, and heavy moan. We can hear how wet Stacey is with each lick. The sounds are driving me crazy, adjusting myself in my pants. I'm not sure how long this little show will go because I don't think we're going to be able to wait all night. Stacey arches her back, so she's lying flat in her harness. The brunette straddles her face

Suddenly Broken

and lets out a hiss as Stacey's tongue connects with her. Fuck. Fuck me dead, this is hot. I think I might ask for this for my birthday.

Suddenly, the wall between the two rooms begins to open. We all look at each other. Was this an invitation to join what's happening on stage, or are they giving us a better view? "Fuck it, it's my birthday." Axel starts to head toward the stage. Jackson and I look over at each other and do the same. The brunette gives us a welcoming smile—maybe it's okay. I tap the blonde on the shoulder, and she moves away. It's my turn to be between those thighs now. God, she tastes so sweet. The blonde is unzipping my fly as I feast on Stacey, who is wriggling now that she realizes someone else is between her legs. The blonde's wet mouth is on me, and I hum against Stacey's cunt. Axel has replaced the brunette and has his dick down Stacey's throat. The brunette has moved over to where Jackson is standing and drops to her knees.

"I love seeing you in the swing," Axel tells Stacey as he plucks her nipples. "Utterly at our control, our whims. You like that, don't you?" Stacey hums against his dick. "You're such a good girl." Axel runs his hands over her body. "You wanted to please me for my birthday day, didn't you?" Stacey's body moves as she nods her head. "I'm very pleased, Stacey, very pleased, indeed."

Stacey becomes wetter, listening to Axel's words. Axel moves away from Stacey's mouth and over to the drawer always stocked with necessities. He pulls out the condoms and lube. He undresses as he returns to the action, handing out the condoms and placing the lube beside me. Moving away from Stacey and the blonde, I quickly undress and sheath myself and grab the lube. Stacey is sitting up, those green eyes watching me. She knows exactly what I have planned for her. We've spoken about it but haven't gone there. Tonight is perfect. She licks her lips and gives me a knowing smile. Axel pulls over one of the bench chairs and positions it underneath the swing, sheaths himself, and the blonde lowers the swing. She moves Stacey's legs so that she's kneeling on either side of Axel's hips.

"Want to wish me a happy birthday, princess?" Axel asks. Stacey nods and lowers herself over him. He moves her hips ever so slowly, making sure she's comfortable. Positioning myself behind her, I squirt the lube onto my fingers. Then I start to circle her puckered hole with my thumb. The blonde is sitting on Axel's face facing Stacey, who leans forward and captures a nipple into her mouth. This will distract her enough for me to get her into position. My fingers work their way through the resistance inside her, she bucks at the intrusion, she's soon humming with satisfaction. I keep working Stacey until she's ready. When she starts pushing back against my fingers, then I know it's time. I pour a generous amount of lube over me and slowly start working my way in, bit by bit, ever so gently until there's no resistance and I'm snug all the way inside her.

Axel would usually like to set the pace, seeing as he has his hands full with the Stacey and the blonde, I start to set the pace. Slowly, I move inside her, and with each thrust, she pushes against Axel. The sound of sex begins to echo through the room. Panting. Swearing. Grunting. Moaning. Screaming. All melding together like a beautiful symphony. Thankfully, she's harnessed because I have lost myself to it all, and the room has turned manic with need as we all chase that euphoric bliss. The blonde is the first to climax, which sets Axel off, which, in turn, has Stacey gripping his dick tightly, making me come.

"Happy fucking birthday to me," Axel shouts.

15

OSCAR

The girls have gone to Paris for the weekend to do wedding shit for Vanessa and Christian's upcoming wedding. We've decided to head up to Big Bear, where Christian bought a holiday home for his bride-to-be.

"Still can't believe you're married, dude." Zander, our tattooist from The California Bros., slaps Christian on the back as he takes a seat across from him on the plane.

"Best decision I ever made, boys." Christian raises his bottle of beer to everyone.

"Here, here." Evan clinks his bottle against his.

"Aw, look, the married boys club," Axel jokes.

"Seriously, bro, don't knock it."

Axel huffs at his twin, "There's no way in the world I'm ever settling down." Finn, Zander, Axel, and I clink our beers together in single-man solidarity.

"Never say never. Y'all aren't getting any younger," Christian warns us.

Axel groans. "Doesn't mean we have to settle down with one woman."

"There's no way on God's green earth I'd ever give up Ness

for the endless supply of pussy you guys are talking about. None of that stuff could ever compare to what Ness and I have."

"That's 'cause you and Evan got the best ones," Zander adds.

"Damn right, we did," Evan agrees.

"Yeah, we got lucky, that's 'cause we stopped searching through the easy pussy to get to the prime stuff."

"You know Ness would kill you if she heard you talking about her prime pussy," Finn tells Christian.

"Yeah, she would, and I wouldn't care because that woman is my life, and one day y'all might meet that one woman who makes you lose your breath and want more from life."

The plane is silent for a minute, then the guys burst out laughing. There's one woman who has taken my breath away, she's not the marrying type, and neither am I. Christian does have a point, though. I do find myself spending more time with Stacey than I have with anyone else, maybe that's because we're friends, not just lovers.

"Y'all are a bunch of fuck faces." Christian flips us off.

"I like husband Christian. His words are poetic and shit," Zander teases him.

"Whatever, I'm saying, there's more out there than short-term kicks."

"Agreed," Evan adds.

"Oscar's been hanging out with Stacey a lot. He might be next." Finn throws me under the bus. Dick.

"Well, well, well." Christian smiles.

"Fuck you, dude. We aren't a bunch of women gossiping about our sex lives," I grumble.

"Hell, yeah, we are. I want the gossip," Christian laughs, enjoying my torment.

"You've been around Derrick too long, and you sound like him." Christian shrugs.

"Time to buckle up, boys. We're about to take off," the hostess advises us before disappearing again. The cabin goes quiet as the rumble of the jet starts, and we taxi down the runway. Moments later, we're up in the sky, the plane evens out, and we all resume talking again. It's less than an hour to Big Bear from LA, so it will be quick.

"Don't think I've forgotten what we were talking about before," Christian tells me.

"Argh, you're so annoying. Fine, Stacey and I like playing at The Paradise Club. We're into the same things, and she's very sexually adventurous, other than that, I'm not looking for anything more." There, it's out. I've told them what they wanted to know, so hopefully, they will leave me alone now.

"So, Stacey is a fuck buddy?" Christian questions me. Urgh. I'm going to kill Finn. I run my hands over my face.

"Yes... no... I'm not really sure. She's a cool chick but has never indicated she wants anything outside of the hookups we have."

"But you hook up with her a lot." Shut up, Finn.

"Like I said, sexually, she's highly compatible."

"She's pretty hot at the club." Axel forgets himself for the moment.

"I know that you know." Why is everyone sticking their noses into my business today? Can't we talk about anything else other than Stacey and me?

"What does that mean?" Of course, Christian would pick on that. Fuck it. They pretty much know everything now.

"They've hooked up before." The plane goes silent.

"What the hell, bro." Christian throws a cushion at him.

"Hey, hey, Oscar allowed it," Axel defends himself.

You allowed it?" The shock on Christian's face is evident.

"Chris, you know Axel and I are into different kinds of kinks than you boys are." Evan and Christian are pretty vanilla compared to the rest of us.

"Why would you share Stacey with Axel? Was she okay

about it?" I knew Christian wouldn't understand. The guy has been in love with Vanessa from day one.

"Yes, of course. I shared her with another because she wanted a certain experience that one man couldn't give her. So I asked Axel, who understood what she was asking for, and who I trusted to give her that experience."

"And now?"

"Axel joins in if she needs more," I tell them.

"And you're okay with doing this?" Christian asks his twin.

"Oscar wanted to fulfill an experience that his woman wanted, I helped, and that's all there is to it."

"So, you don't do anything with her outside of the club?" Christian digs. I'm going to have to warn Stacey because as soon as we get off this plane, Christian will tell Ness, and Evan's probably texting Sienna as we speak.

"We both agreed that we keep what we have in the club."

"And you do?" Christian pushes.

"Yes. Could you imagine if *TMZ* got a hold of this, especially after *Fifty Shades of Grey*? They would have a field day. I don't need my family knowing what I get up to behind closed doors." The boys should understand this.

"And you trust Stacey?" Christian asks.

"Hell, yeah, I do. She's a great girl, plus she's already in our inner circle. She is best friends with your girls so that means something." Evan and Christian both agree.

"So what happens if she goes to the club without you?" Evan asks.

"Then she has fun without me."

"And you're okay with that?" Evan has a severe jealous streak, so I don't think he'd get it.

"Of course, we're not exclusive. We have an agreement. She's mine to do with as I see fit at the club, and I'm helping her explore her sexual side. The one that's started to bloom since we've, you know..." Please make this all stop. I take a sip of my beer.

"So, you're her boss?" Evan asks.

"Kind of. She tells me what she wants to experience, and I help her experience it. When we're together at the club, she's mine, she must ask for permission if she wants to be with another, and I must do the same."

"You're only exclusive at the club and only when you're together?" Evan repeats.

"Yes." This is something that has been a relatively new change the longer we're together

"You don't see her as anything more?" Finn questions me.

"Stacey may be the first woman who has made me question my stance on commitment." The plane falls silent.

"So if you were committed, you would stop sleeping with other people?" Christian asks. I turn to Axel, looking for help in answering that question.

"Like we've said, Oscar and I like things a little different to you guys," Axel explains.

"If I could find a woman who let me sleep with other women, I wouldn't let her go." Zander chuckles to himself.

"It's not ..." Axel starts, and I can see it on his face that he's becoming defensive of our choices.

"I guess as long as you all understand the rules, and no one is getting hurt, then it's all good." Christian smiles at me.

"I know it's not conventional compared to what you guys have. I know it sounds really strange, Stacey isn't a jealous girl. Believe me, I've tested her."

"Stacey is a genuine girl. Just because she might like things a little dirty and kinky in the bedroom doesn't change who she is. So I hope that none of you dickheads look at her any differently or say anything to her. That would be a real breach of trust," Jackson lectures the plane.

"You seem very defensive over a girl you hardly know," Finn questions his brother. Jackson looks over at me.

"She's a friend." Finn's eyes narrow, then his head whips around to me.

"You let him play with your girl." I refuse to answer Finn. "Are you pimping her out to your friends?" What the fuck. I charge at Finn, my hand wrapping around his throat.

"What the fuck." The boys pull me off of him. "How could you say that? How could you?"

"Because you won't let yourself fall for her. She's amazing, and you're putting these walls up." I'm genuinely shocked. "I've never seen you happy before with a girl. She makes you happy. And I'm not talking about in the bedroom."

"Finn. You don't understand."

"I do, Oscar. Believe me, I do."

"Stacey doesn't want a relationship," Jackson adds.

"He's right. She doesn't want to get married or have kids." Evan and Christian look shocked. "She's wired differently than other girls. We call what we have non-monogamously loyal. And that's what we want. It may not be what you all want, and that's fine. Please stop trying to push us together. We're happy. Things might change, or they might stay the same. I have no idea what the future holds, whatever it is, it's between us."

"I'm sorry, man. I thought you needed a push like Evan and Christian did." I shake my head. "I won't butt in anymore."

"Thanks. I hear enough about it at home from Isla. She loves Stacey and keeps pressuring us to be together." Finn nods in agreement.

"Okay, enough of the gossip, ladies. We're fucking men," Zander yells.

16

OSCAR

We've got back from Christian and Vanessa's bachelor and bachelorette party in Monaco. It was wild. We all had the best times. Christian wanted a James Bond theme party. Nate let us borrow his super yacht moored off the South of France. It was basically a floating Paradise Club that we got to stay on for a couple of nights, women catering to our every whim. Nate had even set up this Sex Menu that you could request a blow job wake-up call. Of course, I had to try it. Best idea ever. I ordered one every morning to alleviate the morning wood.

We got to gamble in a private high-roller's room, where I lost a shitload of money. I have no idea how to play blackjack, it sure as hell was fun. The girls later on that night met us at the casino, crashing the bachelor party. A tiny brunette caught Axel's eye, Vanessa's friend, Olivia. She's loaning them her castle for their wedding. She's royal.

Nate took us to his club in Monaco to end the night. The couples left earlier, leaving us singles to have some fun. Nate and Camryn, Vanessa's wedding planner, disappeared because they had 'work' to do. Which I find fishy, that could be because of how my mind works. Stacey and I didn't stick around for long because, if I'm honest, I was horny as hell, and she had been teasing me all night.

There's a knock at our door. Who could it be? Jackson is here with us. He's sitting right in front of Stacey, who is bent over a desk. Her arms are tied to the front legs, and her legs are tied and spread apart attached to the back legs. Light pink marks mar her peachy backside as she watches Jackson get a blow job from a stunning blonde. I move away from the scene and open the door. Axel is standing there.

"Is everything okay?"

"Yes, of course. Sorry to interrupt." *He looks over my shoulder.* "I have a favor to ask," *Axel explains to me about Olivia, the beautiful brunette we met earlier in the night. She's showing the same tendencies as Stacey was and is very curious for more. He asked if we'd be willing to help him out. Of course, I agreed, as he has done for me.*

"She's in the shower," *Axel tells Stacey, who gives us a thumbs up. Axel and I nervously wait for the girls to return.*

"You have never shared a girl you're interested in before," *I mention to Axel.*

"I've just met her tonight. Don't get carried away," *he says defensively. First time Axel has ever been defensive over a girl. It could get interesting tonight.*

"Ladies?" *Axel questions. Olivia looks utterly terrified. Stacey takes her hand, which visibly steadies her. There's a knock at the door, and Jackson joins us.* "Liv, this is all who will be present in the room." *He reassures her.* "I thought it might relax you to know who was here first, then we could work up to your top fantasy." *Olivia's cheeks burn bright, she smiles at him.* "Good. Are you okay with who I have chosen?" *Olivia looks over at Jackson and me, those chocolate eyes assessing us. She nods.* "And are you okay with Stacey?" *Olivia quickly nods her head.*

"I think we should start with this, for nerves." I pull out the bottle of tequila Jackson brought over. I stalk over to where Olivia is frozen to the spot, my eyes moving between her and Stacey, who understands exactly what I'm doing, moving behind her. "Open up." She obeys easily, and I pour the cool liquid into her mouth. "It will help you relax." Giving her a reassuring smile, I do the same. Stacey's fingers run up and down Olivia's arms, making her shiver. "Open." Olivia opens her mouth again, and I give her another shot. The way she hasn't moved, if she wants to get past her fear, a little bit of alcoholic courage goes a long way. Stacey's lips faintly kiss Olivia's neck while her hands roam over her body. Axel takes the bottle from my hand and takes a sip. Olivia's eyes follow him. Jackson moves around to the other side and takes a sip.

"Would you like one more?" he asks Olivia.

"Yes, please." Her voice sounds breathless. Stacey's hands are doing their job, and Olivia is relaxing. Jackson places the bottle back onto the table, and she now has our full attention. Those chocolate eyes bounce between us, slight panic clouds them, some internal conversation she's been having with herself resolves, and she turns her back to us and kisses Stacey, surprising the hell out of Stacey and us. It doesn't take long for the kiss to turn from awkward to hot. They both lose themselves in the kiss, which is a beautiful thing to watch.

"You okay?" Stacey asks as they pull apart.

"Tequila makes me giggly," Olivia tells her. The tips of her ears are red hot, and Stacey smiles at her.

"Follow me." Taking her hand and leading her to the four-poster bed, Stacey touches a panel on the wall, and the bed disappears. She pulls down a padded table from underneath the bed. "Do you trust me?" she asks when she sees Olivia panic. Stacey leans in and kisses Olivia again, her fingers finding the thin straps of her dress and start to pull it down. "Are you okay?" she asks Olivia when she notices her stiffen.

"Sorry, surprised, that's all."

"Axel, maybe you would like to do the honors," Stacey suggests, as she lets her fingers graze over Olivia's hardened nipples.

"You did good, little one." He kisses her forehead as she joins Jackson and me.

"I promise you, Liv, nothing bad will happen to you. I'll make sure of it," Axel tells Olivia. "Now, put your hands on the table." She follows his instruction, placing her hands on the table's soft leather. He kicks her legs wider, her dress exposing her bottom in the process.

"Perfect," Jackson mumbles.

"That ass would look amazing with a shade of pink to it," I add. Olivia gasps at my suggestion.

"Do not move, Liv," Axel commands. "No matter what, don't move. Nothing but pleasure is about to happen, even if there's a tiny bit of pain with it." She flinches at the word 'pain.' "Stacey," Axel calls out. "She will need this."

"What's that?" Olivia asks.

"A blindfold."

"Oh," Olivia replies. Axel whispers reassurance into Olivia's ear and steps away. He nods to me to begin. I take the riding crop and ever so gently start to spank her with it, working her up until I can see her pussy glisten, whispering words of encouragement as she takes each one without moving. She's such a good girl. I look over and realize how turned-on Stacey has been, watching me spank Olivia, that she has fallen to her knees and is sucking Jackson. She's such a good girl too.

Axel places a hand on my shoulder, indicating enough. I step away. My dick is tenting against my tuxedo pants. Axel runs a reassuring hand over Olivia's pink backside, teasing her pussy with each glide until his fingers are sinking into her. Olivia lets out a groan. Axel moves her to a standing position, then shucks off the dress she's still wearing, exposing her beautiful body to the room. Axel kisses her as he picks her up and places her back onto the padded table. He repositions her, and her chest is moving quickly now that her nerves have kicked back in.

Axel asks if she's okay, and she tells him she is. He pushes her legs apart and places her ankles in the restraints making her gasp. He asks her to test them, which she does, and they are perfect. I've undressed, ready and willing. Jackson is slowly undressing while Stacey is kept occupied on her knees. My hand reaches out and caresses her hair, letting her know how pleased I am with her.

My attention is pulled back to the scene set out before me. I tilt my head in Axel's direction, silently asking him if I'm able to sample. He nods, and I move between Olivia's legs, a beautiful, glistening pink pussy spread out before me. I let my fingers trail over her creamy skin, watching as she arches ever so softly against my touch and arching further as they sink inside her. There's movement beside me, and I notice it's Stacey, who links her fingers with Olivia, giving her some moral support. Jackson has joined us, too, standing on the other side of Olivia. He takes her hand and wraps it around his wet dick. She lets out a startled gasp, it soon turns to a smile as she relaxes.

Axel moves to her head and watches the scene before him. Stacey is moving her hand all over Olivia's body. She's so turned on, my fingers move easily. I curl my fingers inside her, hitting those atomic nerves, making her scream. *That's it, princess. Give it to me.*

Axel places the tip of his dick at the entrance to Olivia's mouth, and she opens up wide for him. She's catching on rather quickly. Her hand is wrapped around Jackson's dick, my fingers are in her cunt, Axel is pushing his dick down her throat, and Stacey is… Stacey is riding Olivia's fingers, a tiny moan falling from her lips, the only indication that something is happening. Stacey is still wearing her slip. Axel tells her to remove it, so we can all see Olivia's fingers inside her. Olivia arches her back as I press my thumb over her clit.

"Yes, oh God, yes," Olivia hums around Axel's dick as she orgasms. Pulling my fingers from her, I offer them to Stacey, who licks them clean as I bury my face between Olivia's thighs, enjoying every last bit of her orgasm. Stacey comes moments later, Jackson grabbing Olivia's wet fingers and sucking them clean. Olivia wriggles against my mouth, her body arching as another orgasm comes crashing down upon her. I continue the assault with my mouth until she's begging me to stop. Moving away from Olivia, Stacey practically jumps me, kissing my wet face, savoring Olivia's essence.

"I want the blindfold off," Olivia calls from behind us. Stacey and I continue what we're doing while the conversations continue all around us.

"But I thought ..." Axel sounds concerned. Olivia chews her lip.

"I want to watch. I want to watch all of us." Axel slowly does as she asks and takes the blindfold away. Realization hits Olivia, and she tries to cover herself, the restraints stop her.

"No, no, no. There's no hiding... you wanted the blindfold off." She takes in a deep breath and relaxes. "Good girl, now let me unbuckle you." Axel unbuckles her. She's a little unsteady on her feet for a couple of moments.

"Maybe we should make it a little more comfortable then." Jackson smirks, looking over at Stacey jerking me off. What can I say, she's beyond horny.

"Good idea," Axel agrees, and they bring the bed back down. Axel tells Olivia to get on. He lays down beside her, pulling her on top of him, her peachy little ass pressed against his cock. "Sweetheart, concentrate and watch the show." He points to Stacey and me.

"Come on, little one, give her a show." Stacey gives me an

impish grin. Jackson joins us, bending Stacey in half, legs open, showing the bed her perfect pussy. "Open wide, little one. Show princess how to suck my cock." She purrs against me, taking all of me into her mouth. Stacey can be a bit of an exhibitionist, so she's giving Olivia the perfect show. Jackson drops to his knees behind her and buries his face between them. I wrap my hand around Stacey's ponytail and pull it tight, making sure Olivia can see exactly how much Stacey enjoys it. I watch as Axel fingers Olivia, his hands disappearing inside her, and how she's squirming in his arms. She likes it. She likes watching me fuck Stacey's face. Those chocolate eyes melting with each thrust into Stacey's mouth.

Then her attention is pulled toward Jackson, watching him sheath himself. He's watching her, too, as he enters Stacey. His hands are on her hips as he bucks into her, and Stacey goes wild as he enters her, her mouth sucking down on me harder. I'm closing my eyes because I need to last, Stacey is a fucking pro at sucking my dick.

"Shit, Stace, you know... I can't last when you do that." This makes me smile—saucy little devil.

"Fuck, Stace," Jackson curses as he comes, which sets off Olivia as she follows behind him.

"Such, a good girl. Now I think it's your turn. Get up," he commands her. Axel sheaths himself. "Bend over." She does as she's told, placing her hands on the edge of the bed. Then Axel sinks into her, and they both hiss at the contact. I pull myself from Stacey's mouth, tilt my head in Olivia's direction and silently ask her permission. She gives me a hungry smile and an enthusiastic nod. I know Jackson will look after her.

I kneel on the bed in front of Olivia and offer myself to her, and she takes my dick willingly. Her perfect little mouth takes me, not as far as Stacey can enough to make it feel good. I look over to where I left Jackson and Stacey, and she's riding his face. I knew she needed to finish. She looks so beautiful as she arches her back. Jackson is nothing more than a willing tongue as she controls the tempo, the pressure, and the depth.

A loud crack pulls me from them. Olivia practically chokes on my dick from the momentum, making me laugh. He does it again, and my eyes roll back inside my head. Olivia turns her head as she hears the noises Stacey is making in the corner. I love listening to Stacey come—it makes my balls tingle.

Axel increases his pace, cocking Olivia on my dick, he's too far gone to notice. His fingers dig into her creamy ass as he loses control, and to be fair, this is so rare that I can't help but watch. I think there's something about little miss Olivia that might have caught Axel's attention. I wrap Olivia's hair around my hand like I do Stacey, thrusting further into her mouth. Fuck, she feels so good.

"Your mouth is so fucking hot, Liv. Fuck," Oscar moans. "I'm about to come." He taps her on the shoulder. "If you don't want to swallow, then you better let me go." My dick falls from her mouth with a pop, and I come in my hand as Axel continues to fuck her until they both come.

I come out of the bathroom after cleaning up and see Axel and Olivia are having a moment. I grab my stuff and quietly leave them to it. They don't need us anymore.

"That was fucking hot," Jackson states.

"Can we keep her?" Stacey looks up at me, her arm wrapped around my waist. "She was fun."

"I think Axel might be smitten with her," I say as we walk along one of the corridors.

"I think you might be right," Stacey agrees.

Thank God for spank bank material as I come down the redhead's throat.

"That was…" The redhead wipes her face.

"Jackson," I call my head of security over who is with us at this party.

"This is Julia."

"It's Jennifer." She looks at me crossly.

"Oh yeah, sorry. Umm, this is Jackson. He's ex-special forces and a war hero. And he'd love to fuck you." Jackson's eyes widen, the redhead is sold.

"I owe you." I slap him on the back.

17

OSCAR

Being tied up with wedding preparations as all the girls have, I haven't seen much of Stacey since coming back from Monaco. It's all Vanessa and Isla talk about in the office, which we all steer clear of.

"Hey," I say, popping my head into my sister's office. She's been really funny since coming back from Monaco. I asked her what's going on, she tells me she's fine, which I know is universal for I'm pissed, I don't want to talk about it.

"Oh, hey." She looks up from her computer.

"Can I ask you something?" Isla crosses her arms and eyes me suspiciously.

"Depends on the question."

"Do you know if Stacey is around? I haven't seen her in a while." A huge smile lights up on my sister's face.

"Really, now." I roll my eyes at her.

"I knew this was a mistake asking you." I turn around to leave.

"Wait," she calls out. "I'm sorry. You've never asked me about a girl before." It's the truth—this is all new to me. "So, you're missing Stacey?"

"Missing isn't the right word."

"Fine. You're curious to see what she has been up to?"

"I'm not going to have a kumbaya about my feelings, Is."

"So you agree, you have feelings for her." Ugh, she's relentless.

"I like hanging out with her. I like seeing her. I like fucking her." Isla screws her face up at the last one.

"You don't want to be monogamous?"

"Would you rather me cheat on her instead?" Isla glares at me.

"Stacey tells me the same things. Seriously, you two are the same person. It's really frustrating." Good to know we're still on the same page about our non-relationship, then.

"I wanted to know if she was home tonight. Thought I might pop in and say hi." Isla grins.

"It's cute that you're still fighting what's happening between you both, to answer your question, she's home." I jump up out of my chair. "Hold up." She stops me. "She's not alone." A tiny little jab hits me in the stomach. What the hell was that?

"Oh. That's okay. I can catch up with her another time." Isla bursts out laughing.

"See, I knew it. I saw it on your face, you're jealous."

"No, I'm not."

"Yes, you are. The teeny tiniest bit." That wasn't jealousy. I refuse to believe it. "Fine. Be stubborn. It's only Jackson. Vanessa asked him to drop off something for the wedding at her apartment on his way home." The tension releases from my shoulders.

"Thank you. That wasn't so hard, was it?" Isla laughs.

"You shouldn't deny your feelings, Oscar, because when you finally do, it might be too late." I wave my sister goodbye, ignoring her. She has a white-picket-fence view of the world. That isn't Stacey and me.

There's a pep in my step as I make my way to Stacey's apartment incognito. Picking up a bottle of her favorite wine from the liquor store along the way, I enter her building. The smells of people's evening meals filter through the air. I take the stairs two at a time, которое brings me to her front door in a couple of bounds. My knuckles are poised to knock on the door, I stop.

Maybe I should surprise her and start the night off with a bit of role playing. We've done it once before, me surprising her in her apartment, forcing her to have sex, consensually, of course. It was so fucking hot. Pulling my keys from my jeans pocket, I insert it into the hole and turn it ever so quietly. The television is on, so she's home, which is good. I creep in and close the door behind me. Her apartment is empty. She might be in the shower. Even better. I place the bottle of wine on the kitchen counter and notice two glasses of half-drunk red wine. Isla did say that Jackson popped in, so maybe she offered him a glass. Moving through the living room, I make my way to her bedroom. Her door is open.

Looking around the corner, I wasn't prepared for what I saw —Stacey arching her back as she rides Jackson's dick. A stabbing pain hits me in the chest. I blink a couple of times, not really believing what I'm seeing. Jackson's fingers grip her hips as she bucks against him.

"Yes, oh yes," she cries out.

"You feel so fucking good," Jackson groans. Stacey leans over and kisses him. They lose themselves in the kiss, so much so that Jackson rolls them over and moves them into another position. I… I stand there like an idiot, feeling utterly confused and betrayed.

"Oscar," Stacey screams, noticing me there. Jackson stops mid-thrust and looks over at me, and an oh-fuck look crosses his face.

"I…" Not sure what to say, I quickly turn and walk out of her bedroom.

"Oscar." Stacey runs out from the bedroom with a t-shirt on.

"Hey." She grabs my arm. "I didn't know you were coming over."

"Surprise." Sarcasm is lacing my tone. Her eyes widen at it.

"You sound angry at me." Folding her arms across her chest.

"Why would I be angry, Stace? You're fucking one of my friends." Her mouth falls open.

"One that you have watched me fuck many a time." Jackson appears at the doorway fully dressed. He stands behind Stacey, placing a reassuring hand on her hip. I see red and lunge at him. Stacey screams as I push him up against the wall.

"Go on. Hit me if it makes you feel better," Jackson goads me.

"Oscar." Stacey tries to pull me away from him, she can't move me. She begins to slap me hard across the back until I finally let him go.

"What the fuck do you think you're doing?" Stacey screams at me. "How fucking dare you!" Why is she pissed at me? I'm the one who busted her with another man. Did I? I mean, we aren't in a relationship. I've been fucking other women too. Last weekend, I let some redhead blow me at a party. I rake my fingers through my hair in frustration.

"Fuck." Stacey lays a hand on my arm.

"Sit down, Oscar. Please. Let's talk about this." She gives me a sad smile. I nod and take a seat, hanging my head in my hands. "Don't think you're going anywhere," Stacey tells Jackson. "You can sit too." Pointing to the chair opposite me, he does as he's told and sits. "Now, let me pour us some wine and talk like civilized adults. Okay?" Jackson and I nod.

"Now." Stacey takes a seat in front of us both. "Let me start with saying, Oscar, I'm so sorry that you walked in on us like that." She reaches out and touches my knee. "What you saw wasn't planned." She looks over at Jackson, who nods his head. "We had a couple of glasses of wine. It had been a stressful day." She should've contacted me to help destress her.

"I offered her a massage," Jackson confesses.

"Gee, as if that wasn't a line." I sneer at him. He takes a sip of his red wine, ignoring my tone.

"It started out as a massage." I stare at the floor. Stacey gets up and sits beside me. "Oscar, will you look at me, please?" Letting out a heavy sigh, I look up at her. "It was me who made the first move, not him." That stabbing feeling hits me again. "I told him that I didn't think you would care if we had some fun together. I had no idea that you would." How could she know that I'd act like this? I didn't even know I would react as I did. "I'm sorry I hurt you." She grabs my hand and links it with hers.

"This… this feeling is really foreign to me… seeing you with him outside of the club. I don't know… it felt… weird."

"I'm sorry," Jackson apologizes, and I accept it. "I might go and leave you guys to it." Stacey stands up and walks him to the door. They have a whispered conversation before he leaves. Once the door closes, Stacey presses her forehead against the wood, sucking in a deep breath. Does she like him? It hadn't occurred to me that she might be hanging out with other people. I know she dates, I didn't know she'd have a close friendship with someone else in the group like she does me.

Stacey walks back into the kitchen and pours herself another wine.

"Do you like him?" I ask the question, not sure I want to hear the answer.

"Jackson's nice." That doesn't really answer it for me.

"No. I mean, do you want to have a relationship with him like you do me?" Stacey comes back over to the couch and sits beside me.

"Are you asking me to choose between you and Jackson?" Am I? Maybe. I don't know. It's confusing as fuck.

"Maybe." She leans back against the couch and stares at me.

"When was the last time you messed around with someone outside of the club?"

"Last weekend at some party, a girl gave me a blow job. It wasn't very good because I had to think about Monaco to get off." *Maybe that was too much honesty, Oscar.*

"How many since Monaco?"

"None. Except for that girl. And you." I brace myself for her response.

"None, except for tonight." Why do I feel relieved? "What about at the club?"

"I haven't' been because you weren't with me," I admit, making her smile.

"Me either," I agree, making me smile. I take her hand in mine and kiss her knuckles. "We're a fucked-up pair, aren't we?" We chuckle. She rests her head on my shoulder. "I had no idea that what happened tonight would upset you."

"I know, Stace." I run my thumb over her hand. "I didn't think it would upset me, either." We sit in silence, absorbing the conversation.

"I'm guessing we might have to update the rules."

"Yeah? Such as…"

"Dare I say it…" She looks over at me and smiles. "Outside the club, we're exclusive, inside we only play together." My chest tightens in a good way.

"So you would be happy to give up dating to hang out with me?"

"The same question could be asked of you? Could you give up the groupies for me?" Honestly, I think it's a no-brainer.

"Yes." Her eyes widen. "As long as we're still allowed to play with others at the club." I reiterate making sure that's still the agreement. She grins.

"Of course. I don't think either of us would like to give that up." Reaching over, I pick her up and deposit her in my lap, and she straddles me. My hands cup her face.

"You're the first girl I have ever wanted to try more with."

"You're the first guy I have wanted to try more with." Leaning forward, I give her a chaste kiss.

"I have to know, what happened tonight? I mean, the massage story seems like a convenient excuse." Stacey rolls her eyes at me.

"It was a convenient excuse for me."

"So, you wanted him?"

"Yes. I haven't had sex since Monaco, and I've been flat out with work and this wedding, and I needed some stress relief. Jackson dropped in. I offered him some wine. He told me I looked stressed. I said I'd kill for a massage, and then you walked in." My dick twitches to life. How is my dick responding to what I saw earlier when I had such a negative reaction to begin with? Feelings are confusing.

"I need details, Stacey." She raises a brow at me.

"Are you sure? Because you didn't like it when it was happening." Grabbing her hand and placing it on my dick.

"He wants to hear more."

"Before I do. I need to tell you something." I don't know if my feelings can handle any more surprises. "It was always you, Oscar. You're the one I want to hang out with, spend my time with, explore this world with." My stomach churns as if a million butterflies have taken refuge in there. "I needed you to know that. Jackson was the person who happened to be here tonight in my moment of weakness. I won't play with him at the club anymore." A frown creases my brow.

"From this moment onward is what counts. Agreed?" Because it's the truth. I can't blame Stacey or Jackson for what happened tonight because I haven't been honest with Stacey about how I feel toward her. She can't read my mind, I'll tell Jackson the new rules in the morning.

"Agreed. But…" Huh. There shouldn't be a but in this conversation. "Let's not tell our friends we're semi-exclusive.

You know Isla will try to have us married off within the month." She's right.

"Or the boys will be asking me to join Dad club" A cold shiver races through my body, making us both laugh. "What's going on between us stays between us."

18

STACEY

I've never been to England before. The rolling green hills, the gray skies, and the history are amazing. We're staying at Olivia's family estate in the north of the country. Her home borders Scotland, and there's nothing but green all around. There's a charming little village not far from the castle that looks like it stepped out of the pages of a storybook. Her family owns that too.

Once we arrived, Olivia disappeared. I guess she's busy getting everything sorted for Vanessa and Christian's wedding, plus Christmas there. Last year, I caught up with my family for Christmas, then flew back for the wedding. I'm missing Christmas with them this year, I'll be flying home after New Year's for a two-week visit.

Oscar isn't really happy about it, he has to go to New York with Finn to lock in a new location for Dirty Texas Records. Otherwise, he'd have come with me. I told him we weren't quite ready to meet the parents, even though I've met his multiple times. I guess that's different because I met them before we ever got serious.

Things between us have gone from strength to strength. We

still hang out like we used to and still have fun at The Paradise Club together, even if Axel has been missing in action since Monaco. I told Oscar it was because he fell for Olivia, he thinks that's bullshit.

Axel is even worse than him when it comes to commitment. None of us have seen him at the club, and he practically lived there before Monaco. Oscar isn't convinced.

Isla's been acting weird as well. I thought that maybe she was upset with me because she might have found out about my indiscretion with Jackson, thankfully it wasn't me. Something happened with Finn in Monaco, and she doesn't want to talk about it. It has me a little worried, they have been hot and cold with each other most of their life. Maybe this is all they know.

Speaking of Jackson, he and Oscar are cool now. He even invited him to play with us one night to show him that everything was forgiven. I thought it was a terrible idea because of how he reacted that night, I had nothing to worry about. Oscar was back to his usual self, especially when I bought him two gifts to help him that night—his fantasy twins. He thanked me long and hard after that present. I'm such a good non-girlfriend.

We had an amazing welcome dinner prepared by Sienna's friend, Sebastien Ramirez. I've met him a few times over the years when we used to visit Yvette, his sister, in Barcelona and Paris, shopping for Sienna's old boutique. He's one of the hottest chefs in the world at the moment. The boys have retreated to the games room where they play pool and drink whiskey, basically pretending they are lords of the manor. We girls have retired to the parlor, where we're roasting marshmallows around the fireplace, sipping hot chocolate in our winter pajamas, and watching the snow fall outside.

"I still can't believe it," Derrick says to Camryn, who is the wedding planner and one of Vanessa's closest friends. She found out her boyfriend was cheating on her by organizing his engagement party. Brutal.

"You and me both." Camryn weakly smiles at him.

"And he seriously had no idea you were organizing it?" Sienna asks. Camryn shakes her head.

"His father had set it all up," Kimberly, her business partner, explains. "Camryn has been busy with organizing your wedding and other things, so I took the initial call. If I had known, I'd never have done it."

"At least it was the talk of the town for being the best engagement party of the year. So, I guess it kind of backfired because we're getting so much business off his party." Camryn smiles. That's pretty good revenge.

"Karma," Isla suggests.

"I know it might be too soon, but what eligible bachelors are coming to this wedding?" Derrick asks.

"Derrick…" Camryn jokingly warns him.

"I'm sorry, Cammie, I want to know. It's not all about you," Derrick tells her. "We have the Sons of Brooklyn boys," Derrick rattles off.

"Except Blake," Charlotte whispers.

"Yes, yes, sweetie, he's all yours." Derrick smiles.

"And we only have Axel left in Dirty Texas, then again, if the serious fuck-me eyes he was throwing Olivia's way was any indication, then probably not." I knew it. I want to shout, but sip my hot chocolate instead. Nothing gets past Derrick. I look over to where Olivia is sitting. She's staying really quiet, her cheeks look awfully flushed. "What about Nate? You know you would be in for a good time with him. I bet he's kinky as fuck," Derrick speculates.

"I bet he's a playboy. He looks like one." Sienna rolls her eyes.

"The California Bros. boys are coming as well," Isla adds.

"So they will all be free unless Isla is hooking up with Wes on the sly." Derrick looks at Isla, who stays quiet. How the hell does Derrick know all the tea? "Wait…" Derrick picks up on her non-communication. "You've told us that nothing has happened between Wes and you?"

"You know I'm a hot mess," she groans.

"Isla." Derrick's voice lowers. "What's going on?"

"Fine, I was never going to tell you guys because… well, because of your interrogating."

"I thought you didn't like Wes like that?" Vanessa asks.

"I don't, I can still appreciate a hot-as-fuck guy, plus we're friends."

"Friends who obviously fuck," Derrick adds.

Isla rolls her eyes at him. "True, we have taken our friendship to a different level."

"Why?" Sienna asks.

"We got drunk one night, and one thing led to another."

"Issy, you aren't telling us all the juicy stuff," Derrick adds.

"Fine, he had broken up with this skank he was seeing, who worked in his bar. I told him it was a stupid idea to hook up with his staff, you know men, they are mesmerized by boobs." So true. "Anyway, he caught her stealing from the till, and he also found out she had a boyfriend who she liked to bang on the bar counters after hours."

"That sucks," Ivy, Camryn's sister and Olivia's best friend, comments.

"Sure does. He came over and told me all about it, and I decided I'd cheer him up."

"By using your pussy. Good idea." Derrick laughs.

"It wasn't like that." Isla makes a face at Derrick. "We got drunk, and one thing led to another, and we slept together."

"Finn is going to be pissed if he finds out," I tell her. That's the one thing I keep from Oscar in our relationship—the secret I know about Finn and Isla.

"Whatever, remember I'm on a Finn detox, so it doesn't matter." I know it does to her. She's not as tough as she appears sometimes. "Seriously, Isla, how the hell do you get yourself into such predicaments?" Vanessa chuckles, and Isla's shoulders sag.

"I know. I'm a hot mess. I'm kind of a disaster, and I have no idea why?" Isla states, poking fun at herself, making the group giggle.

"Umm, it starts and ends with your feelings for Finn," I tell her.

"Urgh, my feelings. Feelings get in the way and are annoying." She lets out a heavy sigh. "Look, Finn is an idiot, so am I." She looks around the room, giving us all a sad smile. "I know that the chances of Finn and I being together are slim. I know you all think I'm naïve, things between us are a little more complicated than what looks like an old teenage crush." She looks defeated. "I now know I'm not enough for Finn," she says sadly. "We've had this thing between us going for so long, it has kind of become normal. I've tried to fight it, we keep falling back into old patterns. I need it to stop."

My heart is breaking for her at the moment. Finn is a dick.

"Maybe it's time for a change," Charlotte tells her. "Like moving out of the home you share with Oscar." That's probably a good idea.

"I haven't really lived on my own," Isla responds.

"Maybe a new job as well," Charlotte adds.

Isla stills. "You mean, leave Dirty Texas?"

"Yeah, you have worked there your entire adult life. You're with them twenty-four seven. I've known you most of my life, Isla, and don't forget I'm the one who saw the two of you as kids. I know I was young, I had eyes. Is being the band's assistant always what you wanted to do?"

Wow, we're going deep tonight. Maybe it's the fresh English air, making everyone see life a little clearer.

"I think Charlotte is being Dr. Phil." Derrick smirks.

"I think she is…" Isla pauses, "…I kind of think she might be right."

"I am?" Charlotte seems shocked, and I'm right there with her.

"Yeah, all my life I've been at the boys' beck and call. Maybe it's time I find myself, find out what I want outside of Dirty Texas."

"Well, we need help," Sienna adds. I agree, especially with Sienna having another baby.

"That sounds awesome, maybe I need to move further away from Finn. You know, instead of next door." Boo, she's probably right.

"Sebastien needs an assistant. He's so busy and needs someone he can trust," Yvette suggests.

"Working with Sebastien?"

"Yeah, you would be based in Europe, so that's pretty far from Finn."

"And you think he'd hire me? I mean, I don't know anything about food or chefs or Europe."

Isla seems a little excited about this idea. Oscar is going to lose his mind. Fuck. I hate being stuck in the middle of those two —they both have my loyalty.

"I'm pretty sure working for Dirty Texas all these years, you're way over-qualified for him." Yvette chuckles.

Isla turns to Vanessa. "Am I fucking things up for you and Dirty Texas Records if I think about leaving? I mean, you're going to be having a baby soon, and…"

"Isla, don't worry about me, I can find a replacement. I want you to be certain this is the right thing for you to do. Leaving Dirty Texas? Leaving Finn?"

"We know someone who can take over the PR for Dirty Texas," Camryn adds.

"Who?" Vanessa asks.

"Harper. I don't know why I didn't think of it sooner, she'd be kind of perfect. She's coming to the wedding, so you could talk to her about it?"

Apparently, this Harper girl runs a successful PR firm in New York, and she's friends with Camryn and Kimberly, the wedding planners. She's heir to the Rose's Hotel chain, and her brother, Sam, is actually helping the boys find Dirty Texas new offices in New York. This upper-crust world is truly a small place. Everyone knows everyone.

"She could even work from New York. I know the boys are looking at adding an East Coast office to the mix next year," Camryn adds.

"I think that would work, depends on what the boys say," Vanessa tells her.

"So, does that mean Isla can go on an adventure with sexy Sebastien?" Derrick asks.

"I can't see why not. I don't think Finn or Oscar will like it, I think Isla deserves a break from all things Dirty Texas that she has been dealing with over the years. Why not have a change? Maybe then Finn might realize what he has when Isla is not around anymore," Vanessa reassures her.

"This is kind of crazy, though?" Isla looks around at everyone.

"Yes, you need a new adventure," Stacey tells her.

"Forget Finn and start living," Derrick adds.

"This is your time now, no regrets. This is about you, not them anymore," Charlotte gives her a pep talk.

"Okay, well, if Sebastien is okay with it, then, yeah, I think it's time for a new adventure."

We all cheer with our hot chocolates. I'm not looking forward to Oscar and Finn finding out.

19
STACEY

We've had the rehearsal dinner for Vanessa and Christian, and we've continued celebrating in the dining hall. Everyone else has retired. We've all had one too many glasses of champagne, we're all in a jovial mood. Isla stands and taps a knife against the crystal glass. *Tap, tap, tap.* This silences the room.

"I have an announcement to make." Reaching under the table, I grab Oscar's hand and entwine our fingers together because I know what's about to happen. "For the past ten years, I have been working with the amazing guys of Dirty Texas." She looks out at everyone, and her hands are shaking. "It's been a crazy rollercoaster ride, and I have loved every moment of it…" Oscar squeezes my hand. I'm suspecting he knows something is about to happen. "But… I have decided to pursue a new adventure." Shock hits the room. Oscar stills beside me. My thumb rubs his hand, hopefully soothing him. "I'm going to be Sebastien's new assistant."

Oscar doesn't move. I look over at him, and he's frozen, absorbing the information. Looking over, I see the devastation that's written all over Finn's face. He looks crushed, he knows he can't say anything because that will out him to Oscar, and he won't risk that.

"I'm so happy for you." Derrick is the first to congratulate Isla, which, in turn, prompts the rest of the room to do so too. One by one, everyone hugs her, pats her on the back, and thanks her for always being there for them, Oscar still hasn't moved.

"Are you okay?" I lean over to him.

"I think so." Oscar slowly stands up and makes his way over to where Isla is standing. The room has gone silent. All eyes are on them at this moment. Please don't lose it, Oscar, please. Oscar then surprises everyone and pulls his sister into a tight hug. Tears begin to well in Isla's eyes.

"If this is what you want, Is, I'll support you." She breaks down in his arms, the stress of telling him evident. She hugs him tightly again. I'm so proud of him at this moment. "I'm going to miss you. You know. We've been side by side for so many years."

"I know." She sniffles. "That's why I have to do this." He kisses her forehead.

"I'll support you no matter what. You know you can always talk to me. I had no idea you were so unhappy." Isla's face softens at her brother's concern.

"You're pretty overprotective." Oscar huffs, which makes us all laugh because it's the truth.

"I know. Go see the world. Enjoy life. Have some fun. Find yourself." They hug again, and now I can breathe a sigh of relief. I'm going to show him how proud I am at how he handled this situation tonight when we get back to our room. Oscar then turns and points directly at Sebastien.

"Hands off my sister." Ah, and there he is. Sebastien fidgets in his chair uncomfortably nods in agreement.

"Oscar!" Isla yells at her brother. "You can't talk to my new boss like that." Isla looks over to where Sebastien is sitting and mouths, 'Sorry.'

"Congrats," Finn mumbles. Isla looks over, giving him a small smile before turning back to the group. Finn looks devastated. Something has happened between them. Did this trigger her need to get out of town? Derrick and Finn are whisper-yelling between each other. Finn looks angry and hurt. Whatever is going on between them, Derrick looks pissed. He eventually turns his back on Finn and starts talking to someone else. I feel for Finn at this moment. Something has happened. He jolts up quickly, his chair scraping the floor, echoing throughout the room and makes everyone look up.

"I need my beauty sleep, guys. Got to look fresh for the wedding tomorrow." He plasters a big smile on his face, his eyes tell the real story. People wave him goodbye, and Isla doesn't even acknowledge his leaving, then he rushes out of the room. I follow after him. No one else seems to care, I do.

"Finn," I call down the corridor. He stops and turns around. His eyes are bloodshot, and his face is wet. I rush to him and pull him into a big hug. He wraps his long arms around me and cries.

"I don't know what's going on, but please let me help." He shakes his head. The man looks broken. I grab his hand and pull him into one of the rooms off to the side of the hallway. It looks like an office of some sort.

"Sit." I point to one of the old leather chairs. "Tell me what's going on. I know something has happened between you and Isla. I think in Monaco." His eyes widen. Bingo. "She won't tell me a thing, I did notice she's been a little distant with you." Finn leans forward and rubs his face with his hands.

"I can't tell you." He looks up at me.

"Why? Because of Oscar?" He nods. It's something he doesn't want me to tell Oscar about.

"You know Isla confides in me about you?" This surprises him. "I know pretty much everything. Don't you think Oscar would've kicked your ass by now if I had told him?" He nods in agreement. "If it's something important, Finn, I promise I won't tell him. It looks like you could use someone in your corner right about now." I tap his knee.

"Please, Stace. I mean it. Please don't say anything to Oscar. I know he'd murder me." He's a little dramatic, I get what he's saying.

"I'm guessing you know everything up until Monaco." I nod my head. "While you guys were having fun at The Paradise Club, so were Isla and I." Didn't need to be a detective to work that out. "She knows that we all have our kinks, and she seemed down with exploring things." This surprises me, everyone is entitled to getting a little crazy sometimes. "I took her to the room."

"Oh, Finn."

"I know. It was stupid. It freaked her out." The room is basically one massive orgy. You have no idea who is touching or fucking you. The lights flash every couple of minutes, and all you see are bodies. It's so much fun, not really for the inexperienced. "That was the beginning of the end between us." His shoulders slump in defeat. "Because what happened next really put the nail in the coffin." Oh no. "I have a secret, Stacey. A secret no one really knows about." This sounds serious.

"Whatever it is, Finn. It won't change the way I see you. I promise." I reach out, holding his hand and reassure him that I'm there for him because I think he feels very alone at this moment.

"Isla found out about it, and now I disgust her." Tears fall down his cheeks.

"Hey. No. Isla could never be disgusted with you. I mean, look at Oscar and me. We're together but screw around with other people, and that's her brother. You'd think she'd be disgusted over that, she's not. She doesn't get it, she's certainly not disgusted. Plus, Isla loves you." Finn shakes his head.

"Loved me. Past tense. I fucked up, Stace. I really fucked up."

"It might feel like that now, but …" He shakes his head.

"She's running halfway across the world to get away from me." See, I knew it. I knew something else had encouraged her to make this decision.

"It's going to be okay."

"She caught me in the shower with someone." She's caught him plenty of times before, so I don't understand how this time it would make her run. "It was a man." Oh. My eyes widen. Oh. Wow. I had no idea.

"Are you gay?" Is that why he's not into her? Finn shakes his head.

"I'm like you, Stace. I like playing with the opposite sex, I don't want to date them."

Oh. I see. I know I shouldn't be thinking this now because Finn is so devastated, but Finn with a man is all kinds of hot. Standing up, I walk over and hug him. I get now why Isla has been so indifferent toward Finn. She probably feels like a fool, pining after this man for so many years and then realizing he's not into her because she doesn't have the right bits.

"You need to talk to her, Finn. Explain the situation. I know it's going to be hard, you can't let her go to Paris with all this hanging over you."

"She really hates me, Stacey."

"It's not hatred, Finn. I honestly think she's embarrassed. She's pined after you for so long. You give her hope each time you're together. Then she stumbled upon you with a man. She's probably second-guessing everything you have ever had. She's probably really confused." Finn nods, his head in understanding. "Talk to her. Get it all out in the open, and whatever happens, happens."

"You're right." At least he doesn't look as defeated. "Thank you for listening." He gives me another hug. "Can I say this? I like you and Oscar together. I've never seen him happier."

"Aw. Thank you. We may not be conventional, but it works."

I walk Finn out of the office, and he heads back up to his room.

"There you are." Oscar surprises me. My heart almost jumps out of my chest.

"What were you and Finn doing?" He asks, wrapping his arms around me.

"He seemed upset over Isla leaving, so I wanted to check on him." Oscar's ice-blue eyes narrow in on me.

"Didn't think he'd care?" Oh, Oscar Eriksen is digging for gossip.

"Well, he does." Oscar pulls me tighter into him.

"I'm not blind, Stace. I know they've hooked up in the past." My eyes widening, a little shocked because they both have no idea. "I think it will be good for them both to have time apart. I want Isla to be happy."

"And you think that's far enough away from Finn?"

"Yes. He can't give her what she wants or needs." Does Oscar know? He must. They are best friends.

"Come on. Let's forget about our friends' problems, and let me take you to bed." I distract him with my lips.

20

OSCAR

I'm picking Stacey up from LAX Airport. She's been in Australia for two weeks with her family, while I've been in New York with Finn looking for new digs for Dirty Texas Records. I've missed her so badly, especially going out in New York with Finn and Sam, who's a friend of Nate's and has been helping us find commercial space while in New York. His family owns hotels or something. He seems like a nice guy.

He took us out to some clubs, honestly, I wasn't interested, especially not in the women who wanted to get close with me. None of them could compare to Stacey. I graciously palmed them off to Finn and Sam, and most nights, I left them to it and went home. Who the hell have I become? Christian did warn me that one day a woman would turn my life upside down and that no one else would matter except her. Fuck. I'm at that point. Stacey has utterly pussy-whipped me. And I don't even care. Not even the slightest.

I patiently wait my turn in line with everyone else. Then I see her. Her blonde hair is pulled up into a ponytail, and she's dressed in leggings and a long sweater. She's texting on her phone. I honk my horn which gets her attention, and when she sees it's me, her whole face lights up. I don't dare get out, I probably look like a dick, I don't want anyone to see us. She opens the back door to my truck, throws her suitcase into the back, and closes it again. She jumps into the passenger seat and gives me a long kiss, horns honk behind us, pulling us from the moment. Thankfully, my windows are tinted, and no one saw what happened. Taking her hand in mine, I merge back into traffic and straight into a traffic jam.

"It's so good to be back in LA," she jokes.

"Not the best welcome home." I grin. Our fingers staying locked together. "I missed you."

"I missed you too. It didn't look like you were very lonely?" Raising a brow at me. Shit, is she pissed about the paparazzi photos because we spoke about it on the phone when I found out about them? They were nothing serious, just photos of girls all around us.

"Babe, I told you I was so sorry about that. I…" Stacey bursts out laughing.

"Oscar," I turn and look over at her. "I'm playing with you." She gives me a blinding smile. Oh, thank God. I thought I was about to be sick over it all. "Oh, babe. You were seriously worried about those photos, weren't you? I can see it on your face."

"I didn't want you to think that I was doing something I wasn't." I squeezed her hand.

"Oscar, I trust you. I'm sorry I made a really bad joke about it." She kisses my knuckles. "Let me make it up to you when we get home, okay?" My dick twitches to life.

"I think I need to make it up to you." I look over her hungrily.

"I guess we're both going to be winners when we get home." Home. That has a nice ring to it. Then I realize she means her apartment; not my place.

"Hey, what's that face for?"

"When you said home, I automatically assumed my place."

"It's your home."

"I kind of thought it was ours at that moment." She looks over at me, surprised. "I don't know if I want you going back to your apartment. I've missed you so much since you've been away. I kind of want you in my bed." Stacey tilts her head to the side as she stares at me.

"I can stay over if you want, we can't, you know, fuck on every surface in your home because Issy is there." She has a valid point.

"She leaves in two weeks."

"I guess we can christen your home properly then." I like the sound of that.

"Move in." The words fall out of my mouth.

"Wait. What?" Stacey seems surprised.

"When Isla leaves, I want you to move in with me." I've shocked her. I can see it on her face.

"But… I… we're about to start working together." We asked Stacey if she wouldn't mind working with us until we find a replacement for Issy. Sienna and Derrick's business has expanded twofold, and they have hired a heap of new staff, which means Stacey is delegating work now instead of doing it. Sienna will take over while Stacey is helping us, then when she goes on maternity leave, *again*, in six months, we'll have someone trained, and Stacey can go back and be boss while Sienna pops out another Wyld child.

"Don't you think working and living together might strain our relationship?"

"No."

"I only bought the apartment." Her apartment went on the market before Christmas, so she bought it, which means she was truly going to stay in LA. I always worried that she'd one day pack her bags and move back to Australia because I know how much she misses it.

"It's a great investment. You could rent it out."

"And you seriously don't think this is going to ruin what we have? You're that confident?" Okay. Maybe I'm not that confident, all I do know is that I want her with me.

"These last two weeks have got me thinking about us, in a good way," I say, reassuring her. "Made me realize that what we have is something good." She smiles at me. "Made me think more about the future and what I want." She squeezes my hand. "I mean, you and I have been together for a year now."

"A year?" she questions me.

"Sienna and Evan's wedding is the first time we hooked up, and that was a year ago," I remind her. She nods her head. Honestly, it doesn't feel that long. "Seeing Evan and Christian happy with settling down and moving on to the next phase of their life has kind of shown me that I shouldn't be scared of committing to someone." Stacey's eyes well up. "I know we'll never be as traditional as those guys nor do we want to be, but… I do see the appeal with having someone to share things with both in and out of the bedroom." I wink at her.

"Oscar." She's crying. Oh no. I've made her cry.

"Are they happy tears?" I'm feeling a little worried.

"They are."

"Does that mean you might think about it?"

"I don't need to think about it." My stomach sinks. I knew it. I pushed her too far. "I'm all in." Huh? What? "I'm willing to take a chance on us."

"You are?" There's a slight surprise to my tone. She kisses my knuckles. "Fuck, I love you." Oh, shit. The words tumbled out without me even thinking about it. It's too much. I've come on way too strong. She kisses my knuckles again.

"I love you, too, Oscar."

She loves me.

She loves me.

She loves me.

I want to fist pump to the moon. "Hurry up and take me home, so I can make love to my man."

Her wish is my command.

I'm back at the airport this time, dropping my sister off.

"I'm going to miss you." I hug her on the sidewalk.

"I'm going to miss you too." Tears are falling down her cheeks.

"Stay safe. Call me any time." I don't want to let go of her.

"Oscar. You're crushing me," Isla mumbles against me.

"Sorry." I let her go. Isla and Stacey teary hug too.

"Look after him for me," Isla tells her.

"I will." Stacey places her arm around my waist.

"I guess I better go, love birds." She sighs, picking up her bags.

"Have so much fun," Stacey tells her.

"Not too much fun," I warn her. I don't like this Sebastien character—he's too good-looking and Latin. That's a winning combination to get women into his bed.

"Ignore him." Stacey slaps me on the chest. "He can't stop his big-brother mode." Isla waves us off and disappears into the airport. My heart hurts as I turn around and jump back into my truck.

"No, Oscar, you can't jump on the next plane to Paris." Stacey knows me so well.

"We could go for Valentine's Day. It would be totally romantic." Stacey glares at me. "Okay, fine. I promise I'll stop being overprotective."

21

STACEY

For the past five months, life for the Dirty Texas crew has been a whirlwind.

Let's start with Olivia and Axel—that has been some kind of telenovela romance. Olivia chose duty over love, and when it came to walking down the aisle, she couldn't. Plus, she found her sister in bed with her soon-to-be groom on her wedding day. Her sister announced she was pregnant with Eddie, Olivia's arranged groom's baby. *Scandalous, right?* Olivia decided enough was enough, and she jumped onto the first flight to LA, turning up on Axel's doorstep, declaring her love for him. Like something out of an epic romance movie.

Finn has been going wild, losing himself in endless hookups while utterly devastated by the European tabloid stories linking Isla and Sebastien together. I keep telling him it's not true. I left out the bit where she did accidentally sleep with him, but Finn won't listen. He wants to wallow in groupies. Each to their own, I guess.

Christian and Vanessa are gearing up for the twins' arrival. They announced over Christmas that they would be having twin girls. I pray for them every day.

Sienna and Evan found out they were having another boy, which, of course, Evan is happy about. His vision of a football team is slowly coming to life.

Oscar and I? Well, we have been going from strength to strength. I moved in the day Isla left. Oscar had my stuff ready to go. We spent the night christening every single surface of his home. It's a big home. We still occasionally play at The Paradise Club, not as much as we used to because Oscar's house is huge, and we keep finding new places to christen.

We've been working together for the past couple of months, and honestly, it's been fun. Mostly because he likes surprising me during the day for what he calls 'stress breaks,' which is basically us screwing around in our offices—discreetly, of course. Oscar is excited because Isla is coming back. Sebastien has been offered a television show and has a meeting with the network this week. If everything goes well, then Isla will be back in LA. I'm not so sure Isla is as happy as Oscar is to be back in America.

"Congratulations," I say, walking into the maternity suite to visit Sienna and Evan after the birth of their son, Levi. Handing Evan the bouquet of flowers, I kiss Sienna. "He's so cute," I gush, looking down at the little blue bundle.

"He's perfect, isn't he?" Sienna is glowing.

"Isla texted me. She's arrived."

"Can't wait to see her." Oscar puts his arm around my shoulders. Isla and Oscar have caught up via Skype most weeks. Oscar kept pressuring her to let him come over, she said she was too busy to entertain him. "Levi's pretty cute," Oscar whispers to me.

"Don't tell me you're getting clucky, Mr. Eriksen." He makes a gagging face. The creak of the suite door alerts us to more arrivals. The room falls silent when Isla walks in, hand in hand with Sebastien. All eyes are on them. What on earth is going on? Why is she wearing such a hideous dress? It's practically a kaftan, and she's swimming in it.

"What the fuck?" Finn says from across the room as Isla and Sebastien greet the new parents. His eyes zero in on their hand-holding. Shit. Are they together? Oscar is going to lose his mind in a second.

"Holy shit, you're pregnant," Derrick calls out, silencing the room. Isla and Sebastien freeze. She looks like a deer caught in headlights. Her face turns pale, and Sebastien looks mighty uncomfortable. Now that I look closer, she's pregnant and not a tiny bump. We're talking baby kicking around in there. Why the hell has she been hiding this?

"You're pregnant?" Oscar's voice rises as he takes a couple of steps toward Isla and Sebastien. I place my hand on his forearm. Now isn't the time for him to lose his shit. We're in the middle of the maternity ward. This is supposed to be a happy moment for them.

"You seriously thought you could disguise yourself in that hideous outfit?" Derrick is oblivious to the room, and now isn't the time for jokes.

"Sienna, Evan… congratulations," Sebastien says loudly, breaking the tension as he hands over a large bouquet of flowers to them.

"Issy, are you pregnant?" Oscar asks calmly as he moves closer to her.

"Yes," she whispers, a single tear falling down her cheek. Shit. She doesn't look happy about it.

"Excuse me." Finn bolts from the room. Shit. This is an epic cluster fuck.

"Why didn't you tell me?" Oscar sounds hurt and confused.

"Because…" Isla pauses for a moment to catch her breath. "Because I was ashamed. It was a one-night stand. A mistake."

"I'm still your brother," Oscar pleads.

"I know, I just…"

"Do Mom and Dad know?" Isla shakes her head. Oscar doesn't look happy.

"So you have kept this from all of us for what, the past four or five months?"

"It was easier."

"Easier for who?" You can hear the hurt in his voice and the silence in the room.

"It was a shock. It wasn't planned… I …"

"Were you ever going to tell us? Or would you have turned up one day saying, 'Oh, by the way, Oscar, here is your niece or nephew?'"

"Nephew, it's a boy," Isla quickly adds.

Oscar's face softens a little, he's still really hurt, and I don't blame him. What the hell was Isla thinking?

"You're having a boy?" Oscar asks. Isla bursts out crying. "Shit, Issy." Oscar pulls her against him, and she wraps herself as far as she can around the hulking Viking.

"I'm sorry, I am so sorry I didn't tell you," she mumbles into his shirt, and he brushes her hair from her face.

"Shh, it's going to be okay. You're home, and it's going to be all okay." Isla stiffens.

"I'm not staying. My life is in Europe, not here."

"What? Are you seriously going back to Europe when you're about to pop out a child?"

"I've hit five months, Oscar. I'm only halfway." Oscar frowns at her.

"Oh shit, it was a wedding baby," Derrick adds. Isla shoots daggers at him. "Sorry." Derrick holds up his hands.

"Is this true?" Oscar asks.

Isla waves her hand at him. "I'm not answering that, it doesn't matter. What matters now is that we're here to celebrate Evan and Sienna, not me and my drama." She turns and looks at the new parents, walking over and hugging them both. "Sorry about this." They both shake their heads at Isla, indicating it's fine. Oscar storms out of the room.

"Sorry, guys," I tell Sienna and Evan, rushing after Oscar.

"Babe, wait." I run after him. His face is furious. I keep running after him to his truck. As soon as he gets in, he starts hitting the steering wheel and cursing before he starts crying. I jump into his lap and wrap my arms around him.

"How could she…" I've never seen him so devastated before. "How could she do that to her family, Stace? Her fucking family." He bangs his chest.

"I suspect she's scared. Embarrassed."

"She knows she can tell me anything. I'm her brother." The pain is etched so deep in his face. "Mom is going to be so upset."

"I'm sure once the shock has worn off, she will come around, and you will too."

"Derrick said it was a wedding baby. What was he talking about?" Oh. Shit. He remembered that.

"She said it was a one-night stand."

"If that fucking little shit, Tyler, knocked her up. I'll fucking kill him." Isla had a little fling with Tyler from Sons of Brooklyn, they are friends.

"There will be no killing Tyler. I saw him with someone else at the wedding." Oscar nods.

"I'm going to kill whoever knocked up my sister, leaving her alone like that."

"If she didn't tell her family, do you think she'd have told the father?" Oscar sits up straight.

"You think she hasn't told the father?" I nod my head. "That's so fucking cruel. Why is she being so cruel?"

"Babe." I run my hand over his cheek. "We may never know why Isla kept it from everyone in the beginning, we all know now, and that's what matters. You're going to be an uncle." Oscar tilts his head and stares at me.

"And uncle?" I nod my head, and a small smile curls on his lips. "An uncle to a little boy." Yep.

"I'm going to buy him his first bass." I let out a sigh of relief. "And a football, so we can throw it in the backyard."

"See. So many positives to dwell on instead of the negatives."

"You're right, Stacey." He leans over to kiss me. "You are so fucking perfect." He kisses me again. "I'm so lucky to have you in my life." He kisses me again and again and again.

"Umm, babe. We're in the hospital parking lot. You're going to have to remove those hands from my boobs unless you want us to get arrested."

OSCAR

"Good luck, babe." Stacey kisses me. "And don't forget, listen to her."
"I'll try."
"And don't shout at a pregnant lady." Stacey points her finger at me.
"I'll try not to." She gives me the evil eye. "Love you, babe." I blow her a kiss and head over to Derrick's place.

Butterflies take off in my stomach as I walk up to Derrick's front door. I rap my knuckles against the wooden door, and he opens it dramatically.

"Behave, you hear me," he warns before I come in. Agreeing and following him inside, I see Isla sitting on the couch, her baby bump on display. "I thought this would be a safe environment. Sit, Ragnar. And if you upset the pregnant lady, I'll kill you." And with that, he disappears into the kitchen. Isla and I sit awkwardly together, both of us stubborn as the other.

"I'm sorry, Is." She looks at me, shocked. "The way I spoke to you at the hospital, I... I was in shock." Isla's face softens.

"I know I sprung it on everyone." She lets out a heavy sigh. "You need to know that I have a little person coming into my life who is my sole responsibility. You can help, be the baby's uncle, you'll not control my life like you used to." My heart breaks at her words.

"You think that's what I've been doing?" My gut twists in knots.

"Yes. You have controlled every aspect of my life. Why do you think I left?" Her words are like daggers to my heart.

"I thought I was protecting you. I had no idea I was pushing you away, Issy. I thought I was helping." Fuck. How did I get this all so wrong? Isla moves over to sit beside me, and she wraps her arms around me in a hug. I take it.

"I know you thought you were doing the right thing, but…" I see things a little clearer now. All these years trying to protect her, I pushed her away instead. I let her down. You're such an idiot, Oscar.

"I need to butt out." She gives me a weary smile. "You know I love you, Issy, and I want what's best for you." I hold her hand in mine.

"I know you do, your love seems a little controlling at times."

"Shit." I hang my head and feel utterly ashamed.

"Why have you not told me this before?" She gives me a skeptical look. "I would have… I'd have at least tried to stop it. You're my family. I never want to lose you." Isla cuddles me again, tears falling down her cheeks. I guess the hormones are kicking in. I've never seen her cry so much in my life.

"I love you, Oscar. I'm about to start a new phase of my life, and I need you to respect it. Respect my choices." I can do this. I hug her tighter.

"Damn you, Ragnar, you beautiful beast." Derrick comes out looking at the two of us and places a few bottles of water on the table. Then there's another knock at the door.

"I'll be right back." Derrick flitters off.

"I'm sorry, Is."

"I know you are. I should've spoken up over the years." Footsteps echo down the hallway, and I see Finn standing there. What on earth is he doing here? Did Derrick ask him to be the moderator between us all? I think Issy and I are sweet now.

"What are you up to, D?" Finn asks Derrick, who ignores his question and waves him into the living room. Finn takes a seat the furthest away from the two of us—that's strange.

"Okay. Thank you all for coming here today. I'll be your interrogator... no, sorry, your mediator." Derrick chuckles.

"Why is Finn here?" I ask as I look between them all. Derrick is shooting daggers at Isla, who is shooting them right back at him. Finn looks like he'd rather be anywhere else other than here. Isla lets out a heavy sigh.

"I need you not to freak out." Those words don't sound good. "All those nice things you said to me, I need you to mean them." Stacey's warning of not yelling at a pregnant lady sticks in my mind. Count to ten, man... one... two...

"What's going on?"

"Finn is the father of my baby," Isla says quickly. What in the absolute fuck did she say? She looks dead serious. I look over at Derrick, who is nodding. Then my attention turns to Finn, who can't even look at me.

"You motherfucker!" I launch myself at my best friend. That fucker. How dare he? How could he? Someone is grabbing at me as my fists lay into Finn, who is defending himself. Isla is screaming in the background, all I see is red. "I told you to leave her alone." He promised me he wouldn't touch her. He's going to break her fucking heart like he has for years. He was supposed to stay away from her, and now he's fucking knocked her up and abandoned her.

"Fuck off, man, I fucking love her." This stops me in my tracks. Derrick pulls me off him, and I notice Finn's lip is bleeding.

"You're going to pay to fix this shit, you hear me, Eriksen."

Derrick glares at me. I look around the room where I have smashed a lamp and done some damage to his couch.

"I told you if you went near her, I'd tell your secret," I threaten him. I don't care that Finn likes dudes, I do care that he will cheat on my sister and break her heart.

"She already knows," Finn snaps at me.

"I don't care. I'm honestly more upset that you have tried to keep us apart." Isla points her finger at me. I'm confused. She doesn't care? She already knows.

"I didn't want him to break your heart." Why can't she see I was trying to protect her?

"So you broke it for him?" That hit like an arrow to the heart. "I've loved him all my life, Oscar. From the moment we saw each other as kids. There has been no other man in my life that I have loved more than him."

"I thought I was trying to protect you."

"You pushed us apart. You put so many barriers between us, Oscar. You gave us so much baggage that you destroyed our love." Fuck. I rake my hands through my hair. I had no idea. I look over at Finn, who looks devastated. Shit. What have I done? "Finn proposed to me when we were in England, because I was so sick of being under your control, I chose to run. I left him when my heart wanted to stay. I broke him that night, and I don't think I'll ever be able to fix what I broke." Derrick sniffles beside me. "I was so scared to tell you that he was the father that I kept it a secret, and I denied him those months of being with his son."

"Issy…" Her words have ripped my heart out.

"I can't blame you for everything that has happened between Finn and me over the years, you were to blame for a lot of my pain. Finn pushed me away out of loyalty to you. He was so scared that you would tell his secret to the world that no matter how much he loved me, it wasn't enough. He was so scared to hurt his family if his secret came out."

Fuck, fuck, fuck. I start pacing around the room. I fucked up so badly. I had no idea they loved each other so much. I thought it was a phase.

"I did all this." Thumping my chest. I nod. "Fuck!" Nearly pulling my hair out. "Fuck!" I roar through the room, tears falling down my cheeks. "I did it to protect you. I thought it was the right thing. I…" Issy runs into my arms and holds me tight, both of us crying over the mistakes we both have made with each other. "I'm sorry, Issy. I had no idea I was hurting you so much."

I look over to where Finn is, looking so very lost. I let go of Issy and make my way over to my best friend, and he flinches when I open my arms. "I'm sorry, man. I am so sorry." Pulling him into my arms, I slap him on the back. "I fucked up. I fucked up so much." Finn's grip tightens around me. "Do you still love my sister?"

"I do… but…" He looks over at Issy. "We have a lot to discuss."

All because of me.

"You both have my blessing. I should never have stood in the way. I could see it… how much you both meant to each other. I didn't want anything to fuck it up, instead, I did. I messed it all up." Derrick pulls me into his side, his tears drying up.

"I know how you can pay me for all this damage, Ragnar, it requires you to get onto your knees." This makes the room explode with laughter—trust Derrick to break the tension.

23

STACEY

The last half of the year has flown by. Finn and Isla got engaged, had a baby, the gorgeous little Easton, and threw a dart at the globe to choose their wedding destination. Thankfully, they hit Hawaii because going to a wedding in Vladivostok wasn't high on many people's calendars. They are getting married next Valentine's Day—awfully romantic. It took Oscar a little while to get used to Isla and Finn being a couple, seeing them together and how happy they were, soon turned him around, especially when Easton arrived. Oscar is the best uncle—he loves that little dude.

Sienna and Evan are a family of four now with Ryder and Levi. We're all taking bets on when Sienna will be knocked up again. I mean, Levi is six months old. Wyld Jones company is going from strength to strength, especially in Wyld's kids' department. When the girls take photos of their kids wearing the trendiest clothes, they sell out, and the waitlist is insane.

Derrick has also become hot property within the styling world, and celebrities are flocking to him. He's expanded his styling space and employed more staff and junior stylists to help him.

Vanessa and Christian disappeared for the first couple of months of their twins, Ruby and Sadie's life. I don't blame them, those two girls are such a handful, they are ridiculously cute.

Olivia and Axel got married in France in one of her family's castles. How crazy is that? Their relationship is still a juggling act crisis crossing between LA and England. The boys have opened up Dirty Texas Records in London, which has taken off, so Axel spends a lot of time there, so at least he's in the same country as his bride. Olivia made up with her sister, Penny, who was the biggest bitch on the planet. I mean, she had been having an affair with her sister's fiancée for months, then told her family that the baby was his, we found out that the ex-president of France is the father. These British girls are fancy as fuck. They have a gorgeous little girl called Genevieve. Not long after the birth, Olivia's father died suddenly from heart failure. It devastated her, especially as she was the heir to the family's estates. Thankfully, everything worked out in the end so that Axel and Olivia could be together.

And Oscar and me? We're still going strong. Much stronger than I ever thought possible. We still have fun at The Paradise Club, only maybe once a month. Living together has been a breeze, and working together is so much fun, we probably distract each other too much for it to be a long-term solution, so now I'm back working with Sienna and Derrick.

We have decided to spend Christmas together this year with all the family and babies. I'm a little sad that I won't be visiting my family this year because I really wanted Oscar to meet my parents even though they talk via Skype. They are happy for me, especially my nieces, who can't believe I'm dating a famous rock star. I come from a tiny little country town in the middle of the outback. My family has a sheep farm and are simple people. The drought has been tough on them this year, they are made of hardy stock, so they've gotten through it.

It's Christmas Eve, and we have all converged onto Christian and Vanessa's Big Bear property. It is mayhem, the feeling of chaos reminds me of home, so it's nice, and I don't feel as homesick. A cold front came through earlier this evening, dumping a big chunk of snow everywhere. It's nice, looking out the cabin windows and seeing the snow falling—it's bloody freezing still beautiful—maybe because I'm Aussie, and we don't really get snow, especially at Christmas time. We finished a traditional Christmas Eve dinner, all of us stuffed to the gills.

"Time to open one present under the Christmas tree," Christian tells everyone. The Christmas tree is a monster and beautifully decorated too, the piles and piles of presents under is insanity. Boxes and boxes of gifts for kids who can't even walk yet.

"Ryder will hand them out." Ryder's face lights up as he follows Christian over to the Christmas tree. He takes the presents and hands them out to everyone. We all open our gifts one at a time, and the kids go crazy over their new toys, especially Ryder with his new kid-size car. He jumps in, hits the horn a couple of times, and starts zooming around the house. That car is fast. Evan had to sprint after him as he nearly took out the Christmas tree on a sharp turn.

"Stacey hasn't opened her present yet."

"Yes, I have. You bought me this." The light bounces off the diamonds showering the room with rainbow light. I had a heart attack when I opened the box containing an exquisite necklace. It's the most extravagant gift Oscar has given me. It is beautiful, it's too much. He knows he doesn't need to spend money on me to make me happy—all I need is him.

"That was only part of it." What's he up to? I know he's excited this is our first Christmas together, I wasn't expecting him to go crazy. He hands me another gift.

"Open it," he urges me to open the present. I unwrap the box and pull out an iPad. "There's a video." Oscar is almost bouncing out of his seat with excitement. I press play on the video. Oh my God, it's my family. They are all dressed up in Santa hats. They are sitting on an old cart and are singing "Merry Christmas" to me. Mum and Dad pop onto the screen first and tell me how much they miss me, how proud they are of me making a life for myself in LA, and they send their love to Oscar too. Next is my sister and her kids, each one of them doing something silly for the camera. I can't stop crying. I didn't realize how much I missed them until seeing them. "I know you miss your family and wish they could be here." God, I love this man. I wrap my arms around him.

"This was perfect, thank you," I say, sniffling into his chest.

"I think I can do better," he tells me. "Look over there." He points to the large glass window behind us, and I see people standing in the snow.

"Oh my God," I scream, realizing who is standing there.

My family. My family is here in Big Bear. I can't believe this is happening right now. The door opens, and a large gust of wintery air rushes in as my family rushes toward me. Everyone is crying, screaming, talking, and yelling. So many hands are hugging me—Mum, Dad, my sister, Naomi, her husband, Simon, my nephews, Hunter and Lockie, and my nieces, Amelia, Emma, and Becca. They are all here. "How?" I stare at my windblown family.

"Oscar organized it." Turning around, I see Oscar standing there, looking a little embarrassed by the attention. I rush into his arms and kiss him. I can hear my nieces and nephews making gagging sounds and the rest of them hollering as I kiss Oscar within an inch of his life. "I love you. I love you so much."

"I love you too."

"I thought the diamonds were an extravagant gift, but this… how can I ever repay you?"

"You don't. You being in my life is all I need." I can't. I kiss him again. Shit. I haven't introduced my family to him yet.

"Oscar, come meet my family. Officially." Pulling him over

to them, my mum pulls him in for a big hug, thanking him over and over again for his generosity. My father does the same but shakes his hand instead. My sister practically tackles him.

"Wow, he's strong." She winks at me. Her husband shakes Oscar's hand. They introduce him to all the kids, who are a little distracted by the snow falling outside. They have never seen it before or been overseas. Oscar's family comes over and introduces themselves too, then the rest of our friends.

"I don't deserve you, Oscar," I say, taking a moment away from the chaos.

"How can you say that?"

"This. You did this all for me."

"I'd do this and more for you, Stace." He wraps his arms around me.

"I have nothing to offer you. I can't compete with all this." Waving my arms around at the luxury of the life these Dirty Texas guys live.

"I never want you to. It's my job to provide for us." What, the? I never expected him to have such a traditional point of view. "Stacey, I can see it on your face that you're pissed over that comment. I love you. There's no one else I want in this world other than you. You're stuck with me. Forever." I hate it when he's acting all squishy and romantic when I'm mad at him. "I'm a washed-up rock star. I've peaked. This is it for me. I have made more money in one lifetime than people make in twenty. I can't possibly spend it all unless you want me to keep buying you shit." I roll my eyes at him. "Exactly. I live to make you happy, Stace. And what makes you happy is your family. I know you aren't a fan of LA, everyone that you love is here, except for them. So I thought that they needed to come to you. I know it seems extravagant, which it wasn't. I mean, I didn't use the jet or anything." This makes me laugh, him thinking not using his private jet isn't an extravagance. "Look how happy your family is." My family struggles being farmers, so it would never happen for them to ever be able to do this for themselves. He's right, they are happy.

"I'm sorry, I have a hang-up over your money," I confess, snuggling into his strong arms.

"Well, at least I know you're not a gold digger." I slap him lightly. "The empty credit card I've given you is testament to that." When I moved in, Oscar gave me a credit card that had access to one of his accounts. When I saw there was no credit limit, it freaked me out. So, I may not earn millions like him, I do well for myself. If I want anything, I can buy it.

"This life takes a bit of getting used to. I sometimes forget who you are."

"I can remind you more often if you like. I'm kind of a big deal." I shake my head at him. "I know it might seem old-fashioned to people like us who aren't living a traditional relationship, I want to provide for my woman." It's sexy when he gets all alpha. "Do you understand?" Not sure how I got this lucky to have him in my life, I'm so happy he is.

"I'm sorry for being weird about it all. I love what you have done for me. The best."

"Lifetime-blow-jobs best."

"Of course." He fist-pumps the air.

"Does that mean you'll start using your credit card, or am I pushing it?"

"I'll think about it."

"What happens if I told you, thinking about you using it, gets me hard?" Oscar's voice drops low as he nuzzles my ear.

"Maybe, I might have to visit some special shops that could help with this problem."

"Yes, please do." Oscar kisses me.

"Eww. That's gross." Little Lockie interrupts our kiss.

"You won't be saying that in fifteen years, little buddy." Oscar jumps up and tickles my nephew until he's crying from laughter.

24

OSCAR

"**M**erry Christmas." Rolling over, I pull an exhausted Stacey against me. She mumbles something utterly incoherent about being sore and then falls back to sleep again. Not going to lie, it's kind of hot knowing that my dick did that to her. Once we were alone, we ripped each other's clothes off and tested pretty much every bit of furniture in the room. *Sorry, Christian.*

Stacey thanked me over and over again for her presents. She thanked me on her knees. She thanked me on my face. She thanked me via her back door. I'm hoping she will have more energy tonight because the surprises aren't over for her. Nerves begin to kick in as I think about what I have planned for later.

Rolling over, I kiss her and go back to sleep.

It's been pandemonium this morning opening the presents. Paper and ribbon are strewn all over the place, and toys are scattered across the floor with dads trying to locate batteries for the gifts or scissors to get the packaging off. The most delicious smells are coming from the kitchen as the moms are preparing their family's favorites.

My palms are beginning to sweat, so I rub them on my dress pants. I wasn't expecting to be this nervous, as I look around the room filled with our nearest and dearest, it hits me.

What happens if Stacey says no? Maybe I've read the signs wrong. I know we both agreed we weren't interested in getting married or having kids, the more I hang around with this group of pussy-whipped fools, the more I want in on their club, maybe not the kid stuff because Easton puked up a mouth full of milk all over me this morning. I thought I was on the set of *The Exorcist*. He's lucky I didn't join him in his barf-fest because that shit was gross. He's still cute, though. Stacey is having an animated discussion with Isla and her sister, Naomi. I'm curious as to what it is about, so I move closer.

"I don't put too much pressure on Oscar." I hear Stacey say my name. What's she talking about putting pressure on me?

"What? No!" Isla raises her voice.

"No, what?" I ask the group. Finn joins me.

"Nothing." Stacey shakes her head, looking at me with a worried expression on her face.

"Would you mind terribly if Hunter stayed with you for a year on a gap year?" Isla asks me. That isn't at all what I thought they were talking about.

"Please, you don't have to answer that," Stacey tells me, looking slightly panicked.

"I told Naomi that he could intern for all of us." Stacey is shaking her head and shooting daggers at my sister.

"I can rent somewhere with him. You don't have to house him," Stacey adds quickly. What in the ever-loving fuck? Is she being serious?

"Excuse me?" I raise my voice. "Are you telling me you're moving out?"

"I... just... he's my nephew, and I'm responsible for him.

You shouldn't be." After everything we spoke about last night and after everything I have done, she still doesn't seem secure in us.

"Are you telling me that you're not my responsibility?" I ask Stacey. "I love you, Stacey Ferguson. If that means I have to look after a teenager for a year, then that's what I'm going to do." Stacey is slightly speechless. Does she seriously think I don't mean what I say? "I told you when you moved in, this was it, Stace. It's you and me together no matter what." Stacey's eyes glisten.

I need to fix this. I need her to realize that when I said together forever, no matter what, I meant it. I stand up and clear my throat. "Can I get everyone into the lounge room, please?" Startling everyone. Stacey is looking at me, concerned. No one is sure what's going on. I stand by the fireplace. "I have an announcement," I tell the room. "Hunter, it's been brought to my attention that you don't know what you want to do now that you've finished school." Hunter stares at me, looking a little scared. "Well, then, would you like to have a gap year with your aunt and me?" Hunter's bright green eyes widen in surprise.

"Are you serious?" He looks at me in disbelief. "Mum, Dad?" He looks over at them. Naomi has tears in her eyes as she nods her head. "You mean I stay with Aunt Stacey in LA?" Hunter clarifies.

"This is so not fair," Amelia, or Mia as she's nicknamed, his fifteen-year-old sister, shouts with a pout. "Why can't I stay too?"

"When you've finished high school, you can come and stay with us as well," I tell her. The teenager's pout disappears, and she smiles widely.

"Cool." Her cheeks turn a bright pink.

"So, what do you say?" I ask Hunter again.

"Yes. Yes, thank you. Thank you so much." He rushes up and hugs me, then he hugs Stacey.

"There's one more thing." I fall to my knees in front of Stacey. Gasps echo throughout the room. I pull the black velvet box from my pocket. "The moment I met you, Stacey, I knew you were different. I fought my feelings for you until I couldn't anymore. I was scared to take the leap, I'd be more scared of living my life without you." Stacey tears up, her hands are shaking. I can hear sniffles all around me. "Will you marry me, Stacey?" My hands are shaking as I place the yellow diamond ring on her finger. Never in my life have I ever been so nervous. This coming from a man who plays in front of hundreds of thousands of people as a rock star and never gets nervous. "Yes. Yes. Yes." She bounces up and down. Once the ring is secured on her finger and thankfully fits, I pick her up in my arms and kiss her, Hollywood style, which makes the room erupt with hollering, applause, and congratulations.

"The last Dirty Texas man has fallen," Derrick hollers, making the room laugh.

"I can't believe you proposed." Stacey stares at me.

"You're stuck with me, babe. Thought you needed a reminder of that."

"I love you, Oscar Eriksen, and I can't wait to spend the rest of my life with you." Moments later, we're pulled apart by well-wishers.

"You can't stop looking at it, can you?" I sit down beside Stacey, who is staring at her ring again.

"Oscar, this is beautiful. A yellow diamond."

"It's rare, like you." She leans over and kisses me. I like this bubble we're currently in.

"I never thought you wanted to get married."

"We can have a long engagement." This makes her chuckle.

"I like the sound of that." Stacey snuggles into my side, looking at the open fire. "I'm the luckiest girl in the world."

"We're both pretty lucky." She looks down at the ring again.

"Are you sure about taking Hunter in?"

"Of course. If he has no idea what he wants to do, why not? I mean, between us all, he has access to some of the best businesses in the world. What a great place to learn."

"You're right."

"Of course, I am. I do want to ask, though. We're you seriously thinking about moving out?" Stacey looks up at me.

"I didn't want to put pressure on us. You shouldn't have to be responsible for Hunter."

"I know I don't have to, but I do for you. I tell you that all the time."

"Guess I'm a slow learner." I nuzzle her neck.

"I hope you get it now. We're in this together. I don't want separate lives anymore. I want you and me as one."

"Okay, okay. I get it. I get it." She giggles as my teeth find her neck. "I won't ever doubt you ever again."

New Year's Eve

Olivia and Axel missed Christmas because it was the first one after Olivia's father dying, so they agreed to spend Christmas in Europe and New Year's with all of us. Axel was shocked that he missed my proposal, the boys showed him a video someone took. We've all retired to the games room to play pool, smoke some cigars, and drink some whiskey. Axel announced his news, too—he's going to be a father of twins.

"Welcome to the dad club." Evan smiles, slapping Axel on the back.

"I'm still kind of in shock… it wasn't planned."

"Never usually is," Finn adds.

"Now we need the Viking to spread his seed, and the Dirty Texas family will be complete." Derrick makes me choke on my drink.

"Dude, I proposed. Babies are a long way off." Derrick rolls his eyes.

"That's what they all say. And now look at everyone." Derrick points to the rest of the guys.

"We have a menagerie of kids. It won't be long until you're bitten by the kids' bug. I see you with Easton." Derrick raises his eyebrow at me. There's a big difference between being an awesome fun uncle and being a dad.

"Take your time, man, there's no hurry. Enjoy Stacey and Oscar time," Finn explains, a sad tone to his voice.

"Did you miss that with Issy?"

"Yeah, I did, and I wish we had it." Guilt hits me like an arrow through the heart that I kept them apart for so long. Now that I actually see them together, I see it. I get it. He really does love her. "I wouldn't swap what we have for anything, though. Being a father is the best thing in the world, it's also the most draining."

"Stop it, guys. I'm already clucky. Listening to you hot men talk about babies is making my ovaries pop," Derrick groans.

"You don't have ovaries," Christian points out.

"Doesn't mean I'm not clucky. I envy you all. I wish I could find someone to have a baby with, it makes it hard when the person I want doesn't have the right reproductive organs."

"Hello, modern medicine, man." Christian throws his arm around Derrick's shoulders. "You pick an egg or a surrogate, and you have a baby. Heaps of single women do it, why can't you?" Derrick's eyes widen as if he's never considered this before.

"Yeah? Like a gay single man is going to be able to have a baby. They are going to shut the door right in my face." Derrick's shoulders sink. We're all used to Derrick's hair-brained schemes, seeing him physically upset over this is new.

"Money. You have lots of money, Derrick. You're in a great position to be able to do this," Evan tells him.

"I'm so busy at work."

"No one is saying you have to do it now. You have plenty of time. Why not look into it as a Plan B?" Evan presses.

"You never know what the new year might bring. The love of your life could be around the corner," Christian encourages him.

"You're right, Christian. I need to stop being a ho and start looking for Mr. Right." This makes me chuckle.

"I heard my name." Hudson, Finn's older brother, walks in at that moment, surprising us all. Finn rushes up and hugs his brother. He's been in the Middle East working with the troops there. He's a photojournalist who specializes in war-torn areas. Every time he goes away, Finn worries about him and even more so since Jackson's accident. Jackson used to be in the military until he was medically discharged due to an IED attack. Thankfully, he's better, it took a lot of therapy, both physical and mental, to get him back to the man he is today. "I see being a dad has made you soft," Hudson chuckles.

"Fuck you. I'm glad you're safe, that's all, asshole." Finn punches his brother. They always had a rivalry with each other. Derrick rushes up to Hudson and gives him a very enthusiastic hug and a bit of a bum squeeze for good measure.

"Now, where's my nephew? I'm dying to see him." Finn and Hudson disappear to introduce the newest uncle to his nephew.

25

STACEY

This group knows how to throw epic bachelor and bachelorette parties. From Sienna's epic beach party, Vanessa's in Monaco, to Olivia's in Paris, Isla's has kind of topped them all, or maybe for Oscar and me, it seems pretty epic. Nate has invited us all to check out The Paradise Club Resort in the Caribbean. Olivia has been raving about it as she got to see it during its soft launch, so I'm dying to check it out.

"Welcome to the most epic last hurrah ever!" Derrick yells throughout the Dirty Texas jet, a bottle of champagne in his hand. As always, he's the first to get the party started.

By the time we land, everyone is in good spirits, our cheeks are flushed, and our steps are a little wobbly. We take the transfer from the airport to the wharf, where Nate and Camryn are waiting to transport us to the resort.

"Welcome to paradise, my Dirty Texas family," Nate and Camryn greet us.

"I have water bottles for everyone." Camryn hands over the bottles, which are welcome after all the drinks we had on the plane. I think most of us are going to need it, especially in this heat. It's so nice and warm here in the Caribbean with the smell of the salt air, the warm tropical breezes, and the swaying of the palm trees. I'm so looking forward to this trip and naked dips in the ocean with my man, making love under the stars, plus trying out pretty much everything and everyone that is on offer at the resort.

"If you would like to come aboard, we'll take you across to the resort." Nate gives us his megawatt smile, his white teeth shining against his suntanned skin. He looks like he's stepped off an ad for luxury yachts, selling ordinary men his billionaire playboy lifestyle. "I'll be taking you around to your own private area of the resort which is reserved for VIPs and is blocked off to regular guests. It's near my villa, an area I built for my friends to come and stay at the resort," he tells us.

We take a seat on the boat, and the captain starts to move slowly away from the harbor, with nothing but crystal-clear water surrounding us. Once we're safe from the other boats, the captain opens up the engines, and we hurtle toward the resort. Nate reassures us it's not far to the island. Dolphins jump beside the boat as we speed through the turquoise sea. Over the horizon, the closer we get, the more the island comes into focus. On one side of the Island, it appears like bungalows jut out into the ocean.

"I stayed there." Olivia points out to us. "It's beautiful." Nate smiles, looking very proud of Olivia's statement.

"There's a fantastic bar at the end of the pier too." Camryn points
out.

"This place is beautiful," Oscar says into my ear, the wind whipping my hair around.

"I can't wait. The place looks like paradise."

"I'm going to ravage you like a wild beast as soon as we get there," Oscar warns, and a shiver races through my body.

We finally arrive. The boat slows down, and the crew ties up the ropes to secure the boat to the pier. There's a fleet of golf carts waiting to take us to our rooms.

"Your luggage will be at your rooms," Nate advises. "Thought I might take you on a tour first. Is that okay?"

We all nod enthusiastically as we hop into our carts. Nate gives us cordless headphones so we can hear him explain about the resort.

"We're now in the private area not accessible by guests." Nate points this out as we drive through the lush rainforest. "My villa is over to the right, and your villas will be on the left. They all have direct access to the beach don't worry, they are all far enough away that you won't see your friends skinny-dipping in the ocean unless you want to, that is." He chuckles through our earphones. Oscar and I sure know we're up for it, I don't think any of our friends will be so keen.

Nate points out the gate that takes us into the guest area, and the golf carts continue along the dirt paths. The sounds of the rainforest are all you can hear—exotic birds calling to their mates. It looks like any other luxury resort—you would have no idea it's a sex resort.

We continue on the path past the rainforest villas until we get to a more open area. Nate points out this is where the open showers are for people who want to get cleaned up from the beach. I look over at Oscar, and he gives me a naughty wink—he knows those open showers have my name written all over them. We look up at the glass cubes, and we spot our first encounter. A man has a woman pressed up against the glass and is fucking her.

"I think I'm going to enjoy this place." Oscar eyes the couple hungrily.

"I wonder if the others are freaking out yet? I bet Sienna is."

"Evan wouldn't allow anyone to watch Sienna. I bet they stay in their villa the entire time."

"Olivia is slightly bummed that she's pregnant, and she and Axel can't go crazy," I tell Oscar.

"Don't worry, little one. There will be plenty of people to play with, I promise you." I snuggle into Oscar's chest. I'm a lucky woman.

We continue traveling, and Nate points out a waterfall with a hidden grotto you can visit. Oscar and I mentally tick that one on our list. There are pools where people are sunbathing naked. Apparently, clothing is optional everywhere in the resort except the restaurants and bars. Nate also points out the mini-Paradise Club to us. Everything looks like a luxury resort except there are many naked people around—our kind of place. I don't know if Oscar and I will want to leave—this truly is paradise to us all.

Nate continues his tour, telling us about twenty-four-hour room service and that they cater not for food and drink, you can order pretty much any sexual desire you require from them. Oscar and I smile at each other. Sexual room service—I think we're going to have to try everything on that menu.

Nate points out areas dedicated to kinks and fetishes. He reminds us that everyone on the island has signed NDAs to reassure the group that if we want to go crazy, we can, and no one will know unless our friends stumble upon us. Eventually, we make it back around to the resort's private area.

"So, what did you think?" Nate asks as we get out of the golf carts.

"I'm going to have the best time ever." Derrick jumps up and down.

"We have dinner planned for tonight at Nate's villa for around eight thirty. Until then, your time is your own. Oh, and each one of your villas has its dedicated butler," Camryn lets us know. "What you do with that butler is up to you." Nate smirks, and Derrick pretty much starts sprinting to his villa.

"Have fun, guys. See you at dinner." Camryn waves us away.

"Oh, and your colored wristbands are in your rooms. Don't forget to wear them," Nate reminds us. The group nervously says goodbye to each other, Oscar and I can't wait to get paradise started.

"Welcome to your villa," the beautiful blonde greets us, opening the door for us. "My name is Marnie, and I'll be your personal butler during your stay. If you require anything, all you have to do is call for me any time of the day or night." Marnie is dressed in a white polo that's pulled tight across her breasts, which Oscar has noticed, and navy shorts that are molded to her perfect butt.

"So, we can call on you at any time of the day or night?" Oscar asks. Her blue eyes sparkle at him.

"Yes. I'm here to service you both." My eyes fall to her wrist filled with colored bands letting us know what she's into. I spy pink amongst them, meaning she plays with women too. Good, Oscar can't have all the fun. "We have a twenty-four-hour room service menu, where you can order food and drinks as well as anything else you so desire."

"Such as?" I question her.

"We have blow-job wake-up calls, our erotic masseuse, male or female or both, you can order extra people for play, you can order voyeurs to come watch, and so much more." I look over at Oscar, raising a brow at me. This is going to be fun.

"Babe, I could do with a massage. My body is feeling awfully tense after that long flight." Oscar grins.

"I can arrange that for you," Marnie advises us. "Would you like male or female masseuses?"

"Female for me," Oscar tells her.

"Male for me. Might steal the female off you once you're finished with her." Running my hand down Oscar's chest, his hand grips my wrist.

"Wouldn't expect anything less." He leans over and kisses me. His large paw grips my ass tightly. Slowly, I untangle myself.

"Can we also organize some beers and champagne as well as some chocolate-dipped strawberries? My fiancé loves them." Marnie nods and leaves the room.

"She's hot," I say, looking up at Oscar.

"She is. I'm assuming you want to play." I nod my head. "I think I am loving this place already." I give him the biggest smile, and not ten minutes later, two beautiful people arrive at our door.

"We're here for your massage." Two gorgeous-looking Scandinavian-looking man and woman stand waiting. This should be fun, and I open the door for them to enter. "My name is Elias, and this is Astrid. We're certified Swedish masseuses." So not only am I going to get a happy ending, I'm going to get a proper massage too. Winning. "Would you like us to set up outside or inside?" Oscar and I look at each other. We hadn't thought about it.

"Maybe inside first. Don't want to scare our friends," Oscar tells the couple.

"Would you like the tables to be in the same room or separate?" I look over at Oscar—his call. We do have a three-bedroom villa.

"What would you like, little one?"

"Is there enough room in here?" I ask, looking around the living room.

"Yes, of course," Elias tells us.

"Okay, then right here is fine." They busily set themselves up in the main living area.

"I have one last question before we start. Do you require the half service or the full service? Half service is erotic massage with orgasm or would you like erotic massage with orgasm and penetration too?" Oh my God, so many decisions. Best holiday ever.

"We're on holiday, babe." Biting my lip, my eyes roam over the Swedish god that is Elias. I can see Oscar is as equally enchanted with Astrid.

"Exactly. I think a full service would be the way to start it off right." The blondes nod in agreement and begin to undress from their white uniforms. Elias slowly pulls his polo off, exposing a tanned, muscular body. His arms are insanely defined, probably because he gives good massages. Then I watch in slow motion as he removes his shorts. A long thick dick springs free. He was commando. That's a pretty dick.

Looking over, I see Astrid has undressed, exposing her perfectly toned body and beautiful breasts. Oscar is biting his lip, and I can see hunger written across his face.

"We ask that you both undress and make yourself comfortable on the table," Elias tells us. We both quickly undress and lay down on the table. This is a weird massage table—there's a hole for my face, then the end of the table is cut into a U-shape, so someone can stand between my legs. I look over at Oscar's, and his has a hole for his dick. This is going to get interesting.

We lay down on the table on our stomachs first. Once I'm comfortable, Elias starts to pour oil over my body, and his hands start to glide all over, his strong fingers digging into my tense muscles. This is so good even before he's even got to the fun stuff. He starts with my shoulders and makes his way slowly around my body, his hands gliding over my thighs, working the fatigued muscles, and his long fingers gliding across my inner thighs. The silky oil adds to the thrill.

Bit by bit, he works me up, teasing me never intimately touching me. It's driving me crazy. He moves between my legs, and the first sweep across my clit nearly sends me jumping off the bed, as I'm incredibly sensitive. Those strong fingers begin to work me over, sliding between my folds with ease, working me gently. He is so good. Then a finger slips inside me, and I moan at the intrusion. Another joins it soon after, curling inside me, massaging the delicate nerves until my whole body is shaking. Elias pushes through, and I swear I see stars when I orgasm. His strong fingers still thrust inside me until I can't take it any longer, my body arching against them. Yet, he still pushes on until I can feel another orgasm coming from deep within. I'm so relaxed that the second orgasm makes me squirt and come. He pulls the most unusual noises from me as he transports me to a whole other realm.

I turn my head once I get my composure back and see Astrid riding Oscar on the massage table. He turns and finds me staring and gives me a wicked smile, as Elias enters me. Closing my eyes, his heavy thrusts catch every sensitive nerve ending inside me. Astrid is making the most beautiful noises as she rides Thor's hammer. I know he's thoroughly fucking her which makes my body shiver. Elias's hands are all over me, still massaging areas of my body while fucking me. It's utterly impressive that he's able to multi-task like that. My body is so sensitive that it doesn't take long for me to come again. Elias and Oscar come not long after each other. My body is like liquid. Elias picks me up and moves me to the bedroom, and moments later, Oscar is joining me. Both of us wearing a satisfied grin on our faces.

"Best massage ever."

"We need to get some of those tables for home." Oscar nuzzles into my neck.

"Yes. They were fun," I agree sleepily.

We have been invited to Nate's private villa for dinner. He's put on the most beautiful feast for us. There's also an island band playing for us in the background.

"How did everyone's day go?' Nate asks the table. There are cheers from the boys and blushes from the girls. I think it's safe to say everyone got lucky.

"I'm never leaving this island," Derrick adds. "Do you even realize that your butler will suck your cock for you at any moment of the day?" Everyone bursts out laughing at him. "Ernesto has a magic mouth. Can I take him home? Pretty please." Derrick flutters his eyelashes at Nate.

"No. Ernesto is one of my top staff members," Nate tells him. Derrick pouts.

We enjoy the fabulous feast. Obviously, most of us have worked up an appetite. As the night continues, we split off into groups—the boys head off somewhere with their whiskey, and we girls head outside to sit under the tiki torches.

"So, has anyone else explored the delights of this resort yet?" Derrick asks the girls. Everyone remains tight-lipped, sipping their cocktails. "Really?" Derrick eyes us all suspiciously. "I bet you have." He points to Camryn, who raises her brow at him.

"I've tried most things here," is all she says.

"I bet you have with that delicious sex beast, Nate." Camryn bursts out laughing and gives him a high five. "So, Camryn is the only one who did anything? None of you used the pleasures of your on-call sex toy?" He looks expectantly at us all. I don't meet his eyes.

"We didn't. We had a good time by ourselves." Sienna stares at her best friend. "Is that what you wanted to hear?" As I thought, Sienna and Evan have been enjoying each other. I know not everyone is weird like Oscar and I.

"Of course, you did. I wouldn't be surprised if Evan knocked you up again. You're a given, Sienna. You're such a slut for your man." Sienna laughs and rolls her eyes at him. "So, everyone got lucky but nothing kinky?" Derrick is the biggest gossip queen, and even if any of us had a story, we wouldn't be telling him. He can't keep his big mouth shut. With no one else confessing,

Camryn begins to tell us about all the crazy things she has done at the resort. Everyone is listening intensely. I think I might have to pick Camryn's brain about the best spots.

There's a long ruckus, then cheers in the distance, and it grabs our attention. Through the rainforest, I see the rest of our party turn up. The Sons of Brooklyn boys with Charlotte, much to Evan's horror, The California Bros., and Finn's brothers, Hudson and Parker. Jackson came with us earlier, as well as Sebastien and Yvette. It's one big dysfunctional Dirty Texas family get-together.

26

OSCAR

We've arrived at the beautiful Island of Kauai in Hawaii for Isla and Finn's wedding—all our families are here. I even invited Stacey's sister and brother-in-law to the wedding. It's their twentieth wedding anniversary, and Stacey told me how much she'd love to do something for them because things have been really bad back at home. The drought has hit hard where they live, and there's no money for any luxuries.

I was excited that Stacey actually asked me for my help with it. Stacey refuses to use any of the money that I have given her access to. Well, except to buy sexy lingerie, which I'm not complaining about, I wish she'd treat herself sometimes because she works really hard, and I want to spoil her.

After everyone spent the morning refreshing up after traveling, we all meet in the main house for dinner. Hawaiian music is playing as we enter the dining room, and some people are already milling around.

"This place looks like paradise." Naomi comes up to greet Stacey with has a tropical-looking cocktail in her hand.

"I'm waiting for the dinosaurs to emerge from the rainforest," Simon jokes.

"I'm so happy you guys are here and get to experience all of this, Stacey tells her sister.

"You have no idea how much we needed this, Stace. Thank you, Oscar." Naomi pats my arm.

"You're family, guys." I can see how appreciative they are for this break.

"Simon and I had massages today. I can't remember the last time I had a massage. It was *amazing*. Simon, of course, fell asleep, and his snoring was trying to ruin my bliss, I pushed it far, far away." Naomi squeezes her husband's elbow gently. He smiles down adoringly at her.

"You guys totally deserve it. Now, where can I get one of those cocktails? They look amazing." Stacey searches the room before locating the waiter and rushes off in search of a drink.

"We can never repay you for all this, Oscar, and for Christmas too."

"Please. It's all fine. I want to make Stacey happy, and she misses you guys. So what's a couple of flights for you all to be together?"

"You're a top bloke, Oscar," Simon adds. I think that's a pretty high compliment in Australian.

"And for taking in Hunter, he has come out of his shell so much. We speak to him regularly, and he is having so much fun. He's being good, isn't he?" Of course, Naomi wants to check up on her son.

"Hunter is an amazing kid. You both should be so proud. Everyone he has helped has nothing but praise for him. I think he's enjoying his time with Derrick the most. It seems like he has a flair for fashion." Simon and Naomi look at each other in shock.

"I think it might be the models he has a flair for." Simon chuckles.

"You're probably right. I remember me at that age."

"I don't want to know." Naomi chuckles, looking slightly horrified.

"The happy couple is here," Christian calls out, pulling our attention to Isla and Finn arriving. Everyone cheers them as they enter. They are greeted by staff who puts a black bead necklace around Finn's neck and a flower lei in Isla's hair. They greet everyone as they move their way through the room. Isla sees Sebastien and moves away to chat with him, and they start off laughing before it looks like she's telling him off over something. I bet she found out he's been hooking up with his assistant. The girl is very beautiful maybe slightly a bit obsessed with him. We've warned him about it, he keeps thinking with his dick.

Eventually, Isla and Finn come over to where we're standing.

"I can't believe you're getting married." Stacey hugs my sister.

"I know, it's kind of surreal," Isla tells the group.

"I'm a little nervous about what Derrick has planned as he's organized most of it." Finn takes a sip of his beer.

"Camryn would reel him in, wouldn't she?" Stacey questions.

"Yeah. I'd think so. Some of the ideas Derrick has thrown out have been more along the lines of a Derrick Jones' wedding and not a Finn and Isla one." We all chuckle at Finn's comment. I could imagine what Derrick's wedding would look like. Actually, no, I probably couldn't because his mind works in mysterious ways.

"Best day ever," Finn screams as we zip through the rainforest on the zipline. The views are breathtaking—nothing but green foliage underneath us, bright blue sky peppered with fluffy white clouds, endless blue horizon of the ocean, and the heat of the full sun on my skin. We started the morning off with a boat cruise, swimming with turtles and sharks, totally fear factor, epically awesome. We then went off-roading through the mud and rainforests where they filmed *Jurassic Park*, and, of course, this turned into a mock race. We're an overly competitive bunch when it comes to these activities, especially when the girls aren't here freaking out.

"This has been a pretty awesome day, son." Finn's dad slaps him on the back. "I thought I was going to die so many times, which made me feel alive. Don't tell your mother." This makes us laugh as we sit at the bar having a beer in the afternoon sunshine.

"I have one last stop I want to take you all to," Finn mentioned to the group. "It's a secret." We all look around at each other, wondering what he's got planned? I'd probably follow him anywhere after how much epic shit we've done today.

"What are we doing here?" Christian groans.

"This wasn't on my itinerary," Derrick adds.

"I know, I know, today has been kind of awesome, and I've been inspired."

"Did you forget to buy her a wedding gift?" Evan asks.

"No. I have that. I've seen all you fuckers go through this before. I've got it all covered. No. I had an epiphany while we were scuba diving this morning."

"No. That's called shitting your pants," I joke. Finn flips me off.

"I love it here," Finn says dramatically.

"Can't deny this island is awesome," his dad adds. "Best holiday I've had in a long time."

"Good. Because I want to buy this house." What did he say?

"Excuse me, son?" His dad is the first to talk.

"I want us to make more memories as a family," Finn tells him. "I also want to get Easton away from the whole Hollywood scene. My son will grow up wanting for nothing, and this Hollywood bubble he will grow up in isn't the real world. I want to show him there's more outside of all the riches where we live." His dad claps him on the shoulder and looks at him with pride.

"And you think buying a multi-million-dollar home in Hawaii is going to make him realize there's more to life?" Finn's brother, Hudson, mocks. "It's safe here. He can run around and not worry about anything. He will be able to immerse himself in nature. Plus, there's no paparazzi here. No people trying to get photos of him or the threat of kidnapping because of who I am." Hudson's eyes widen. I don't think he realized that he isn't the only one who deals with threats on a daily basis.

"You think someone would do that?" he asks, seemingly shocked.

"The guys live in the public eye, so there are always threats," Jackson, Finn's young brother and our head of security, tells him.

"I had no idea." Hudson shakes his head, a worried look resting on his face.

"It's not something we like to dwell on. Eventually, it would be nice not to have to be in LA," Finn adds.

"That's why we love being down in Australia," Evan adds. "If I could live at our home in Byron Bay all year round, I would. The lifestyle there for the kids is great. The only things I have to worry about are the sharks in the water and stupid killer octopuses in the rock pools." He chuckles.

"That's the same with England. We can kind of go anywhere and not be worried when we're at Olivia's family estate. You notice the difference… the clean air, the rolling green hills, no traffic, and the friendly faces."

"And the rain," Axel's dad adds, making him laugh.

"Yeah, the rain. It kind of adds to the charm of it all. Now that Olivia is pregnant, the lifestyle I was chasing isn't what I think I want anymore. Maybe I'm getting old, or maybe I want to slow down and stop working for a while. I mean, we all haven't stopped since we were teens." Axel has a point—we have been working nonstop—I had no idea the guys hated LA so much.

"You boys have started expanding. If you all want to live somewhere else, why don't you set up offices in those locations and work from there? You don't have to be in LA," Evan's dad advises us.

"We have already started London and New York," Axel states. "I guess we could expand into Australia." Evan mulls this over. If we had an office in Australia, Stacey could see her family more.

"I know Stacey would love to live closer to her family in Australia," I add my two cents into the conversation.

"Your mom would miss you, son," Dad tells me.

"You could always come with."

"I'm not sure about those killer sharks and octopuses Evan was talking about earlier," Dad adds, making us all laugh.

You didn't die when you were there a couple of years ago," I remind him.

True. I don't want to tempt fate," Dad argues back.

"Sounds like big changes are happening for Dirty Texas again," Zander, our tattoo artist from The California Bros., adds. "We'd all miss ya."

"Kids change everything," Finn's dad adds. "You're a family man now, Finn. You have to do what's best for your family."

"Well, how about I start by buying this house?" he announces, pointing to the house behind him. "And then we can work out the rest."

27

STACEY

We're having a girls' day at the day spa in preparation for Isla's big day. Babysitters are looking after the kids, so all the mums can relax for the day. A large tent is set up on the grass area overlooking the beach and ocean. Inside the tent are daybeds, mats on the grass, massage tables, foot spas, and a table set up for manicures. A waiter greets us with virgin cocktails with decorative fruit sticking out the top. We each then choose from the spa menu and disappear into bliss for the rest of the day.

Hours later after we have been pampered into bliss, we all take a seat in the tent together, sipping on fruit-infused waters and champagne. A table is filled with tiny decorative cupcakes, macaroons, and little sandwiches.

"This is the life," Sienna groans as she lies back against the lounge, closing her eyes and sipping on her champagne.

"I feel amazing," I agree with her.

Everyone is utterly blissed out, and who can blame them? I've been steamed, rolled around in mud, and every muscle massaged within an inch of its life until my body turned to liquid. My feet were scrubbed and polished as were my hands.

"I'm so happy Finn's dart hit Hawaii," Vanessa muses. "Could you imagine what we'd be doing if it was Vladivostok?" This makes us laugh.

"We would be all drunk on vodka trying to keep warm," Olivia adds.

"Always seeing the positives in a situation," Ness jokes.

"I'm pretty happy Finn hit here. This place is utter perfection," Isla sighs, sipping on a glass of chilled champagne. "I never really thought about my wedding."

"That it was always going to be with Finn," her mum adds. Finn's mother giggles at the comment. I think they have been hitting the champagne bar.

"Well, it took us a while to get to this point, yes, it was always going to be Finn. He's had my heart since the moment we moved next door to him."

"Well, we can't wait until you're officially Isla Connolly," Finn's mom tells her. "There was no other girl I wanted for him. I knew Finn had a crush on you, he was trying to hide it from your brother. The sly little glances he took of you when no one was watching, the way his cheeks turn pink when you were around." Aww, that's cute.

"Plus, I'm sure Oscar warned him away from you the moment Finn met you." Her mom laughs. "He was always too overprotective of you." He most certainly is.

"He was overprotective all my life. No wonder Finn was too scared to ever take a chance with me." You can tell Isla is still a little upset with Oscar over the lost time with Finn.

"I know your brother regrets it. He thought he was doing the right thing," her mom adds, sticking up for Oscar.

"I know he does, Mom." Isla gives her a reassuring smile.

"All that matters now is we're going to finally celebrate the two of you officially becoming husband and wife," Finn's mom says excitedly. "I'll finally have a daughter of my own and won't be so outnumbered with all that testosterone. Unless you have a daughter, then the numbers will be more in our favor." She winks. It looks like someone wants more grandbabies.

"So, Stacey, any ideas for your wedding?" Isla quickly changes the baby talk, throwing me under the bus in the process. She catches me mid-sip of my champagne.

"Umm."

"Yes. I'm dying to hear your plans," Oscar's mom adds enthusiastically.

"Oscar and I haven't really thought about it." Panic is racing through my body.

"What? You have had your wedding planned since you were young," my sister butts in. "Stacey used to prance around in Mum's old wedding veil." This makes everyone laugh because they know my stance on getting married. "You said that you would get married at the Sydney Opera House."

"Nommie, I was five," I protest, my cheeks turning with embarrassment.

"Well, I'm sure Oscar could make it happen." My sister smiles widely.

"We only got engaged a couple of months ago. Which was a surprise, as Oscar always told me he didn't want to get married, that he didn't see any real point in having a piece of paper."

"That's because he was used to fooling around with groupies and gold diggers," Isla adds.

"And now he's one giant teddy bear," Oscar's mom adds, her face softening at the words.

"What about kids? I want to be an aunty," my sister asks.

"Nommie, stop. You're going to scare him away." Little do they all know it's me who hasn't come around to the mum thing. Sitting in a room surrounded by mums, they wouldn't understand.

"If babysitting Hunter hasn't scared him away yet, then nothing will." Naomi laughs.

"Hunter is a wonderful boy, Naomi. You should be so proud.

He has the most beautiful manners," Oscar's mum tells her. You can see the motherly pride on her face at my mother's words.

"Thank you so much. Your family has been so generous to him. Seeing him again, I can see he's grown up so much in such a short time."

"He's a hard worker," Sienna adds. "He's helped me out so much in the shop and Derrick as well. He gets stuck in there and helps no matter the task."

"He's also helped the boys with their social media as well, getting them get a little more clued in on what the young people are into these days. As much as the boys think they are young, they are kind of clueless." Vanessa laughs. "Especially, with the technology." Naomi has a huge smile on her face.

"Thank you all so much." Her eyes are glassy. "You all live such busy, important lives and taking the time to look after my eldest…" She sniffles. "I don't know how I can ever repay you all for your generosity." I jump up and hug my sister.

"You're family," Sienna adds. "We look after family." Naomi nods and squeezes my hand tighter.

"I can't believe you told that story to everyone." I'm chatting with Naomi as we walk back to the house after our spa day.

"What, it was funny."

"Oscar and I… we aren't like everyone else here."

"I know you've said you never wanted to get married or have kids, I thought that would've changed now that you're engaged." My sister looks at me.

"Getting engaged was a big enough step."

"The way Oscar is with Easton, that man wants kids." I frown at her.

"Can't he be an awesome uncle?" Naomi gives me a look.

"I love you, sis. But look at all your friends around you and how happy they are."

"You think I'm not happy," I question, looking at my sister.

"It's a different kind of happy when you have kids." I knew my family wouldn't understand.

"I love kids... but other people's," I add.

"You're still young, Stace. You have plenty of time. Your biological clock hasn't started ticking yet."

"What happens if it never starts?" I ask her. She stops and looks at me.

"You would be happy never to have kids?"

"I don't know, maybe." Not going to lie, there's a tiny portion of me that's curious to see what our kid would look like.

"All I'm going to say is, never say never, okay?" She throws her arm around my shoulder. "I know you're building your career, look at Sienna, she has been able to juggle two kids and a career. Life doesn't stop." Maybe she's right. I know Oscar has broached the subject that he wouldn't be freaked out if I accidentally became pregnant. Ugh, too much pressure. I'll worry about it another day.

"You know, I have you down as guardian of our kids if anything happened to us."

"Really?"

"Yeah, I trust you, Stace." Wow. I had no idea she trusted me that much. "Now you have Oscar in your life, too, so I know they would be looked after."

"Well, don't let anything happen, please. I'm not ready to be a mum to five kids. I have one of yours, and he's enough."

"Deal." My sister laughs.

28

STACEY

"Babe, your phone is ringing." Oscar nudges me.

"It's four in the morning." I squint at the bedside clock that's glowing right in front of me. "Who the hell is calling..."

"It's Amelia." That wakes me up, quickly sitting up in my bed. Why is my niece calling at this time? I pick it up.

"Amelia, is everything okay?" There's silence on the phone. "Amelia," I say it again. Maybe she pocket-dialed me. Then I hear sniffling. "Amelia. I'm here. Is everything okay?"

"They're dead." She bursts out crying. Oscar stiffens beside me.

"Honey, what's going on. Are you okay? Do you need help?"

"They're dead, Stacey. All dead." My heart is racing a hundred miles an hour. What's she talking about? I'm becoming really concerned.

"Honey. Put your mum on the phone. You're scaring me." Panic is starting to seep through my bones.

"I can't. She's dead." What the hell did she say? This better be some kind of sick joke she's playing on me.

"Amelia, what the hell is going on?" My anger is taking over from the shock.

"There's been an accident." Silence falls between us, my heart racing. "Pop had to grab something in town before picking them up from the airport. I can't even remember what anymore. Gran went, too, because she wanted to get her hair done before some big CWA thing." Amelia is rambling. "And now... now they are dead, Stacey. Mum, Dad, Gran, and Pop." I shake my head. No. No. No. No. This isn't happening. No. Not my family. No. I think I'm going to be sick. Oscar is up out of bed and moving around the room.

"What do you mean?" Shaking my head, I don't believe it. Naomi and Simon were with us in Hawaii for Finn and Isla's wedding. We only said goodbye to them, and they should've arrived today. Today! No. Mum and Dad were picking them up from the airport.

They live in the bush, a four-hour drive from Sydney or a fifty-minute flight to Mudgee. They're farmers, and Dad mostly deals in sheep. Simon had taken over the family business as Dad has gotten older, the drought has been tough on them. That's why Oscar giving Naomi and Simon this trip to Hawaii for his sister's wedding for their twentieth wedding anniversary meant the world to them. We didn't come from money—everything goes back into the farm or their kids' education.

"They..." Amelia starts, she can't seem to finish. "A truck driver fell asleep at the wheel, and..." She couldn't finish the sentence, she didn't need to. "No one survived." No. I can't believe it. I scream and wail. I'm unable to hold it in. My heart has been ripped from my chest. No. Not my family. They can't be gone. Oscar holds me tight as my world falls apart. He takes the phone from my hand when I'm unable to hold it due to my shaking.

"Who's looking after you?" Oscar asks, placing Amelia on speaker. Oh no, they are all alone. All alone.

Suddenly Broken

"The neighbors. They... have come over." No. This isn't right. I should be there. I should be with my family.

"I'm getting on the first plane out of LA."

"We can take the jet," Oscar advises. "I've texted the crew to tell them to get ready." Fuck, I love this man.

"And Hunter? What about him?" Amelia asks.

"Yes, of course. Of course, he, too, will be on the plane." Oscar nods.

"Okay," she says through tears. "Please hurry, Aunt Stacey. We need you."

"I need you too. I love you. I love you all so much. I'm coming. Tell them all I'm coming." My hands are shaking as I hang up. I feel lost.

"Baby, come here." Oscar pulls me into his lap, and I let it all out.

I sit there for what seems to be hours, absorbing all of Oscar's strength.

"You think you're ready to tell Hunter?" Looking up into his ice-blue eyes, I shake my head.

"How can I be? His whole life is about to change."

"I'll be there for you." He kisses my forehead. "I can tell him if you can't say the words. He's going to need you there, I can be the one who delivers the news."

"You would do that for me?"

"You should know by now, little one. I'd do anything for you."

Hours later, we're pulling up at the private airport. Christian's mum, a former nurse, gave Hunter a mild sedative—he didn't cope when he heard the news. That was the worst thing I ever had to do, watching this young kid literally shatter before me.

We get out of the car, and the next thing I see is Sienna and Derrick racing toward me, their arms stretched out, tears falling down their faces. They knew my family. We'd visit them often. Derrick loved to play cowboy out on the farm. They hit me full force and pulled me into their arms. I hold onto them tightly.

"I'm so sorry. So, so sorry." Sienna bawls.

"I have no words," Derrick adds.

"I don't believe it. We only saw them a day ago. They were here, living and breathing and now… now…" The tears fall again, and they pull me close, mumbling words of endearment to me. Eventually, I pull away from them. "Thank you, guys, for coming down to the airport to see me. I appreciate it so much, I better go."

"We're coming," Derrick adds. I still. What did he say?

"Did you seriously think I'd let you go through this alone?" Sienna asks me.

"We know you have your Viking, love, but now you have the two of us too." Derrick gives me a small smile.

"What about the babies?" I ask Sienna. She waves her hands in the air.

"Evan has it covered, plus his parents are down the road."

"What about work?" Derrick waves my concerns away.

"Sweetheart, it's called delegating." I burst into tears because I never expected this from my friends.

"Thank you, guys. Thank you so much."

"What are friends for?" Derrick smiles.

29

STACEY

We arrive in Australia. It's the middle of summer, and the heat really hits you. We then board a smaller private plane to take us to Mudgee from Sydney as the larger jet couldn't land at the regional airport. Thankfully, this time the paparazzi hasn't followed us. I couldn't deal with them with everything else going on. It's a dusty thirty-minute drive out to my family's farm from the airport.

Oscar holds my hand the entire way. I don't think he's let go of it since LA. He is my rock at this moment, the closer we get to the farm, the tighter my chest feels. Derrick and Sienna have been amazing, helping out with Hunter, who has totally shut down. The sedative wore off not long after arriving in Australia, and the closer he gets to the farm, the more glazed his eyes become.

The driver pulls into the long driveway. The red dirt blows up all around us. The once green grass is now a horrible brown color, and in most places, nonexistent. The dirt road leads us up to the white homestead. The house garden is looking green— mum loves her roses and vegetable patch. Because water is tight, she still doesn't want to give up on her garden, so she puts buckets in the shower to collect the water for them. She's also connected the gray water hose to a sprinkler in the garden—she doesn't waste a drop of water. The garden looks fantastic, considering everything else is dead around it. It's like a tiny oasis.

The front screen door swings open as the car pulls to a stop. My three nieces run out—Amelia is fifteen, Emma is thirteen, and Rebecca is ten. Hunter is the first one out of the car, heavy sobs falling from his lips, his sisters equally heartbroken. They all collapse into a pile of grief. My heart is being ripped out at this moment. Oscar pulls me into him as we give the siblings their moment together. I slowly walk over to where they are, and Emma is the first to look up.

"Aunt Stacey." She jumps up and into my arms. She buries her face into my chest, and the other two join her. I reach to wrap my arms as far as I can around them, holding them as tightly as possible. I never want to let them go. The screen door creaks, and Lockie's little shrieks pull us apart.

"Hunnie," Lockie calls for his brother. He kicks and whines in the neighbor's arms. She puts him down, and they run to each other. Hunter scoops up Lockie in his arms, holding him tightly, trying not to cry in front of the three-year-old. The girls stick close to me as I make my way toward the front stoop. Hilda O'Brien, our next-door neighbor and Mum's best friend, looks out to me, her eyes red raw with emotion, she's holding it in for us. I rush to where she is and pull her into my arms, and she's unable to hold it in anymore.

"It's not fair, Stace. It's not fair."

"Thank you for being here. Thank you for looking after them for me," I acknowledge as we untangle ourselves.

"You're family, girl. It's what we do." I nod in agreement.

"Shacey…" Lockie realizes I'm here too. He reaches out for

me, and I take him from Hunter's arms. My heart breaks, knowing how confused he must be. He has no idea that his family isn't coming home. He doesn't understand why everyone is crying. I bury my face into his little neck, making him giggle. I turn my crying into raspberries, hoping it will distract him from what's going on.

"Hey, little man. You have grown so big." My voice hitches as the moment hits me—he's going to grow up, and my sister will never see it. Tears begin to stream down my face. Again.

"No sad. Happy," he tells me, and I try to put on a smile. He reaches out for Hunter again. I turn around and see the girls are wrapped in Oscar's arms, Derrick and Sienna looking a right mess, trying to conceal their red, tear-stained faces.

"Come inside, I've popped the kettle on." Hilda opens the screen door for us. "You're probably exhausted after your long journey."

"Wasn't too bad... the joys of a private jet." I wince, realizing what the hell I said.

"Ah, yes. That does make traveling very comfortable. Your mum didn't stop talking about her trip on it over Christmas. She showed me the photos." I swallow down a sob. "You're probably hungry then. Let me make you all a sandwich or something." I'm suspecting Hilda needs something to do, so I follow her to the kitchen.

Mum's perfume is still in the air. The scent is taking me back to memories of her waking me up to get ready for school. The nostalgia is like an arrow to the heart. We pass my parents' bedroom, and I stop. The door is closed, I can't help myself because this doesn't seem real. I'm hoping she's sitting on her bed reading one of her racy romance books, her glasses sitting on the tip of her nose, her cheeks slightly flushed, caught up in some drama over a sheik or billionaire.

Quickly, I open it, the vision evaporates, and all that's before me is their empty room. Every morning Mum made her bed, no matter what. I run my hands over the quilt, a quilt my grandmother made for Mum for her wedding. An up-turned book is on the bedside table and a half-drunk glass of water with a bright pink lipstick stain on it. A photo of our family at Christmas in Big Bear is taking pride of place on her bedside table. I notice Dad's side next. A magazine about farm machinery sits hap haphazardly on the table. I collapse onto the bed, breathing in their scent, committing it to memory. The bed sinks beside me, and a large hand rests on my side.

"Let it out." His deep voice wraps around me like a beautiful security blanket. Sitting up, I wrap myself around him, purging as many tears as I can because this family is going to need me to be strong for them in the coming days. I can't keep breaking down.

"It's not fair. It is not fair," I scream into his chest.

"It's not." He rubs his hands across my back. Oscar holds me, rocking me, mumbling sweet words until I can't cry anymore. "Let it all out now, baby, because there are some kids out there who are going to need their aunt. And once they are in bed for the night, you can come back here and cry yourself to sleep. I'll hold you all night." He wipes the tears away. Then kisses each of my cheeks. "I promise you, Stacey, I've got you." I let out a heavy sigh. I can do this. I can be strong for those kids. I need to be strong for them because they don't have any other adults in their lives now.

Stepping out of my parents' room, I turn back into the living room.

"Here you go, love. A fresh cuppa and a corned beef sandwich." Hilda places them down in front of me. Emma and Rebecca come up and wrap their arms around me as I sit down on the bar stool.

"We love you, Stacey," Becca tells me. My heart breaks open.

"Girls, would you be able to show us around? It's been years since we have been here," Sienna asks, grabbing their attention. They go with her and Derrick, happy to show them both around. I take a sip of my tea and a small bite of my sandwich.

"The whole community is here for you, sweetheart. Whatever you need, we'll help," Hilda tells me.

"Thank you," I say, taking another shaky sip of my tea.

"If you like, I can talk to Fred down at the funeral home and get started on things while you settle yourself." Shit. The funeral. "You don't have to make any plans at all today. I want to let you know that while you grieve, I can help with that side of things." Hilda and Mum have been best friends for forty years, so I know she'd know what Mum and Dad would want for their funeral.

"It's not fair, Hilda. This whole thing isn't fair." The tears come again, I bite them back.

"I know, sweetheart. I know." She places a steady hand over mine. "Spending Christmas with you all last year made your mum so happy." Her hand pats me. "She was so proud of you. She told the whole town that her daughter was marrying a rock star." Oscar squeezes my shoulder hearing that bit of news. "And Simon and Naomi, it sounds like they had a fantastic holiday in Hawaii. Your mum showed me all the photos and videos of their time there that they had sent through. Giving them that time together, the two of them, was an amazing gift, Stacey." She squeezes my hand.

"I feel so guilty. If they hadn't gone on holiday, then they wouldn't be dead."

"Babe. No. No. You can't think like that. This was a terrible accident. You had no idea the holiday would end like this." The what-ifs still play in my head.

"Stacey. Don't. You can't play those what-if games. It's not healthy," Hilda tells me. "They left us at a time when they were at their happiest. Life's been tough for us out here with the drought. Many people have lost their livelihoods. Your sister was so looking forward to this trip, even Simon, the man who never speaks. They couldn't wait to travel again. They all didn't stop speaking about their time in the snow. Then going to Disneyland. Lockie thinks that's where you live with Mickey Mouse." This makes me smile. "We had no idea that their time was going to be cut short. They died being happy, and that's all anyone can hope for." Tears well in Hilda's eyes.

"What about the truck driver?" Anger fills my veins thinking about the person who took my family away.

"He died in the crash too." I would never wish this heartache on another family, if he had survived, I'd have made sure he'd be spending the rest of his life in jail. "You're the next of kin. The police will want to speak to you at some point as will the funeral home. I know there's a lot to think about, you need to have a plan for after the funeral. I know you live in LA, so I'd be more than happy to look after the kids." My first response is to pull my hand away from Hilda's. How dare she think I would leave my family.

"What!" My voice raises. What kind of person does she think I am?

"I didn't mean to offend you." Hilda back-peddles. "I wanted you to know that I am here if you need anything."

"That's very kind of you, Hilda," Oscar pipes in. He can see the steam falling from my ears. "I think everything is still so raw at the moment. We might get through the next couple of days first before we worry about what's going to happen in the future."

"Of course. Of course," Hilda agrees. "Well, I'll leave you be. You've come such a long way."

"Thank you, Hilda. Thank you for being here for them."

"Anytime." She gives me a sad smile, then walks out the front door.

"Thank you for jumping in on that." Oscar wraps his arms around me.

"I mean it. Now isn't the time to worry about the future. There are so many things we need to get through first before we worry about those kinds of questions." My arms tighten around him. I'm so thankful he's in my life.

30

OSCAR

What the hell is that sound? Is it even morning? My eyes slowly open, and orange streaks of light filter through the blinds.

"Damn chickens," Stacey mumbles beside me falls back asleep again. All I can say is thank goodness the house has air conditioning because this place is like a fucking oven. Yesterday was a big day. Not only from traveling halfway across the world also everyone's emotions were so highly strung. Poor little Lockie, he could feel the tension through the house and was acting up. Thankfully, Sienna was on hand to deal with toddler meltdowns. I was so out of my comfort zone. Give me a stadium of a hundred thousand people and no problems at all, a screaming three-year-old, and I'm beyond panicked.

The kids all wanted to share a room last night which was understandable, so they all pulled mattresses into Hunter's old room. Sienna and Derrick stayed at Stacey's parents' house while we stayed with the kids in Naomi and Simon's house. It's a short walk between the two properties. Once the kids were in bed, I made Stacey a bubble bath, massaged all of her muscles until she fell asleep, which didn't take long since she was exhausted

It's a big day today. We have a meeting with the funeral home to finalize things, the lawyer to read the will, and the police to pick up some belongings. I ease myself out of the squeaky guest bed, grab my phone, and walk outside. As soon as I step out the front door, a wall of heat hits me. I look down at my phone, and it's only 5:23 a.m., and it already feels like it's one hundred degrees. I press my mom's name and wait for the call to connect.

"Oscar, it's so good to hear from you," Mom answers the phone. "How's Stacey?"

"She's holding up. It's horrible, Mom… these kids losing their family. And the little one, Lockie, he has no idea what's going on." My voice strains thinking about that little boy.

"It's such a horrible situation. You need to be there for her. Be her rock when she needs it."

"I will, don't you worry. Today's going to be hard. We have to talk to the funeral home, then go to the lawyer as he has the wills, and then to the police station to pick up some effects that were in the car."

"Oh, honey. I wish I were there to help you both. Do you need me to come down? I can be on the next plane." I know she would be if I asked her to.

"Thanks, Mom, I don't want to overwhelm Stacey's family."

"Of course. Know I'm here for you both, okay?" I kind of want to give my mom a big hug at this moment. When we get back to LA, I'm going to make more time with my family.

"I have a question, though."

"Go ahead, honey."

"Do you think Stacey is going to want to stay?" There's silence on the other end of the phone. I pull the phone from my ear, she's still there. "Mom?"

"Honey…" she says slowly. "I think there's a real chance she's going to want to stay. She's probably their legal guardian. I mean, I can't see she'd leave them with Hunter, he's only turned eighteen. The kids are all still so small. After everything that they have been through, I don't know if moving them halfway across the world after such a horrible tragedy is in the cards." My stomach sinks. It's a thought that has been swirling around me for the past twenty-four hours. "The question is would you stay?" I look around at the red dust bowl.

"I can't see myself living on the farm. I mean, we're literally in the middle of nowhere."

"You love Stacey."

"I do."

"You could always buy something else or maybe even buy something in the city if you feel isolation is too much. Don't forget you can work from home."

"That's true. I know Evan wants to open up a label down here, as they want to spend more time in Australia than LA, I don't think I can be a farmer, Mom."

"You don't have to be one, sweetheart. You could love her, work from home, and keep the kids stable." Maybe Mom is right.

"I know, Mom, but… I love my life in LA." I'm letting myself have a vulnerable moment. I know LA has its faults, it's been my home for the past ten years. My family is there, but Stacey wouldn't be. My heart aches over the situation.

"I know you do, sweetheart. You can't ask Stacey to abandon her family either." I'd never do that, I get what Mom is saying. "We'd visit. We love Australia," she says cheerily. "Look, don't worry about things yet. Help her through the funeral and then worry about the future."

She's right. "Sweetheart, we love you, and we'll be here for you no matter what." I look out across the golden horizon as the sun rises high in the sky.

"I love you too. Thanks for listening."

"Anytime, sweetheart. Love you." And with that, we hang up. I take a deep breath and survey the land. Could I be happy here? I would have no choice because Stacey would be here, and I know for a fact that I wouldn't be happy without her in my life.

I knew the day would be hard, especially for the kids. Little Lockie stayed behind with Sienna and Derrick, the other kids wanted to come. Hilda and her husband, Don, met us at the funeral home. I told Stacey not to worry about the funeral cost, that I'd cover it. She fought me on it long and hard until Hunter interrupted and accepted on the family's behalf. I still think she's angry with me over it, I think she's fighting with me because she's sick of crying.

We then went to the lawyer's office, and the wills were read. Nothing surprising. Her parents left everything to the girls, which, in turn, left everything to Stacey. Naomi and Simon appointed Stacey as guardian to the children. Hunter chose that moment to declare he'd be staying back in Australia. He would take over the farm like he was always supposed to. He then told Stacey that her life was in LA, not Mudgee anymore. You could see that comment stung her to the core. She decided not to argue the fact in front of everyone.

Then, the last bit of our day was collecting some of her family's personal effects left at the scene—wallets, purses, and mobile phones. Stacey handed them straight to the kids, who held them close to their chests.

The journey home was a quiet affair. All the kids have gone to bed, and we're now sitting out on the front deck with Sienna and Derrick, having some beers. The sounds of the bush are coming alive. These insects called cicadas started up, and when they do, they almost deafen you with their song. I can't believe how dark it is out here and how many stars you can see. I was excited to see kangaroos bouncing around the paddocks. The landscape is beautiful, if not a little barren at the moment due to the decade-long drought the state has been suffering.

"I think the kids are pleased to get some items back." Derrick breaks the silence.

"It's not much, but it is something." Stacey plays with the label on her beer bottle.

"Lockie has been really well-behaved," Sienna informs Stacey, who nods. They both give me a concerned look.

"I'm gonna have to talk to Dad's mortgage broker in the morning. Find out how much is owing on the farm and the homes," Stacey states more to herself than to anyone conversing. "And Hunter thinks he's going to be able to pay for it all. The mortgage, the kids' schooling, the bills on some farmer's wage." I knew Hunter's comments hurt her.

"He probably thinks it's the right thing to do," I add.

"And you think that I wouldn't do the right thing?" Stacey's anger radiates at me.

"Of course, you would do the right thing." Those green eyes narrow at me as she manically pulls the label off the bottle.

"You won't be a part of it." Huh? What the—Sienna and Derrick look at me, confused.

"Excuse me... what did you say?" Maybe I heard her wrong.

"I bet you can't wait to get on the first flight back to LA, to civilization, your cozy life, and your precious fucking club." Stacey abruptly stands up, her chair screeching loudly across the deck as she starts heading into the darkness.

"Stacey," I call after her.

"I heard you on the phone to your mum this morning."

My stomach sinks. Fuck. That would have hurt hearing that.

"It's not what you think."

"What, that you could never see yourself in a shitbox like this?" she screams at me.

"I never said that."

"It's what you meant," she screams at me again.

"Leave me alone," she calls from the darkness. Is she seriously walking back to her parents' house? The area is pitch back. There are snakes and shit out there.

"Stacey. Come back. It's dark out there. You'll get lost." Sienna and Derrick follow me into the darkness. A little shiny spec in the distance illuminates the area.

"Got my phone. I'll be all right."

"Wait for me then." I pull my mobile phone out of my pocket and turn on the flash-light mode.

"Don't bother. I'd rather be alone," she yells back at me. I pause in my tracks as if she stabbed me in the heart. Derrick's hand rests on my shoulder.

"She's been through a lot these past couple of days, and she doesn't mean it. She might need to be alone." My head hangs with hurt. Maybe he's right.

"She's had a really hard day today, and from what the girls told me about what happened in the lawyer's office with the will, it seems like she's really hurt. Give her time. I'm sure she's got a lot going on in her head, and she's lashing out at the ones she loves." Maybe Sienna's right.

Stacey didn't come home that night.

"Morning." I surprise Amelia, who's rubbing her eyes. Seriously, how does anyone sleep with all this light? She takes a seat on the bar stool.

"Stacey didn't come home?" I look at her, surprised. How did she know about that? "I heard you fighting." My shoulders sink.

"I'm sorry. We didn't mean for you to hear that."

"What Hunter said at the lawyer's, it wasn't right."

"I know, he's trying to help." Amelia nods.

"What Stacey said to you, is it true? Do you want to go back to LA?"

"No. God, no. My life is with Stacey and now with you guys, wherever that is."

Why did she think you don't want to live here?" Amelia pushes.

"Honestly?" I look at her, she nods in agreement. "I had a moment on the phone to my mom." I cringe saying that because Ameila won't ever get to do that. "It was the first morning here. It was all a little overwhelming. I've never been anywhere like this before."

"So, you would live here?" Amelia waves her arms around the small kitchen.

"Of course. It's what's best for you guys." She nods.

"What happens if we don't want to stay here?" My head tilts, confused.

"What, you don't want to stay in this house?" Amelia nods.

"We can buy a new one if you don't want to stay here anymore," I say, trying to reassure her.

"My sisters and I were talking last night. We don't want to stay here."

"Okay. I can talk to Stacey about it. Let's not make any hasty decisions while you're grieving." I really need to talk to Stacey about all this.

"If we wanted to move to America, can we stay with you?" My body stills.

"You want to move to LA?" She nods her head. "Why?" I ask, confused.

"There are opportunities there."

"Do you not like your town?" Amelia shakes her head.

"Ever since people found out you and Stacey are together, they started treating my sisters and me differently. We're outcasts. Kids are assholes," Amelia states. What! They are getting picked on because of me.

"Do we need to talk to your principal or teachers or something?" This is so far out of my realm of expertise.

"There's nothing left for us here, Oscar."

"What about your memories?" Amelia shakes her head.

"We want a fresh start. Growing up in a small town and having a tragedy such as this... that follows you around. People stare. They talk. They pity you. We'll always be known as the Ferguson kids, who lost their family. They have already started to treat us differently." I did notice it when we went into town, I thought I was reading too much into it. "Can you talk to Stacey about this?"

"Let's talk about this after the funeral." Amelia nods.

"Thanks for listening, Oscar. Stacey's lucky to have you in her life." Her words hit me and my heart blooms with love for this family. Amelia turns on her heel and shuffles back to her room. Moments later the screen door creaks open and Stacey walks in.

"Morning, babe." I keep my voice normal.

"You're not going to yell at me?" Stacey looks at me in shock, tears welling in her eyes.

"Baby, why would I yell at you?"

"Because I was an epic bitch last night." She turns on her heels and rushes back outside again. I chase after her.

"Stacey. Wait." I catch up to her.

"How can you not hate me?" Tears fall down her cheeks. I grab her face between my palms and kiss her salty tears from her cheeks.

"I could never hate you, little one. You're my everything." Stacey collapses into my arms crying. "Shh, baby. Shh, it's going to be okay, I promise." Stacey hiccups on a sob.

"I can't do this without you, Oscar. I can't."

"I'm never leaving you. You hear me. If I have to become a sheep farmer and battle snakes and spiders and whatever other animals that can kill you in Australia I will do that." This makes her smile.

"Wow. You must really love you me." She laughs through her sobs.

"I do, little one, I do. And I'm sorry you heard that moment of weakness with my mom. The stupid chickens had just woken me up, not to mention all the fucking flies that want to impregnate my mouth. I was just a little overwhelmed by all this." I look out over the red barren desert.

"I guess it is a little confronting." At least this gets me a genuine smile. "I'm sorry, babe."

"You have nothing to apologize for. You're going through so much at the moment."

"It's not an excuse to be a bitch to you."

"I can give you a spanking if you want." I nuzzle into her neck which makes her giggle.

"As tempting as that sounds, there isn't a moment of alone time in these houses." This is so true.

"Guess, I will just keep a score of how many spankings I owe you and when the time is right, I'll deliver them." She shivers ever so faintly. Now isn't really the time for getting our kink on but I need her to know when the time does come she better watch out.

"Thank you." She wraps her arms around my neck.

"Apology accepted. But never ever sleep apart from me again, do you hear me?" She nods her head eagerly. "I hated us being apart."

"Me too."

31

OSCAR

"Is everyone ready?" Stacey asks. The kids all nod somberly. Tonight they are scattering their family's ashes underneath the big gum tree which overlooks the dam. Apparently, they used to have family picnics by its banks, and it was the family's favorite spot. The funeral was yesterday, and the whole community came out for it. Hundreds of people attended and paid their respects to the Ferguson/Davies family. The kids held up surprisingly well as did Stacey. Not going to lie, seeing the four coffins before us was heartbreaking. I can't imagine nor do I want to imagine being in Stacey's shoes. The thought of it kills me.

We jump into the farm Ute, and all the kids pile into the back, each holding an urn. We make the journey out to the old gum tree. I help the girls out of the Ute, they dust themselves off and head toward the tree. There's an old picnic table sitting beside the now dried-up bank of the dam. The sun is beginning to set as we all stop and look out over the landscape. Four kangaroos hop buy along the horizon.

"Did you see that?" Hunter points to the kangaroos.

"There are four," Emma counts.

"That's a sign." Stacey smiles. The family all holds hands, taking in the moment. "Does anyone want to say any words?"

"Love you, Mum, Dad, Pop, and Nan," Amelia starts.

"Miss you all." Emma sniffles. Becca shakes her head, too overcome with emotion.

"Look, star." Lockie points to the lone star rising in the orange-streaked sky.

"They're going home." Stacey smiles to herself. "Are you all ready?" she asks, looking nervously at her family. They all nod. "Goodbye, guys. We hope you're happy together. Miss you all. I promise to look after everyone," Stacey says through her tears. Then, one by one, they each pour the ashes out, the wind taking them, scattering across the red earth. The four kangaroos stay on the horizon until the very last spec of ash has blown away. Then they bound off into the darkness.

"I can't believe it's over," Hunter says to the group. His sisters rush around him as they have a moment.

It's been a couple of days since the funeral, and Amelia has asked me to call a family meeting regarding their wishes to leave and come home to America. Thankfully, Sienna and Derrick are still here, they are leaving tomorrow to return home.

"Hey." I stick my head into Stacey's parents' house where she's sorting things out with Derrick and Sienna. "The kids want a family meeting in five." Her eyes widen, she follows me.

"What's going on?" The concern is evident in her voice.

"It's all good. The girls want to talk to you." I don't think that relaxes her. We walk back into the other house, where the girls sit at the dining room table, and Hunter plays cars with Lockie on the floor. He has no idea what this meeting is about either.

"Is everything okay?" Stacey asks them.

"We want to talk about what happens next," Amelia tells her. Stacey looks over at me, and I indicate for her to sit down.

"Hear them out before you say anything," I warn her and Hunter. This gets Hunter's attention, who moves from the floor to the table with them. Derrick and Sienna decide to sit with Lockie to entertain him while they all chat. The girls look nervous.

"We've been talking…" Amelia starts and looks over at me for help. "Oscar, can you…"

"The girls would like to talk to you about maybe living somewhere else."

"What the fuck!" Hunter raises his voice.

"Hunter," Stacey scolds him.

"You can't be serious. They want to move. Our parents have only been gone for two weeks, and they are ready to forget them." The girls burst out crying. Stacey quickly consoles them.

"Hunter," my voice raises loudly. He shrinks a little at my tone. "I asked you to listen to them. It took a huge amount of courage for them to talk to me about this. Now I'm asking you to respectfully hear them out." I look over, the girls are now really upset. Hunter was way too harsh on them. "The girls would like to talk to you about maybe considering a move back to LA." The room falls silent. Hunter looks shocked.

"You want to leave?" he asks his sister.

"You have no idea, Hunter. We're sick of being bullied and the kids making fun of us. We want a new life," Amelia shouts

"You're getting bullied?" Stacey asked them.

"Because we're different now," Amelia tells her.

"What do you mean?"

"Because you're with me," I tell her. Stacey's eyes widen.

"People are bulling you because of me?"

"They think we're too good for them because we hang out with 'celebrities,'" Emma adds.

"You know how small this town is, Stace. Any little thing

that makes you different makes you a target." Amelia snuggles closer into Stacey.

"I had no idea."

"Mum never wanted to tell you. She thought it would make you feel bad," Emma confirms.

"Of course, I feel bad. Why wouldn't I? I'm the reason people are bullying you."

"Tell her," Becca whispers to her sister.

"No," Amelia says back.

"Tell me what?" Stacey looks between them.

"I swallowed some pills last year."

"What!" Stacey's voice raises.

"It was stupid. Nothing happened. I didn't know what to do."

"Oh, Mia. I'm so sorry. So, so sorry." Stacey cries.

"I don't want to go back to school, Stacey. Please," Amelia begs. Stacey turns to me, looking lost. "It's going to be so much worse. Everyone is going to treat us differently."

"I don't think your mum would want me to pull you from school," she tells her niece.

"They couldn't afford the private school. They looked into it."

"Why did they not ask me for the money? I'd have helped."

"The same reason you won't let Oscar help you. Being stubborn is a family trait," Amelia tells her aunt.

"Where do you want to go?" Hunter asks quietly.

"I said they could live with us," I tell them.

"Oscar." Stacey gasps.

"I told them it would be up to you to make the decision, they are welcome to live with us. We can even look at maybe purchasing a new house."

"Oscar," she says my name with a shocked tone.

"It's not his fault, Aunt Stacey. We asked him," Amelia confesses.

"I think Oscar and I have to talk about this." Stacey glares at me.

"You can't be serious?" Hunter questions her. "You're seriously thinking about moving everyone to LA?"

"I said I need to talk to Oscar about it."

"I don't understand." He rakes his hand through his hair.

"You can stay," Amelia tells him. Hunter glares at her before turning on his heel and walking out the door.

"I'll get him." I rush after him.

"Hey, buddy." He ignores me. I grab his arm, and he goes to take a swing at me. "You wanna hit me, tough guy?" He takes a swing at me again, his punch getting me in the side. "Come on. Again," I goad him. Hunter swings violently at me, I easily defend myself. Over and over and over he swings until he can't lift his arms and falls into a puddle of tears. I wrap myself around him as he sobs. "Don't be angry at them."

"How can they leave it all behind?"

"They want a fresh start. It sounds like they have been having a tough time." He looks defeated.

"What about Mum and Dad? Gran and Pop?"

"We can keep this place. It will always be yours. Just because they aren't with us anymore doesn't mean the memories fade."

"I feel like we're abandoning them."

"No, you're not. They will always be with you no matter where you are."

"You know Amelia is going to want a car? She's turning sixteen this year." This makes me chuckle.

"She's going to have to get that past her aunt first. I'm the easy one." Hunter smiles.

"I'm sorry about hitting you."

"It's all good. Go easy on your sisters. It took a lot of courage today for them to tell everyone about what they have been going through." Hunter hangs his head.

"I had no idea it was that bad or that Amelia was so unhappy."

"Yeah, that was scary to hear." We sit in the dirt in silence.

"I guess it wouldn't be so bad to go back." I raise my brow at him.

"Really?" He nods.

"I guess as long as we're all together, that's all that matters." I ruffle his hair.

"You're a good kid, Hunter Davies." He smiles at me.

32

STACEY

The kids have gone to bed early after such an emotional afternoon. I had no idea the girls were getting bullied because I'm with Oscar. I'm even more shocked that Amelia took a bunch of pills because of it. God, Mum, I wish you were here to guide me. On the one hand, I want to make the girls happy, on the other, I wonder if I should change the girls' school instead of their country. Sienna, Derrick, Oscar, and I are sitting on the back veranda drinking beer and looking out into the darkness.

"That was a bit intense." Derrick starts the conversation.

"I feel so bad for the girls," Sienna adds.

"I don't know what to do."

"You should get married and adopt the kids," Derrick states, sipping his beer. Oscar practically chokes on his, and I'm as shocked. "What? You're already engaged. You go to court next week to finalize the guardianship of the kids."

"It's not that simple, D," I tell him.

"Yes, it is. Oscar has enough money to hire good lawyers to speed up everything. The kids are having a crap time at school. It seems Amelia has already had a bad brush with depression. The kids are telling you they want a fresh start. Don't you think they deserve that? I've seen the way people in town look at your family. Everyone is awkward. You can see the pity. The kids pick up on all that shit. They've been through so much already." Does Derrick actually have a point?

"You would have support back home with all of us being there. You wouldn't be alone." I look over at Oscar nodding in agreement. That has been a fear of mine being stuck out here, Oscar and me. We don't know how to parent, but I will say he has done some awesome parenting with the girls, especially since they felt comfortable enough to talk to him first about this.

"It will take a month or two to get your paperwork for the states ready. In that time, apply for a marriage license, you can get married after thirty days. It's done. You're a family. Then you can make a new life in America." Has Derrick gone slightly insane?

"It might help our case being married," Oscar adds.

"Ragnar, what the fuck? That's not romantic," Derrick tells him, and Oscar turns to me.

"Stacey Ferguson. I love you with all my heart. What we have been through these past couple of weeks has only brought us closer together. It's made me realize what's important in my life, and that is you." Oscar is down on one knee again. "Will you marry me in thirty days?" My heart is racing. He can't be serious.

"Do it. Do it. Do it," Derrick chants.

"Yes. Let's do this." Derrick and Sienna cheer to us. Oscar picks me up and kisses me.

"You sure about this?" I ask him one last time.

"Fuck, yes."

33

STACEY

I watch as the bright orange streaks light up the horizon. The birds' morning call echoes all around us. I sip my freshly brewed coffee on the front veranda overlooking the garden. Oscar is out there collecting the eggs from the chickens—his morning ritual. He's really started to embrace this way of life, working the land, seeing the fruits of his labor. Every morning he's up at dawn, the bright sunlight making it hard to sleep in any longer. While it's still cool, he gets dressed and goes for a run around the family's garden that connects the two homes via a wonderful green path. It's about a couple of acres in size. He's mentioned he isn't brave enough to venture further after he and Don, our next-door neighbor, ran into a brown snake while moving a wood heap. Oscar defiantly milks that 'near death' experience, as he calls it, with me, I'm happy to get on my knees for him because that man has been my rock through all of this.

I might not have been able to see it through my consuming grief this past month. It's been there in the simple things he does, like putting the kettle on in the morning, so it's boiled by the time I get up. Taking the kids to school most mornings, helping me sort through my family's clothing and belongings, and holding me when I'd catch a whiff of my mum's perfume amongst her clothes, the grief overwhelming me again, and by being my rock.

Oscar and I haven't really had many tests in our relationship until now, not that we needed one. What we have is good. Yes, it was focused a lot on our sex life, we don't have kids, unlike all our friends, so we've been more selfish with our life and time. Now we've gone from a couple who wasn't interested in the traditional life to being all about that life. And honestly, I think it suits us. It's hard, don't get me wrong, those ratbags do give us joy, especially Lockie, with his finger painting and the crazy things he says.

Before our lives got turned upside down, there was a tiny thought deep down that I worried maybe all Oscar and I had was a deep sexual connection, that without the kinky side of life, maybe one of us would stray. Since we've been living together, our time at The Paradise Club hasn't been as frequent, but we still went. This is the longest we have gone without going there, and to add to it, we haven't really had anything sexual for the first two weeks we were here, which is a long time for us. It worried me. It added to my stress about everything and made me want to push him away. He wouldn't listen, and he wouldn't go. He'd tell me I was stuck with him forever. That, yes, he loves sex, but he loves me more, and he would be a real dick for pressuring me into sex while dealing with the awful tragedy.

That man surprises me every day with the depth of his love and commitment, something I should never have questioned during my weakest moments. Our sex has slowly gotten back on track, maybe not as wild and kinky as it used to be but still as satisfying. Now, I understand why Sienna and Evan continually bang at work.

Trying to find special time with your partner with kids is hard, especially when Lockie jumps into bed with us in the middle of the night. The first time he did, it was a shock, especially as Oscar likes to sleep naked. I've never seen Oscar move so quickly in his entire life to put some boxers on. Lockie then proceeded to tell everyone around the breakfast table in the morning that he saw Oscar's penis. We quickly explained what happened there. Oscar now sleeps with boxers on.

"Morning, gorgeous." Oscar comes bounding toward me with a basket full of eggs.

"Morning." A smile forms on my face.

"The girls have been laying really well this week. I think I'm going to have to google some egg recipes because we have dozens." That's right, ladies, my man can cook too. It's a new skill he has acquired recently. Most nights, he gets dinner for the family, the girls pitching in after they do their homework. It's quite a domesticated scene with everyone finding a new routine around each other. Oscar takes the kids to school as he gets up so early. He has learned how to drive on the 'wrong side of the road' as he calls it, and Hunter picks them up in the afternoons. He then goes and helps Don in the paddocks, getting the sheep ready for market. Unfortunately, we aren't going to get a good price for them because of the drought, and everyone is selling their stock as it's too expensive to keep feeding them, so there's an oversupply in the market.

We're experiencing one of the worst droughts in history at the moment—some places haven't seen rain in years. Farmers who have worked this land for generations are shutting up shop and trying to get new jobs or are leaving town. The effect this has on the community is devastating because then the little businesses in town that rely on the community don't have enough business to get by. Then slowly, one by one, shops close, people move away, and it becomes a ghost town. I know this was a fear my family has had. They've been working on this land for four generations—our family's farm has been passed down with each generation.

We've decided to keep the farm and rent it out as we have the two houses and could generate some income for the kids in their trust funds they will have access to when they are twenty-one. The money from the sheep sale will go to that too. I know that's what their parents would want, to set them up.

"You look so beautiful sitting there." Oscar bends down and kisses me on the forehead as he walks past me into the house. His words wash over me, extinguishing my anxiety. I finish my coffee and walk back inside, placing my cup in the sink.

"You look happy." I catch Oscar humming away as he cleans the eggs, placing them into the cartons.

"That's because I am. This makes me happy. Who knew?" Oscar smiles at me.

"Washing eggs?" I chuckle. He rolls his eyes at me.

"This… collecting the eggs each morning and picking fresh fruit and vegetables from the garden. I don't even have to go to the store to get anything since it's all here." His eyes light up with wonderment.

"I can't believe you got Lockie to start eating his vegetables." Oscar gives me a proud shrug.

"Can we do this when we get home?" he asks. I tilt my head in confusion at him.

"What?"

"All this. The chickens. The gardens. The animals." When we first arrived, Oscar hated the chickens. They were so loud and would wake him up every morning.

"You want to be a farmer?"

Oscar grins. "I guess. A little. I like having all this fresh produce at our doorstep."

"We live in LA. Not sure there are any farms there."

"People live on acreage in Malibu, or we can go further north to Ojai."

"You don't want to live in LA anymore? What about work?" I watch as he continues to scrub the muck off the eggs.

"Evan and Sienna are spending more and more time in Byron Bay. Evan loves the lifestyle, and he's thinking of opening up Dirty Texas Records in Sydney." I knew they were thinking about it. Sienna did mention that she was looking into a boutique space in Byron. "Axel and Olivia spend half the year in London, anyway, I think Axel has really embraced the whole lord-of-the-manor thing. They are spending more and more time there, especially with the London office taking off."

"Christian and Finn are still in LA," I mention.

"Yeah, Finn and Issy love their place in Hawaii, and Christian and Ness commute up to Big Bear a lot of the time too."

"So, you don't want to live in LA anymore?" This concerns me because isn't that the reason we're moving back there because all our family and friends are there?

"Hey." Oscar notices the worry on my face. "Why are you frowning?" He looks at me with concern.

"Well, isn't that why we're moving there, because everyone is there, if everyone isn't there, then why are we moving?" This stills him.

"Babe." He pulls me into his arms. "Sorry. I didn't mean to worry you. I was thinking out loud. Dirty Texas Records is still so busy, and there are so many things we all want to do with it. I think, over the years, as the kids get older, then maybe our group might start to splinter off more and more around the world, at this very moment, everyone will still be together."

"Okay." Oscar kisses my forehead as he turns back to his eggs.

"I've been thinking we should upgrade the house. I've found some great properties." Wow, who knew collecting eggs would have Oscar contemplating the future so much? "I think we need more room."

"You want to move?" My voice rises.

"Mom and Dad have been staying with Issy and Finn in the guest house, helping out with Easton, he will be one in a couple of months. I was thinking they could have our old place, and we can have something a little bit bigger to accommodate everyone, especially something with more bathrooms. Who knew girls would fight so much over them?" This makes me smile.

"You're serious?" He nods as he continues to wash the eggs. "And you want to upgrade to a farm?"

"No. I think the farm should be our holiday place, somewhere we go to escape the city. You know, like Finn and Isla's beach house down in Malibu."

"So, you want to buy two new places?" He shrugs as if buying real estate is no big deal. I guess to him, it isn't.

"I wouldn't mind a place down there, but, in the mountains, we could have something with a perfect view of the Pacific Ocean, then acres and acres of land we could cultivate." You can hear the excitement in his voice. "We can have a pool, tennis court, ATV track, and the girls can have horses. Lockie could have a little dirt bike and ride around." He's really selling this to me. "We can have an orchard, vegetable gardens, and maybe some bees." My eyes widen in surprise—he's actually serious. "Maybe even some sheep so it reminds the kids of home."

He gives me that rock-star grin. How the hell did I get so lucky? I wrap my arms around his back as his hands are stuck in the sink and hug him. He stops what he's doing and turns around in my arms. He wipes his soapy hands on his shorts and cradles my face. "I love you, and I want what's best for this family." Butterflies flutter in my stomach at the word 'family.' He's already thinking about these kids as his family. My heart overflows with love for this man. "The kids want a new life, and I think we deserve one too."

Suddenly Broken 215

"Okay." He stares at me in surprise.

"Just like that. No arguing. No pouting. You're going to agree with me."

"Yep." He doesn't quite believe me.

"You're not usually this agreeable, especially this early in the morning."

"Maybe it's your impressive selling skills."

"I am impressive." He grins.

"That you are." Standing on my tiptoes, I kiss him.

"Eeewww." Amelia comes into the kitchen, busting us. We break apart laughing. "Who knew collecting eggs turned you on." She rolls her eyes at us both. Oscar and I give each other a knowing look.

"Hey, Mia," Oscar calls out, returning to his egg-cleaning duties. She busies herself in the kitchen getting breakfast, but she's listening. "I was thinking of maybe purchasing a farm when we got back to the states," he tells her cautiously. She stills. He has her attention now.

"Would we not be living in LA?"

"We would, it would be a second house." Her eyes widen.

"Are you that rich?" Oscar chuckles.

"I've done okay for myself." Amelia's eyes narrow.

"Are there farms in LA?" Oscar looks over at me. Hey, we're not trying to stereotype.

"Yes, out in Malibu."

"Isn't that the beach?"

"There is land in the hills, or we can look further north."

"Why?" Typical teenager response.

"Because I thought that you guys might like a little slice of home over there." Amelia looks over at me for my reaction.

"Oscar really wants it for himself. He really loves chickens." Pointing to him cleaning the eggs makes Amelia laugh.

"If it makes you happy, Oscar. Then sure," she agrees, filling up her cereal bowl. Oscar looks happy with himself.

"Also…" he starts, "… I was thinking of buying a new place in LA. One that would have room for us all."

"Umm. Hate to break it to you, your house is already huge," she tells him sarcastically, pouring milk into her bowl.

"I know, I kind of wanted a fresh start for all of us. A chance to make it our own." The sincerity in his voice grabs Amelia's attention.

"You would do that?"

"Of course. We're family. You're moving halfway across the world to start all over again. It's a big deal. If having your own room will help you all settle in better, then I'm willing to do it." Amelia stills. She looks up at Oscar, her green eyes a little glassy, and the next thing he knows, she's wrapping herself around him.

"Thank you." She sniffles into his side.

"Hey, baby girl." He wraps his large arms around her, dripping soapy suds all over the floor. "I'd do anything for you guys," he consoles her. She hugs him tighter, showing him exactly how much his words mean to her. *My heart is overflowing with love for this man.*

"What's going on?" Emma and Becca walk into the kitchen and look around at the scene before them.

"Oscar is buying us a new house," Amelia announces.

"Really?" Emma questions. He nods.

"How about tonight after dinner, we have a look at some houses, and you can tell me what you like."

"I want a pool," Becca tells him.

"Done," Oscar agrees. Emma and Becca's eyes light up as they start listing off their requirements for a new home. *I don't think he understands what he's started.*

34

STACEY

"What the hell are you two doing here?" I'm staring at Camryn and Yvette, who have turned up on my doorstep unannounced.

"Derrick sent us an SOS that we have a wedding to get ready for in less than a month." Camryn embraces me, hugging me tightly.

"And a bride needs a dress," Yvette greets me. I'm genuinely in shock. These two have flown halfway across the world to help me. Tears begin to fall.

"Hey, no tears," Camryn tells me. "We don't have time for tears. There's so much to do. Derrick told me it's going to take a lot of work to get all this…" she waves her hands around, "… to be ready for a celebrity wedding."

"I kind of thought we'd tie the knot at a local registry office or something." Camryn's eyes almost pop out of her head. She shakes her head furiously.

"Seriously, Stacey?"

I hadn't thought much about it, we did send off the paperwork to get our marriage license a while ago—Derrick kind of forced that before he went back home. We had the court case this week regarding the kids' guardianship. Even though the will states me, the court could decide that I'm not the right person to be raising these kids. It was hard. They were worried about Oscar's celebrity status and all that brings. Thankfully, we had an amazing family lawyer who was able to spin that around into a positive. The court agreed, and when they finally confirmed that I was the kids' legal guardian, an enormous weight lifted off the kids and me, so we could all slowly start to breathe again.

"Never really put much thought into my wedding." Camryn clutches her chest and looks at me with horror.

"Thank God, I'm here. It sounds like you need all the help you can get." Yvette nods in agreement.

"But… I…"

"What the fuck?" Oscar steps out onto the veranda and spots Camryn and Yvette.

"Derrick sent them," I tell him. His eyes widen, and a smile falls across his face.

"Of course, he did." He chuckles.

"Apparently, we're having a celebrity wedding." I roll my eyes at him.

"Like fuck we are." Oscar's voice raises. "Sorry." He calms himself.

"Maybe we should sit down and have a chat about what it is you both want? Because I have Derrick's ideas, by the sound of it, those aren't yours at all." Camryn nudges us.

"I hate to think what Derrick had planned."

"You don't want to know." Camryn chuckles.

We all settle into the living room, and Camryn pulls out her laptop and a couple of wedding magazines as does Yvette. She has samples of material and lace for me to look at.

"I have one request, though," I mention to the girls. "I want you to use local businesses where possible." Camryn's eyes widen. "This community has been hit hard with the drought, and something like a wedding this size would save a lot of them. So, hairdressers, florists, event hire, cake decorator, and umm... local wines, local produce. I want the community to celebrate with us. They have been so great after everything, and this would be a nice way to give back and maybe even help show the world the amazing treasures that are here in Mudgee."

"Okay, we can do that." Camryn states.

This eases my anxiety over the event. Oscar takes a seat beside me and places a reassuring hand on my knee.

"I never planned on getting married..." Oscar looks over at me, giving me a small smile, "... until I met Stace." The girls gush at his sweet words. "So, whatever you want, babe, I'm all in on." He squeezes my knee. "No budget too." He looks over at Camryn, who nods and tells him what a good man he is.

"I don't want to waste money on a wedding." This stills the room. Camryn looks like she might have a heart attack at any moment by my comment. "It's going to be us," I remind them.

"Um..." Camryn shakes her head. "Derrick has organized with everyone, and they are all tentatively booked in to be here for it." Oscar and I look at each other surprised.

"Really?" My throat tightens at the thought of everyone wanting to come and celebrate with us.

"Yes. No one wants to miss your day. They all want to be here with you both." Oscar's hand squeezes my knee again, tightly, the emotion getting to him.

"Okay then." Camryn smiles at my agreement. "I want it to be a celebration then. Because in essence, this party will be like our farewell. Once the visas and passports come through, we'll be moving back home."

"So, you want a non-traditional wedding, then?" Camryn asks.

"Yes. Exactly that. I don't want anything flashy. Honestly, a barbecue in the backyard with all our family and friends, I'd be happy with that."

"How about a sophisticated barbecue?" Camryn suggests. I look over at a smiling Oscar. "Yes. Exactly that."

"I think we should get married underneath the weeping willow on the side of the dam where we scattered the ashes. That way, your family could be there with us." I suck in a breath at Oscar's comment. Then there's that pang of reality that hits me every so often, reminding me of all the things my family is missing out on. "The kids would love it, too," he adds. I reach out and grab his hand in mine, the emotion getting to me.

"We can easily do that," Camryn agrees, giving me a moment to compose myself. "Maybe, you could show us around later on, and we can get some ideas." I nod, trying to get the knot in my throat to untie itself. "This is a fantastic start, guys. We can easily put together an elegant yet simple country celebration, where it's more about making memories than anything else." That's exactly it.

Not going to admit it out loud, I might be a little excited.

"And what about the dress?" Yvette asks.

"I'll stop you there, ladies. Babe, I don't want to hear anything about it until I see you walking down the aisle or whatever it is you'll be walking down," Oscar tells me. "So, I'll leave you all to it. I've got some things to do out back anyway." He stands up and kisses my forehead before running away really quickly.

"He's a real softy under all that gruff, isn't he?" Camryn muses.

"He's a giant teddy bear." I smile.

Oscar comes back into the room with his hand over his eyes.

"Is it safe?" We all laugh at him.

"Yes," we call out.

"Good. I didn't want to see something I shouldn't. "I'm off to pick up the kids." He rattles the keys in his hands. We say our goodbyes, and he's out the door. Camryn and Yvette stare at me in bewilderment.

"What?" I ask, looking between them both.

"Domestication looks good on both of you." Camryn smirks. "For a couple who didn't want the traditional life, you two seem to be coping well with it."

"This wasn't in our plans at all, somehow we're fumbling our way through it all, and it works."

"The man is doing the school run," Yvette adds.

"I know." I smile. "He's talking about buying a farm when he gets home." Camryn chokes on her tea. "I know. He even spent the other night searching through hundreds of homes with the kids until they found one that suited all their needs and then bought it." Camryn and Yvette look at me with disbelief. "Just like that. The kids think he's fucking God now." This makes us chuckle.

"He sounds like a changed man," Camryn adds.

"Yeah, he has. We both have, I worry."

"Worry about what?" Yvette questions.

"I worry that maybe one day he's going to wake up and resent this new life."

"No way. The way that man looks at you, he's all in," Camryn tells me.

"I know. I just... I'm overthinking things, aren't I?" They both nod their heads at me.

"I don't think Oscar would be buying a new house, one that's perfect for the kids if he weren't all in," Camryn reminds me.

"You're right. I need to stop worrying."

"It's understandable to worry. I mean, Stacey, your world has been turned upside down, and things are all happening really quickly. Of course, you'll be overthinking everything," Camryn explains to me. "Don't be so hard on yourself." She's right. "And also talk to Oscar and don't bottle up your fears because us women like to do that. Don't be scared to voice any concerns you have to him. He's a good guy."

"Thanks, guys." I'm feeling a little lighter.

"Come, show us around. I have so many ideas, and I need to see if they will work." Camryn enthusiastically wiggles in her seat.

We jump into the Ute, and I start giving Camryn and Yvette the grand tour of the farm. They are both quiet as we travel along the dusty, dirt-lined roads, taking it all in.

"What's that?" Camryn points to an old rusty tin shed.

"That's the old shearing shed."

"I want to see it." I turn the steering wheel and head on over. Camryn jumps out of the car and rushes into the shed. She pulls open the rusted doors, which groan at the sudden movement. It's hot, dusty, and stinks of sheep. I can see it on her face, she has found something that has her excited. "This. This is it." Is she mad?

"This old thing. It looks like it will fall in the next storm." Camryn waves her hands at me.

"Have faith, Stace. I promise you when I'm done, this shed is going to look like a million bucks."

"Okay."

"I don't think I heard you. Say it again." Camryn smiles.

"Okay." I raise my voice.

"Hell, yeah," Camryn squeals, pulling me into her arms and hugging me. "I promise you, Stacey, I'll make your family proud." Damn her. The waterworks start again.

"We're home." Oscar stomps along the veranda, letting us know they're home. "Can I come in?" he calls out.

"Yes," we call from the living room. All the dress ideas have been put away.

"What's going on?" Emma asks, looking at us all huddled around Camryn's laptop.

"We're organizing your aunt's wedding," Camryn answers.

"I wanna see." Becca rushes over, then Amelia and Emma join us on the couches. The girls ooh and aah over the pictures Camryn is showing them.

"What are we going to wear?" Becca asks.

"Well, what would you like to wear?" Becca's eyes light up.

"Can I wear anything?" She looks over at me.

"Of course, you can," I tell her. She can wear a clown suit if it makes her happy.

"Oh my God. I have so many ideas," she gushes. The talk turns back to fashion.

"I'm taking the boys over to the other house," Oscar tells us, leaving us to chat about our dresses.

"What does your dress look like, Stace?" Amelia asks.

"Umm, well… it's not really traditional at all." The girl's eyes widen. "It's kind of me, I think?" I click on the folder that holds the inspiration for my wedding dress. The gorgeous emerald green velvet 1940's-style backless dress fills the screen. Everyone is silent for what feels like forever.

"You're going to look like a princess, Aunt Stacey," Becca says with awe.

"I was thinking maybe a jewel-tone kind of wedding. That maybe you girls might like these dresses." Pulling up the gorgeous rich navy dresses with the gold embroiled stars falling across the dress as if they had fallen from the sky. The spaghetti-strap dress has a full short tulle skirt, which I thought would make the girls feel beautiful on that day.

"Are we bridesmaids?" Emma asks.

"Yes, I was thinking Lockie and my friends' little ones could be the pageboys and flower girls. That the little girls could wear the ballerina style tulle skirts with a top, and the boys could be maybe in a dress shirt and pants with little bowties." Emma and Becca nod excitedly.

"What will the older bridesmaids wear?" Amelia asks.

"I was thinking of maybe a deep berry-colored evening dress or something like that." Yvette shows Amelia a simple bridesmaid dress.

"Can I wear that?" Amelia asks quietly.

"Of course, you can." Her eyes light up at my answer. "Then I love it all. You're so cool, Stacey." Amelia surprises me with her compliment.

"This is going to be the bestest wedding ever," Becca adds. Well, I'm glad they were all happy with my choices.

35

OSCAR
A MONTH LATER

Honestly, I can't believe how much Camryn has achieved in such a small amount of time. Somehow, she was able to get the shearing shed back to its former glory. She's arranged for luxury cabins to be set up all around the farm so our guests could stay with us and not disrupt the town with the paparazzi that follows us everywhere.

Stacey was very strict about using local businesses for our wedding, which thankfully, Camryn has adhered to. I know this because every time I go into town, someone tells me how excited they or their family member is to be working on our wedding. We even told the local paper that they were going to be the only publication allowed on the day to cover the event. Any photos purchased by other media outlets around the world and any money received from it, Stacey would like that money to go to the drought relief programs in town. She wants to help the farmers in her local community, as well as mental health programs for families dealing with the strain of the rising debt from the drought. God, my fiancé is a good woman. Not many people would give the huge amount of money the media wants for our wedding to people in need. She's someone really special.

. . .

Everyone is running around crazily today because all our friends and family are arriving. The finishing touches to the cabins are being done, the Dirty Texas jet has touched down in Sydney, and they are taking a couple of private planes out to us here in Mudgee. Then a fleet of cars will bring them to the farm, which should be any moment. It will be so exciting to be catching up with everyone again, especially my family.

"Someone is here," Emma squeals as I notice the first plume of red dust swirls up into the sky.

"Battle stations," I cry because I know everyone has been freaking out.

"Couldn't help yourself, could you?" Stacey joins me on the back deck, watching the cars pull up the long driveway.

"You've all been freaking out all morning." I place my arms lazily around her shoulders.

"That's because I want everything to be perfect." Stacey elbows me in the ribs.

"And, babe, it's perfect." She lets out a frustrated sigh. The rest of the guys join us, Lockie grumbling to get up into my arms. I pick him up and throw him onto my shoulders, making him giggle. He loves it up there, my neck and shoulders not so much—the little dude is heavy. As the first shiny black car pulls into the driveway, stopping in a cloud of dust, we make our way toward it.

"We made it, thank fuck." Derrick steps out of the car, stretching his body. "Oh, sorry little ears, forget what Uncle Derrick said." He rubs his hands on his jeans. "Oh my God, look at you." Derrick rushes toward Stacey, pulling her into his arms. "You look radiant." He nuzzles her neck.

"I've missed you," Stacey tearily confesses.

"I know, my sugar plum. I've missed you too. I hope Ragnar has been looking after you?"

"Ragnar?" Amelia questions me.

"It's Derrick's nickname for me. He's a famous Viking god." Amelia frowns.

"You're a Viking?" She looks a little confused. I guess I haven't really talked that much about where I come from.

"I was born in Germany, my parents are Swedish," I tell her.

"So, you speak other languages?" she inquires.

"Yes. German, Swedish, and English. I know a little Norwegian and Danish as it's close to Swedish."

"I never hear you speak them."

"You will when my family arrives. Sometimes when we get excited, we slip back into Swedish instead of English."

"Will you teach me how to speak your languages?" she asks curiously.

"You want to learn them?" Looking down at her, I give her my full attention. She nods her head furiously. "Okay. Maybe we can find some language school in LA, and we can start teaching you."

"I'd love that. Thanks." A smile beams across her face. Derrick pulls her away from our conversation as more cars pull up.

Insane chaos is what I'd call this get-together. There are tears from both adults and kids. There's a hell of a lot of screaming too. Wave after wave of cars arrive, covering everything in red dust.

"You made it," I scream, seeing my parents jumping out of their car.

"älskling," Mom calls out to me, which is Swedish for sweetheart. Tears are already falling along her cheeks, and she pulls me into a huge motherly hug. "I have missed you so much." My large arms wrap around her too. After everything we have been through since arriving in Australia, this is what I have missed the most. Mom. "You're looking well, baby." She gives me the motherly once-over.

"It's been tough, I think we have come through to the other side." Dad is next to greet me. Then I see Isla with Easton on her hip. Excusing myself, I head over to my nephew. It feels like a lifetime since I've seen him.

"Hey, little buddy." I grab him out of Issy's arms. "Oh my God, you have grown so much." Nuzzling into his neck, my beard tickles him, making him giggle.

"I think he's missed you, too," Issy tells me with a welcoming embrace. All of a sudden, something hits me in the leg and starts screaming. I look down and see Lockie crying. I hand Easton back to Issy and pick up Lockie.

"Hey, little buddy, what's the matter?" The tears are falling over his chubby cheeks.

"Mine. You're mine." He wraps his little arms around my neck. Issy's eyes soften at the sobs coming from the little guy.

"I'm not going anywhere, little man," I try to reassure him, but he clings to me even tighter, not wanting to let me go. I guess over these past couple of months, he has had me all to himself. I guess Stacey and I thought he was too young to realize what happened with his family, I'm guessing now we were wrong.

"Looks like someone is jealous," Issy whispers to me. I nod my head in agreement. I think I need to find Stacey or Hunter quickly.

"I'll be back," I tell my sister and weave my way through the crowd with a little crying koala clinging to me.

"What's the matter?" Stacey spies me, reaching her hand out to me as I pass.

"Is Hunter or Amelia around?" She points to them standing to one side playing on their phones. I walk over to where they are standing, and they look up as I arrive.

"What's the matter?" Hunter asks, noticing Lockie.

"He got super jealous of me holding another baby."

"Mine." Lockie almost chokes me as his arms tighten around me. Stacey joins us and looks at me with concern.

"Hey, buddy." Hunter holds out his arms to Lockie. "Remember how we said we were having a party for Oscar and Stacey? All these people are here for them." Lockie nods against my chest. "Well, they want to say hello to some people. Is that okay?" Hunter uses a calming voice. Lockie looks up at me and then over to Hunter.

"Hey, Lockie. Did you see there were some kids here for you to play with?" Stacey tells him. His eyes widen, he looks over my shoulder and into the crowd. "Want me to introduce you to Ryder? He likes cars and motorbikes, too," Stacey tells him. He eyes her suspiciously and reluctantly hands himself over to her. He wraps himself tight around her, and they disappear back into the crowd.

"Sorry about that, guys. I kind of panicked." I rub my neck.

"Seems he's really bonded with you," Hunter tells me.

"Is that healthy?" I ask them, because I have no idea about this kind of stuff. Amelia and Hunter shrug. *They are just kids, Oscar. How would they know?*

"I think he might have been a little overwhelmed. I mean, there are heaps of people here. We're not used to having that many people at our house," Hunter informs me. Maybe he's right. I mean, I feel slightly overwhelmed seeing everyone, my old and new life reconnecting again.

"Is that why you two are over here on your phone?" I ask, staring at them both.

"I don't know what his reason is." Amelia points to her brother. "But... you do realize there are a heap of famous people in our home?" I look out over all the people and realize what it must look like to someone who isn't used to being around these guys.

"Come on, let me introduce you to everyone then."

"No." Amelia's answer comes out quickly, and her cheeks turn a bright shade of pink.

"Mia is obsessed with Sons of Brooklyn, and they are like there." Hunter points to the boys who are chatting away.

"Oh." Looking at how embarrassed Amelia is and remembering she's a fifteen-year-old girl, I guess her celebrity crushes are standing in her home. Now is the time to adult, Oscar. You've got this. "Who's your favorite?" I ask her.

"Tyler," Hunter answers for her. Amelia nods quickly, her ears turning pink at the thought of him.

"Would you like to meet him, one on one first?" She shakes her head no. "Mia, he's a nice guy." I can't believe I'm saying that about those little turds.

"Okay," she whispers. "Just him for the moment."

"Okay, stay put. I'll grab him." Turning quickly before Amelia decides to run away and probably pukes from nerves, I head on over to where the boys are chatting.

"Congratulations, man." Blake bro-hugs me. The rest of the boys follow suit.

"Thanks, guys." I smile back at them. "Tyler, I have a favor to ask of you."

"Sure, man," he says.

"Okay. Stacey's niece, Amelia, is apparently a big Sons of Brooklyn fan."

"Most of the world is," Johnny quips. I ignore him.

"And you're her favorite, Tyler." I roll my eyes as I say it.

"She's only human." He smiles at me cockily.

"She's also only fifteen." I give him my best authoritative stare, which makes him balk.

"Right, okay," he answers.

"Would you mind coming over to say hi to her? She's a little overwhelmed by everyone here and is hiding out."

"Of course." I let out a nervous breath, then Tyler follows behind me. I can see Amelia's eyes go wide as we approach, her face is turning a bright red. Hunter is sniggering beside her, and I give him the same stare, and he stops immediately.

"Hey, Amelia." Tyler holds out his hand to her. She doesn't move. I've seen that face before—she's gone into fan shock. Tyler's hand falls through the air. "You live in a cool place," Tyler continues chatting away, accustomed to this level of fandom. "Can you believe this dickhead is going to be your uncle in a couple of days?" I clip him behind the head.

"Ow." He rubs the spot I hit. This makes Amelia burst out laughing.

"Nah. Oscar's a pretty cool guy," she tells him, coming to my defense.

"I guess so. He's technically my boss, so I should be nice to him." This makes her giggle. "I hear you're moving to LA soon?" She nods. "Are you looking forward to it?"

"Um. Yeah. I think so. Oscar bought us a new house which looks pretty cool. I can't wait to see it."

"Really? Wow. We must be making him a lot of money then." He cracks a joke, which makes me grumble. Amelia is laughing and slowly relaxing so that's the main point. "I hear you're a bit of a fan?" Amelia nods her head. "Would you like a picture then? Show all your friends at school."

"Really?" Her eyes light up.

"Of course. You're part of the family now." I don't think anything could wipe the smile off her face now. I watch as they take a couple of photos, and Amelia furiously types away on her phone.

"Would you mind speaking to my friend, Tanya. She's like totally obsessed with you, and she'd like die if you called her."

"I'm happy to make my fans' dreams come true." Hunter and I look at each other and gag at Tyler's comment, as long as she's happy, that's all that matters.

36
STACEY

Once everyone has settled into their cabins, we've organized an amazing barbecue in one of the many tents set up around the paddocks for our guests to chill out in.

"Chuck a shrimp on the barbie, Oscar," Christian calls out at him.

"It's called a prawn, you dickhead," Oscar yells back as everyone at the table falls into fits of laughter. Thankfully, Camryn has organized caterers to look after dinner tonight and basically every meal because catering to fifty-plus people before the wedding was a little too much for me.

"It's so beautiful out here." Isla sits down beside me, a glass of water in her hand. I eye her suspiciously. She catches my look. "Oh, for fuck's sake, how did you know?" She moans.

"The water is a giveaway, plus you're glowing," I say, smiling at my friend.

"We've only found out, so it's early, and we didn't want to tell anyone."

"Oh my God, I'm so excited for you." I hug Isla.

"You going to be a new aunty then." What does she mean?

Isla notices my confusion. "Because we're going to be sisters." Oh my God. Yes. It hadn't really clicked yet.

"Sisters. We're going to be sisters." Isla reaches out and takes my hand, making me giggle.

"I can never compare to Naomi, but know that I promise to be as awesome as she was to you." Tears begin to well in my eyes as I reach out for my friend to hug her.

"Thank you. I can't wait for us to be family."

"Me, too, Stace."

"Hope we're not interrupting a moment," Sienna asks, standing with Derrick, Olivia, and Vanessa.

"Come sit," I say to the gang.

"It's so great being back home." Vanessa muses. "The girls screamed when they saw the kangaroos bounding through the paddocks. They also may have scared the crap out of your chickens chasing them." This makes us all laugh. Then I notice Sienna sipping on water. Seriously? She can't be pregnant again.

"You're knocked up again." The words tumble out before I can stop myself. Sienna's eyes widen in surprise, and her cheeks turn a light shade of pink.

"Fucking hell. Is it really that obvious?" Sienna rolls her eyes. The group squeals with delight as we congratulate her. "Look, we found out, so we weren't going to say anything," she tells us.

"I found out, too," Isla squeals and stuns the group.

"You too?" Sienna asks Isla. They both jump up and hug each other excitedly.

"You guys keep getting knocked up at weddings. It's like it is some kind of powerful aphrodisiac or something," Derrick moans. "Damn rock stars and their potent sperm," Derrick mumbles.

"Your time will come soon." Olivia tries to reassure Derrick.

"I know, my little lady bug. I've started to speak to some agencies about looking into adoption, as a single gay man, it doesn't look good, even with my wealth. Plus, there's a part of me that would love to have at least one child who shares my genetics. Because, let's be honest, look at me, all this needs to be in the world." We chuckle.

"What about surrogate?" I ask him.

"That's my next step. I think that's going to be the easier option. It's going to take some time to find the right woman," he tells us.

"Well, this is exciting, D," I say, and he waves me away. "Enough about me. It's all about you?" I smile.

"I can't believe how much Oscar has changed," Isla comments. "Never knew someone under the age of sixty that loved to garden as much as him." I smile again. "He was chatting with Dad about buying a farm or something down in Malibu." Isla looks at me as if she's heard it all.

"Yep, he sure does. He wants somewhere outside the city for the kids, really it's for him," I say, taking a sip of my beer. "He's taken on the role of guardian so well with them. Especially the girls, they seem to confide in him way more than me."

"He's always so good with Easton." Issy smiles.

"He is such a good uncle, he can always give him back." I laugh. "He's stuck with these ratbags."

"He looks like a natural," Sienna adds, making me smile.

"It's not at all how we saw our life turning out." Playing with the label on my beer bottle, I continue, "I mean, we never spoke about getting married or even having a family, life has pushed the fast-forward button, and we're getting married and instantly have five kids."

"So, no little Vikings in the works then?" Derrick pushes.

"Hell, no, Derrick." He's giving me a heart attack. "We have all the family we need. Plus, I have teenagers. Like, I have no idea what they talk about half the time. They make me feel instantly old." The group chuckles. "This teen world is so confusing. I mean, it doesn't feel that long ago that I was one, apparently, this is all in my head because I'm very much older."

"Well, either way, you and Oscar are doing brilliantly," Vanessa states. "The fact that everything you have been through has brought the two of you closer together."

"In a strange way, it has. It's very much made us re-evaluate things," I tell her.

"So, no more play in The Paradise Club?" Derrick asks. I shish him, worried one of the kids might hear, which makes him laugh. "That's such a mum thing to do."

"They don't need to know anything about that life," I warn him. "I can't imagine we'll go back there for a while anyway." Derrick's eyes widen.

"So, you're going vanilla?" I roll my eyes at the gossipy queen.

"There will never be anything vanilla about us, Derrick. Because we may not go to…" I quickly look around the room, making sure the coast is clear, "… sex clubs," I whisper, "… doesn't mean we do missionary all night."

"Having a family changes things," Olivia pipes in. She and Axel have an experimental sex life like us, so hearing what she has to say is interesting. "For Axel and I, we have hit pause on The Paradise Club, as it doesn't fit into our life at the moment, it doesn't mean we won't ever enjoy it again," she adds, giving us a cheeky smirk.

"Good to see my naughty little princess is still there." Derrick gives her a high five.

"Things will eventually settle down for you and Oscar, don't worry if things don't go back to the way they were. You're both living your new normal," Olivia advises me.

"Thanks," I whisper to her.

Derrick stands up, raising his glass. "We're here celebrating the last Dirty Texas man falling." Everyone raises their glasses. "When Sienna and I started this wild journey all those years ago, who knew that good friends would soon become family." Aw, man, don't make me cry. "I'd not be where I am today if it weren't for Sienna and Stacey. You two have helped me launch a career that I only ever dreamed about. You have helped me set up a business that's creating an income that I never thought was possible. You two are like sisters to me, and every day I'm thankful you're both in my life." Dammit, Derrick. Tears well in my eyes.

"To my Dirty Texas bitches, Ness, Issy, and Liv." He turns and looks over at them. "Thank you for welcoming me into your lives and becoming my family." Glassy eyes form in all of their eyes. "I would do anything in the world for all of you. I mean, I'd even sleep with you if you asked, and you all know how much I hate vaginas. Actually, it would be more like I'd have a threesome with you and your husbands. I'd stick it in 'ya. That's how much I love you girls." We all crack up. It's a very Derrick way of saying how much we all mean to him.

"I mean it, ladies. Without you all in my life, I honestly don't know where I'd be. Before y'all, I was never accepted, I was never loved, and I never fit in. Then this blonde bombshell over here…" Derrick points to Sienna, "… took a chance on this old queen and saved my life because what she didn't know was that I had decided to end my life if I didn't get this job. Not because it was my dream job but because I couldn't take any more rejection."

"DD." Sienna jumps up and hugs Derrick, tears streaming down her face. "I never knew that."

"I know, you saved me. So, I never wanted to think about that dark time ever again. You gave me love, acceptance, and you made my dreams come true. You're my guardian angel." We're all crying at his words. Damn him.

"I love you, Derrick." Sienna sobs. We all get up and hug him.

"We love you, D," we all tell him.

"Sorry, I actually didn't mean to make it about me. I know, first time for everything," he jokes. "I'm caught up in the love and everything. I did have a point in there somewhere." He taps his finger on his champagne glass. "Oh, that's right. I wanted to say to you, Stacey, that nothing can ever replace your family. Know that you aren't alone anymore. You have your Dirty Texas family, and we'll always be there for you, no matter what, through thick and thin."

Oh shit, Derrick. Really. Hitting me with all the feels at once. I'm completely overcome with emotion. "It takes a village to raise a child, and this Dirty Texas village is going to help you raise the shit out of those teenagers." This makes me smile. "And gorgeous little Lockie, well, he's young enough that we can mold him right."

"Thank you, D. And thank you guys for coming all this way for us. I didn't realize how much I need all your strength until you got here." Looking out over family and friends, Oscar's dad is swinging little Lockie around, making him giggle. The girls are playing with the babies, Emma and Becca are taking turns to push the prams around, trying to get the kids to sleep. For the first time since losing my family, a sense of calm falls across me.

We're going to be okay.

37

OSCAR

It's been so good showing my family and friends around the farm, impressing them with my farm knowledge. Dad laughed when I told him that I learned how to build a fence and ride a horse to round up the sheep. I also told them the story about my run-ins with the brown snakes and my many 'near-death' experiences, which made them laugh. The grandparents have decided to take the kids to bed, leaving us all to catch up, which is nice.

"I can't believe how many stars there are," Christian muses, looking up in the pitch-black sky, the silvery shiny stars lighting up the sky for as far as the eye can see.

"And it's so quiet," Finn adds.

"It's nice," I tell them, sipping my beer. "It's taken a while to get used to, I think I'm liking the peace and quiet."

"Going to be a culture shock when you get back to LA then," Evan adds.

"Yeah. There's a bit of me that actually isn't looking forward to it, especially the constant media attention. I haven't had to worry about that here. The locals ran them all out of town for us." This makes them chuckle. "It will be good to be back with everyone again. I know I'm a grown-ass man, it's good having the parents around," I acknowledge, sipping my beer.

"They are great with Easton, and I know they can't wait to help you guys, too," Finn adds. "Look at them with Lockie tonight, it's as if he's already theirs." They really did spend a lot of time with him, making him feel like part of the family. After the start of the day where Lockie really wanted to stick close to me, he was happy to start going to anyone and hanging out with them as the day progressed.

"Teenage girls, man, that's going to be hard," Christian adds. "I'm dreading the days Ruby and Sadie are that age. Hormones, man." He chuckles, drinking his beer.

"Funny enough, the girls have been pretty good, except in the mornings when they fight over the bathroom, it's like the fucking hunger games." Everyone chuckles. "That's why I made sure they all have their own bathrooms in our new home. No fighting in the morning."

"How are you feeling about that, moving back?" Evan asks.

"I'm excited to get home also a little worried. You know about the kids. They have all been so adamant that they want a fresh start, what happens if it fucks them up and makes things worse? I worry that I'm going to mess up." The boys go quiet and stare at me.

"Fuck, man, you sound like a parent already." Axel slaps me on the back. Do I? Shit. I do.

"You're doing the right thing, putting those kids first," Christian adds. "If things don't work out, then you can always come back here or somewhere else."

"Like your farm in Malibu," Finn mentioned. I nod in agreement. Maybe they are right.

"There are enough parents around if you need help. I mean, they have all been through the teenage years with all of us, and they seemed to have survived." Evan laughs.

"I never expected this to be my life. I'm not the guardian of five kids. I'm buying a fucking farm. I'm obsessed with chickens and gardens and shit. I haven't even thought about The Paradise Club."

"Wow," Axel says to that.

"I know, right?"

"See, I told 'ya, pussy-whipped man. Best feeling in the world," Christian says cockily. "Remember those times, you three." He points his beer bottle to Finn, Axel, and me. "You used to make fun of Evan and me, and now look at you all." He smiles. "You're fucking practically royal and about to pop out twins." He points at his brother. "And you." He turns to Finn. "You fell for your best friend's sister, such a cliché, and knocked her up."

"And knocked her up again," Finn adds.

"What?" My voice raises. "Issy's pregnant?" Finn nods, a huge grin on his face.

"The girls picked it up early, so they already know. It's only early."

"Oh, man. Congratulations." I get up and hug my best friend and brother-in-law. "I'm going to be an uncle again." Pride radiates from me.

"Sienna's pregnant, too," Evan adds.

"What the fuck?" The words are out before I register them.

"What can I say, fellas? I have potent swimmers." We all flip Evan off then congratulate him. The Dirty Texas brood is growing bigger every day.

"And you, Oscar. The one who never believed in marriage or kids or settling down." Christian smiles smugly. "You're now getting married and have an instant family of five. You are doing the school run and braiding hair. I think we're going to be coming to you for advice soon." He tips his bottle of beer at me.

"Okay, okay. I was wrong for giving you and Evan shit. I get it now. The love of a good woman does change you. And yes, I didn't believe in all those things before Stacey, shit happens, and you soon realize what's important in your life, and it's her. She's my everything thing, and I don't care that it makes me sound pussy-whipped because I guess I am, and I love it." I raise my beer high.

"Hell, yeah," Christian calls out. "To being pussy-whipped." The boys cheer and hold their beers high in the air. We all burst out laughing. It's so good to have the guys back.

The girls eventually join us around the campfire. Stacey snuggles into my lap, her head resting on my shoulder. We all sit around in silence, simply taking it all in.

"Wow, how the nights have changed for Dirty Texas," Tyler from Sons of Brooklyn pipes up, joining the group.

"Your time will come, young Padawan," Evan promises him. Of course, Tyler scoffs at him, turning around to his bandmates, who agree with him.

"No woman can tame all this." Johnny waves his hands all around him. We shake our heads because we, too, were cocky like that in our twenties. You never know what life is going to throw your way.

Eventually, jetlag kicks in for our overseas visitors, and they all head off to bed. Stacey and I head back to ours too.

"It's been so good having everyone here." Stacey snuggles into my side.

"Didn't realize how much I missed the boys." She smiles up at me. "Don't tell them, they already have big enough egos as it is." This makes her chuckle.

"It will be nice having them all around when we move to LA." I nod in agreement. "Can you believe Issy and Sienna are pregnant again?"

"I know, I'm going to be an uncle, and you're going to be an aunty," I say.

"How weird is that?" Stacey shakes her head.

"I think it's going to be good for the kids to be surrounded by all the littles ones. Emma and Becca seem pretty smitten with the babies."

"I know. They asked me if they could babysit them when we move to LA. I told them they needed to be a little older before they could, which totally bummed them out." I chuckle. "Sienna offered Amelia a part-time job at the shop."

"Really?" I didn't realize this.

"Yeah. Amelia was asking a lot of questions about fashion. Sienna said they got into deep conversations about it, and she's pretty into it. So, she offered her a weekend and holiday job working in the shop with her. Sienna said she was so excited, she nearly cried." Stacey's fingers trace over my chest as she talks. "Amelia was so excited when she told me about the job. She said she couldn't wait to move."

"I really hope the reality is as good as what they have in their heads," I confess my worry to Stace.

"Me, too," Stacey agrees. "I also hope they like their schools and that it's not too much of a culture shock for them."

We arrive during spring break, so the girls will start in their new schools for a couple of months and then summer break starts. Stacey and I know nothing about schools, so thankfully, Mom and Dad have gone and looked around the schools we were interested in. Stacey, of course, fought me on it, I wanted to send them to the best schools, no matter how much it cost. I think we owe that to their parents if we're taking them halfway across the world, and we'll give them the best damn education they can get.

Stacey is a little worried about how they will assimilate because they haven't grown up with much, and then we're going to throw them in with all these rich kids. I get her concerns, kids are kind of resilient, and what she doesn't know is that I've got credit cards made up in each of the kid's names, except Lockie because he's three, for emergencies and shopping. I know how hard it might be for them to try to compete with these kids and their lifestyles, and I know Stacey is trying to make sure they don't turn into Hollywood brats, these Hollywood brats are brutal. They are already going to have a target on their backs because of their accent, so I don't want them to have to worry about not having the right things, making it impossible for them to fit it. I'll wait until I'm married to tell Stacey that plan.

I've been speaking to Hunter about maybe going to college and wondering what he'd be interested in doing. He's thinking of maybe a business degree as he loves the aspect of running a business. So, we have enrolled him for the summer. It took a little bit of convincing for Stacey to come on board for Hunter to live on campus, I told her he needs it, especially for making new friends. I explained to her that he knows no one his age in the city, and he might get homesick if he doesn't meet people. She agreed. So, Hunter is going to be working on an MBA at UCLA, which isn't far from us still far enough that he has his own life. He's pretty excited.

"They will be fine," I say, kissing Stacey's forehead. "I promise if they aren't happy, we can pack up and move back to Australia or anywhere in the world, or they can try another school or even be homeschooled."

"Thank you." She kisses me.

"I know how you can really thank me." I wiggle my brows at her.

38

STACEY

A flurry of activity wakes me up, and I turn over to realize Becca and Emma have left my bed. They wanted to sleep over the night before the wedding because they didn't want me to be alone for the night since Oscar had gone and slept at my parents' house to get ready with Hunter and Lockie. Jumping out of bed, I walk out into the living room and see hair and makeup all set up, ready to go. The beautiful bridesmaids' dresses are hanging up, steamed and pressed. Then I catch my wedding gown, the emerald green beauty taking pride of place. Reality hits me.

"You're awake," Camryn greets me. "Grab some breakfast. You're going to need your strength today 'cause you're getting married." She guides me over to the breakfast buffet set up in the kitchen. I grab some fruit and Danish pastries. "Here, a mimosa." Camryn hands me the glass.

"Aunt Stacey." Emma and Becca charge at me, wrapping their arms around me as I try to struggle and not spill everything in my hands. "You're getting married," they squeal excitedly and are practically buzzing.

"Come, girls. It's time for hair and makeup," Camryn tells them, ushering them into their chairs.

"Can I have one of them?" Amelia points to my mimosa.

"Ah no," she pouts. "You can have a couple of sips of mine." I give her my glass. "That's it. You're too young for alcohol," I warn her. She nods and quickly takes two big gulps before spitting them out in the sink.

"Gross." She washes her mouth out. "How can you drink that?"

"You'll appreciate it when you get older." I smile, happy she didn't like the taste.

"Come, Amelia, you have to get hair and makeup, too," Camryn calls for her. I take a sip of my mimosa and a bite of my croissant.

"The party has arrived." Derrick practically kicks down the screen door. "My little possum, you're getting married today." He squishes me in his arms.

"Congratulations." The girls sing-song after him, each of them taking their turn to greet me and give me their best wishes.

"Guys, if you want to grab some food and then take a seat, so we can get you ready." Camryn ushers people into position. How on earth does everyone fit in this house? It's controlled chaos.

"Congratulations, Stacey," one of the hairdressers says to me.

"Lisa? Lisa Stuart?" I realize one of the girls doing our hair I went to school with.

"The one and only." I hug her.

"Oh my God. It's been years. How are you?"

"Great. Really good. I married Liam Fraser, remember him?" That was her high school boyfriend. "We have three kids now, and I own one of the hair salons in town."

"Wow. That's so awesome."

"Thank you so much for using us today. I'm so happy that I can be part of your day. We don't get many celebrity weddings in town, so it's kind of exciting." I shake my head, about to say it's not a celebrity wedding, then I stop myself because, to them, it is. I forget how immersed I am in this life that it isn't actually normal.

"I'm so happy you're here." Turning to Camryn, I say, "I know this is super last-minute, can we add Lisa and the hairdresser to the wedding, please. I'd love for them to see their handiwork in the flesh." Camryn pauses for a couple of moments, obviously running the whole event through her head quickly.

"Of course." She smiles probably is cursing me as we speak. "Oh, Stacey. No, you don't have to do that."

"You should be able to see all your hard work in the flesh."

"Thank you, thank you so much." She looks at me gratefully, which gives me an idea. I reach out to Camryn, stopping her as she passes me.

"Can we add the florists and cake decorator, too, anyone that we used? I wanted to say thank you for helping us." Camryn's face softens. "I'm probably making it worse for you, aren't I?"

Camryn shakes her head. "You're very kind inviting those people. I can add some extra tables, it's not a problem at all."

"Thank you."

"It's your wedding, Stacey, and if you want them to celebrate it with you, then I'll make sure that it gets done." Then she rushes away. I pop a strawberry into my mouth.

"Do you think Oscar is freaking out over there?" I ask as we get our hair and makeup done.

"On the outside, I think he's going to look cool, but, on the inside, he is stressing out." Isla laughs.

"I'll text Chris and find out," Ness volunteers, typing away on her phone, and she gets an instant reply. "He's freaking out." This makes everyone laugh. Grabbing my phone, I send him a quick text.

. . .

Stacey: *I can't wait to marry you.*

Moments later, my phone beeps.

Oscar: *We should've eloped.*
   Oscar: *And I can't wait to marry you too.*
   Stacey: *Nervous?*
   Oscar: *Surprisingly, yes. You better not stand me up.*

Shit, is that why he's freaking out? Does he think I'd stand him up?

Stacey: *Never in a million years. You're stuck with me.*
   Oscar: *Good. Cuz I'd probably hunt you down and force you to marry me if you didn't show up.*

He probably would.

Stacey: *Would you tie me if you did?*
   Oscar: *If I did?*
   Oscar: Oh… I get it.
   Oscar: *I would hunt you down to the ends of the earth, and once I found you…*

My heart begins to race. What would he do to me?

. . .

Oscar: *I would force you to your knees and demand you to apologize to me via your mouth.*

I squirm in my seat.

Oscar: *I'd make sure that you choked on my cock, over and over again until you begged me to stop, and I would ignore every last one of your pleas because you deserved it. You deserved to be choked by my cock for running away from me.*

Fuck. This is turning me on. I can feel my cheeks burning up. Thankfully, they haven't done my makeup yet.

Oscar: *Then once I was finished with you, and you sucked every last bit of my cum from my dick. I'd drag you by your hair into my lair.*

Oh, role play, I like it.

Oscar: *You would be pleading with me not to hurt you and that you would do anything. Which you know gets my dick hard hearing you say that. You still deserve punishment for leaving me at the altar like that. You needed to suffer the utter humiliation as I did.*

. . .

I bite my lip and nervously look around, feeling like everyone can see what's happening on my phone.

Oscar: *I would bend you over a desk. Tie your arms and your legs to it, making sure your legs are wide open. Then I'd leave you there, waiting for someone to come by and fuck you. Punish you. Defile you. You would have no idea if it was me or a stranger. And then, once you have been thoroughly fucked, I would cradle you in my arms and know that you were mine, forever.*

Fuck me dead.

Oscar: *Shit, little one. I have to go rub one out now. How the fuck am I supposed to get dressed with a fucking boner? You owe me. Love you, babe.*
    Stacey: *Love you too.*

Placing my phone down beside me, I'm beyond turned on, wondering if I could sneak next door and have a quickie?
    "Stacey, it's time for your makeup." Camryn pulls me from my dirty thoughts. "Are you feeling okay? You look flushed." Shit. I fan my face with my hands.
    "Just nerves," I lie.
    "Let me grab you some water." Camryn rushes to the kitchen.

"You look so beautiful, Stacey." Yvette looks up at me, messing around with the bottom of my hem. "Oscar is going to be blown away." My stomach does loop de loops thinking about walking down that aisle to him. Lisa, my hairdresser, comes in and places my gorgeous Australian native floral crown on top of my head. My blonde hair falls in light waves down my back, showing off the gorgeous backless dress.

"You ready?" Yvette asks me as she opens the door. I step outside, and the room turns silent.

"You look like a princess." Becca sighs.

"So do you." Becca and Emma are dressed in beautiful navy dresses with gold stars falling from top to bottom, and in their hair are gorgeous little star tiaras. They look so stunning and grown-up.

"You look beautiful," Amelia tells me, and I try to hold in my tears as I look over at her all dressed in a gorgeous deep berry evening dress, her light brown hair in a messy braid with a berry-colored native floral crown.

"Mia, you look so grown up." She gives me a shy smile, nervously straightening out her dress. Naomi would've loved to see her daughter dressed up like this. I suck in a deep breath as my emotions take over. I look out to my friends—Sienna, Vanessa, Isla, and Olivia—all dressed like Amelia, looking like bloody supermodels. And then there's Derrick, dressed in the same deep berry velvet as the bridesmaids but in a suit version. He looks like he could be walking the runways of Milan or Paris.

"Oh, my goodness, look at them," I shriek, noticing the little flower girls for the first time. Sadie and Ruby are dressed in their navy ballerina-style dresses. The small amount of hair that they have is pulled up into a tiny little pigtail. They are so adorable.

"I think this call for champagne," Derrick calls out, busying himself in the kitchen, popping champagne for us all. I'm thankful when I finally get the glass in my hand, taking a sip to calm my nerves.

"Are you ready?" Camryn asks me.

"I didn't think I'd be this nervous," I confess.

"Totally natural. The boys are already down there, so they won't see you. Charlotte wants to take some last-minute photos of you before you get onto the horses. One of our neighbors loaned us their vintage open-horse carriage for today to escort us from the house to our dam, where the ceremony is being held. We pose for some photos and then slowly attempt to get into the carriage. Thankfully, it's one of those long rectangular-shaped ones. Otherwise, I don't think we'd fit in.

Oscar and I decided to get married close to dusk, and we wanted to be pronounced husband and wife as the sun started to set. The light over the landscape is incredible at that time, and there's something magical about the outback at dusk, plus it's a little cooler. Charlotte joins us and takes some photos.

The closer we get, the more my nerves seem to want to play havoc with me. I can see all our family and friends in a semi-circle around the large weeping willow tree, I haven't had a chance yet to see Oscar. Derrick helps me out of the carriage, the gorgeous Clydesdale horses doing their job and getting us to the altar in time. Lisa, the hairdresser, gives us all a quick once-over as we were a little windswept from our journey. As I look up at the horizon, I see four kangaroos standing there watching us. A sense of calm falls over me.

"Look." Emma points them out. "It's Mum and Dad," she squeals with delight.

"And Gran and Pop," Becca adds excitedly, and she gives them a wave.

"They're here." Amelia gives me a sad smile. I nod in her direction, trying to hold in my tears. The girls are right, though, I feel them all around me. It makes me happy that they can share in this day with us. Then I see Hunter, looking so handsome and grown up in navy suit.

"You look beautiful, Stacey." He comes and kisses my cheeks.

"You're so handsome, Hunter." A blush falls across his face. Kimberly, Camryn's business partner, brings the pageboys over.

"Shacey." Lockie runs toward me, burying his little face into my dress. He looks so cute in his dress clothes as does Ryder, who tootles over to Sienna, and she gives him the once-over. We put Ryder on his little ride-on-tractor with Ruby, Sadie, Levi, and Easton in the back of the cart, and there's a Here Comes the Bride sign on the back. We have been practicing it all week and fingers crossed Ryder makes it to the end without losing one of the babies out the back.

"Ready to send the little ones down?" Kimberly asks.

"The Gypsy Sisters in place?" Camryn asks her, and Kimberly nods. Oscar asked the girls if they wouldn't mind signing a song he wrote for me to walk down the aisle called "Forever." I love those girls. They are so talented, and when they sing acoustic, I get the chills. Kimberly gives the band the thumbs-up, and they start playing. Ryder eagerly starts his ride-on-tractor as the first strings begin, and slowly peddles the little ones down the aisle made of Persian rugs. You can hear the crowd cooing at the sight before them. Then it's Lockie's turn, holding the wedding rings in a little glass treasure box. We watch as he slowly and carefully walks down the aisle, followed by Becca with Emma close behind. Next, it's Amelia's turn, then the bridesmaids, and last, but not least, Derrick.

"You ready?" Hunter asks me as he links his arm with mine.

"Yes." Holding onto him, I take my first step onto the beautiful aisle layered in rugs and look up at my groom for the first time. An overwhelming sense of love for him hits me. He looks so handsome, dressed in a navy suit with a white dress shirt, no tie. His blond locks are pulled up into a messy man bun, his Viking beard trimmed nicely. Ice-blue eyes lock on me as I begin to walk toward him. That's when I notice the first tear falling over his cheek.

39

OSCAR

I have been a bundle of nerves today. The boys have been trying to keep me chill, nothing was working. I mean, I'm used to playing in a stadium full of people, so you'd think standing up here in front of a couple of hundred people wouldn't be so bad. Nope. The scariest thing I have ever done until I locked eyes on Stacey. Everything else vanished—my nerves, my anxiety, the people in the crowd, the music, even the voices of my friends congratulating me on my gorgeous bride.

Turning around and seeing her for the first time was as if someone had stolen my breath away. She looks like a vision with the sun slowly setting behind her, showering her with bright shards of light. Then I notice her gorgeous green wedding dress. Wow. Unexpected but totally her. She looks like an elfin queen gliding toward me, then the first tear falls, then another. I don't care if I'm crying because I can't believe how lucky I am to be marrying this woman today and that she wants to spend forever with me. Then she stops before me, Hunter doing the honors of handing over his aunty to me for safekeeping. One of the girls takes Stacey's bouquet so we can join hands. As soon as our hands link together, that's it, my soul knows it's home.

. . .

"I now pronounce you man and wife. You may kiss your bride, Ragnar," Derrick tells us. And I do. I have never craved Stacey as much as I do at this moment, cupping her face and pulling her to me, kissing her with all the love I have. Our friends and family holler as we seal our new life together. "That was hot," Derrick remarks over our kiss. Yes, that's right. Derrick married us. He got ordained over the internet. He said it was a dream come true to marry us, and honestly, he did an amazing job.

"Ladies and Gentlemen, let me introduce you to Mr. and Mrs. Eriksen," Derrick introduces us, and as we take the first steps as a married couple, with the sun setting around us, on the horizon set against the burnt orange of the sun, there are the four kangaroos, the same ones we saw the day we scattered Stacey's family's ashes. I had been watching them over Stacey's shoulder throughout the ceremony. They sat and watched the entire thing, and once Derrick announced us and we took the first steps as a married couple, they hopped away. I kind of hope that means Stacey's family is able to move on, and they can now rest in peace knowing we've got this.

"You saw them, too, didn't you?" Stacey whispers to me as we wave and accept the congratulations from our guests.

"Yes, they were with us the entire time," I tell her.

"But they've gone now."

"Yes."

"I hope they are happy wherever they go." She shakes someone's hand.

"I think they are." As we reach the end of the aisle, I pull Stacey into my arms and give her a Hollywood-style kiss, making everyone erupt in cheers.

. . .

The reception has been amazing, I have no idea how Camryn could get the old shearing shed to resemble a luxury wedding venue, she did. Tables upon tables lined the old corrugated iron shed, fairy lights twinkle above us, and beautiful native flowers fill the centers of each table.

When Stacey saw the room for the first time, she cried—it was truly magical. We wanted a casual dinner, plus being out in the middle of nowhere, a five-course degustation menu wasn't going to work. So, we blended the two barbecuing cultures of Texas and Australia and had a massive all-you-can-eat barbecue buffet. Sienna's dad, who is a celebrated vegan chef, was ever so kind to help the caterers with some nice vegan and vegetarian options for the Hollywood crowd. An entire section was set up for kids with toys, coloring books, petting farm, magician, video games for the older kids, along with a couple of the dads.

Once everyone had finished dinner, it was time for our first dance. We had set up a wooden dance floor outside under the stars, and Gypsy Sisters again delighted the crowd with another song that I wrote for today called "My Heart." I sang it to Stacey as we danced across the wooden floor, lost in our own little world, nothing but the stars above us, surrounded by the night. As the last keys of the song ended, fireworks went off in the paddock behind us. The kids enjoyed that.

Then the party really kicked off. Large tents were scattered around the paddocks, where one was dedicated to a bar, another was for chilling out, there was a whiskey lounge and cigar area for the men, and a champagne lounge for the women. There were oversized tic-tac-toe boards, Connect Four, ring toss, and even glow-in-the-dark bowling between the hay bales.

The entire community came out and supported us, and that made Stacey so happy. The kids' friends were all there too, and they disappeared off to one of the teen tents where they can sit and play on the phone and not talk to each other.

"Hey, wife." I grab my wife as she walks past me.

"Hey, husband." She giggles. Stacey is tipsy. She wraps her arms around my neck. "I like the sound of that. My husband." She giggles again. "Back off bitches, that's my husband." I laugh.

"Looks like you're having fun."

"This is the best wedding ever." She waves her arms around.

"Totally not biased or anything." She rolls her eyes at me. I pick her up and twirl her around until we're strategically outside in the darkness. "I was hoping that maybe we could find some alone time together," I whisper into her ear.

"Ooh, eager to consummate the marriage, huh?" she asks seductively, pressing herself against me.

"I'm eager to get my cock into you. You have been teasing me all day looking so fucking hot." Stacey bites her lip at my dirty words.

"You're the one sexting me while I was getting ready." She points her finger into my chest. Okay, she got me there.

"And my balls still hurt from that. Come on, be a good wifey," I plead with her.

"Fine." She tries to sound annoyed but fails.

"Come on, then." Grabbing her hand, I pull her away from everyone.

"Where are we going?" she calls out into the darkness.

"I noticed some trees over here before the sun went down." I grab the torch on my phone and shine it on the ground. "See, here."

"If I step on a snake and die, I'm coming back to haunt you," she tells me.

"The only snake around here is my dick." This sets her off into a fit of giggles. It was a bad joke, I'm fucking desperate. "Here, put your hands here," I instruct, pointing the torch to the tree.

"Check it first," she tells me. I shine the light over the bark to make sure there are no creatures anywhere, then I check the ground. Nothing but red dirt.

"Lift your dress, little one."

"Don't ruin this dress, you hear me." I hear the warning in her tone, *do not mess up the dress*. She lifts her dress, places her hands against the tree, and spreads her legs for me like a good wife. She's wearing nothing but a barely-there G-string. Fucking perfect. My fingers slip between her folds, and she is ready for me.

"Fuck," I curse, swatting away the little bugs. "I have to turn the light off as the stupid bugs are attracted to it." She grumbles something incoherent. I plunge us into darkness, shutting off the light. I place the phone back into my pocket and unzip my trousers. I place my hand on her rump, basically to see where she is because I can barely make out her silhouette in the darkness. My hand slides over her soft skin and every curve of her body, like second nature as I move behind her, my fingers dipping between her legs, sinking into my wife's cunt. "I've missed this." I continue to move my fingers inside her. "I've missed feeling you. I've missed tasting you. I miss fucking you without a care in the world."

"Take me, baby, please," she begs. I pull my fingers out from her, suck her taste from them, and replace the space left behind with my dick. "We have to be quick," she tells me as both of us hiss as I enter her.

"I don't do quick, little one," I say, slowly moving.

"You're going to have to now. People will be looking for us." She's right.

"Okay, it's going to be rough, dirty, and quick."

"Yes," she groans. My hand moves around to her front and finds her clit as I start to increase my tempo. "Harder, baby," she urges me on. "Harder," she pleads, so I give my wife exactly what she wants. Furiously thrusting into her, I have never been so thankful for my skilled fingers than I am right at this moment, as I'm able to bring both of us to climax. I think that's the quickest I have ever come in my life.

"I'm so sorry that was quick, baby." Stacey slowly starts to fix herself up. I tuck myself back into my trousers and pull out my phone again to check that everything is back in place with each of us. Stacey wraps her arms around my neck and kisses me.

"You fucked me up against a tree, in the middle of the Australian bush, at night, in darkness, during our wedding. That's pretty impressive, husband."

"Don't get used to it. Next time I want to take my time with you." I kiss her back.

"Come on, let's get back before we're busted."

40
STACEY
ONE YEAR LATER

What a year it has been.
    The kids settled perfectly into life in LA. Hunter moved into the dorms at UCLA to study business, and he's coming up on finishing his first year. He's been working with everyone learning the ropes of all kinds of businesses. He's also been interning at Dirty Texas Records answering phone calls, getting coffee, sorting mail, and even helped the guys search through social media for the next new thing.
    Hunter and his friends went to a couple of festivals over the summer, and they had a blast at. He's got himself a great bunch of friends. He bought himself a new car and insisted he buy it himself from his trust money and not from Oscar, who was really insistent on buying him a cooler car than he got. Hunter said he didn't need anything flashy, something to get him around. I was so proud of him.

Amelia, on the other hand, gladly took the car Oscar insisted on buying her for her sweet sixteen birthday—a Mercedes G

Wagon. The car is the same price as a house. Those two have become thick as thieves. Oscar loves to take her shopping, they get their hair done together, and they are always out having massages. They planned her sixteenth birthday together, and I don't think he said no to any of her outlandish requests. I found out later from Camryn, who organized the party, that most of the ideas came from Oscar. It's like he let his inner sweet sixteen girl free.

Amelia got her first boyfriend, Clay, the school's quarterback. He seems like a good kid, and both his parents are doctors. Amelia also joined the cheerleading squad and has become rather popular. I remember one night her pulling me into her arms, crying. I thought oh no, this is it, she hates it here, she was so happy because for the first time, she felt normal, accepted, popular—something she had never felt been back in Australia. She's happy and has her life in order, even if I feel like I'm on the set of *90210*.

Amelia is also obsessed with fashion and interns with Derrick, soaking up everything he has to offer her. Oscar has also taught her Swedish and German as well, which are the two languages he speaks. She has picked it up quicker than I have. Finn and I have been having lessons because we're sick of Isla and Oscar chatting away, and we have no idea what they are talking about. Emma, Becca, and Lockie have all learned as well. Languages are so amazing for kids, especially when they are spoken at home, which we try to do. I fail at it, the rest of the family all understand what's being said.

Then there are Emma and Becca. They spend most of their time horseback riding at our place in Malibu. They love it. Emma has been training hard and has started entering competitions, whereas Becca isn't as competitive as her sister and loves animals. Emma is a freshman this year, so she's feeling pretty mature lately, becoming more and more independent.

And little Lockie starts school this year. He has really bounced back—he goes to daycare and loves it, and he also spends so much time with Easton and Oscar's parents while we're at work. As soon as Easton started calling mormor and morfor which is Swedish for grandma and grandpa, Lockie started to do the same thing. They speak to him in Swedish like they do Easton and baby Mia, who are also learning the language. Lockie loves having Oscar's parents as grandparents. I think he really missed that bond he had with Mum and Dad. He sometimes asks about them and blows kisses to the photo of his parents and mine every night before he goes to bed, whispering little things to them before falling asleep. Because he was so young, we didn't want him to forget about them.

And what about us? Oscar and I are celebrating one year of marriage. Well, it's been pretty bloody fantastic. Oscar's love of farming has taken off. Since he bought an old farm, we've spent the past year fixing it up. It has an orchard, animal sheds for the horses, dairy cows, dairy goats, and a couple of alpacas. Then there's the chicken shed, where we have ducks, geese, and turkeys too. He has a beautiful vegetable garden, pretty much anything and everything you could think of he grows down there, and it is the most amazing fresh produce. He also has bees and makes his own honey.

The Dirty Texas boys have started to slow down on going into the office as much. They hired a heap of new people as they expanded offices worldwide—London, Sydney, New York, Los Angles, and Stockholm.

That Stockholm office was for us. Oscar surprised his parents for their thirtieth wedding anniversary with a gorgeous home in Sweden, a place where we could go as a family and immerse our families into the culture. I love Sweden. Even though it's freezing in winter, I love everything about it. It's slowly becoming our second home.

We celebrated our first wedding anniversary with a big party at our farm in Malibu and also celebrated the launch of our restaurant, The Nordic Table, which has been Oscar's passion this past year. It's a great fusion of Nordic and Australian cuisine in Malibu. We use a lot of our produce in the restaurant, plus we sell great coffee. I never expected my life to go this way, being married to a rock star, a semi-mum to five kids, a farmer, and now a budding restauranteur. My life is pretty fantastic.

The question is, have we gone back to The Paradise Club? *Of course.* Once we had settled into our new life in LA, Oscar's family and the kids insisted that we have a honeymoon because we missed out on one as we were moving back home to LA instead. We took two well-deserved weeks off from everything and spent one week in the Turks and Caicos, and the other week, thanks to a very insistent Nate, we spent it rediscovering our kink at The Paradise Club Resort. It was like all this pent-up sexual frustration came out of us during that week. We may have gone a little crazy, but, boy, it was so much fun. We now try to include a once-a-month date night at the club, the one night we allow ourselves to enjoy our desires fully. It's hard trying to have time for Oscar and me to have sex. Usually, we have to be creative and quick, doing it whenever and wherever we can.

And that's how I find myself in the predicament I'm in now.

"Stace, are you okay?" Oscar knocks on the bathroom door. I hear the creak of the door opening and his footsteps across the tiled floor. Lifting my head from the toilet bowl, I give him a sad smile. "Oh, little one." He crouches down beside me, his fingers pushing back my blonde hair from my face.

"I don't feel good." My voice croaks.

"I know, baby." He gives me a small smile.

"I don't know what happened." His brow raises at me in surprise.

"You haven't been feeling well most mornings lately." What's he saying? "This is the first time you have physically thrown up."

"You don't think?" He shrugs. "Fuck." My stomach somersaults as I throw up again into the toilet, his large palm rubbing my back.

"Remember, last month when we had a quickie before getting the kids, then we went out for dinner, and we all got food poisoning?" I nod my head slowly. "Do you think maybe something happened with your pill because you were so sick?"

"Shit, babe." I realized I threw up for twenty-four hours straight. "There's a test under the counter." Oscar looks at me strangely. "Derrick gave it to us as a gag gift for our wedding anniversary." Oscar grabs the packet for me and hands it over. "Let's check." I slowly move off the floor and do the test. I place it on the counter beside us, waiting for it to do its thing.

"You think I'm pregnant, don't you?" I ask, looking up at him.

"I do. Your love of the toilet this morning makes it suspicious."

"What the hell are we supposed to do?" Panic laces my skin.

"Babe..." Oscar holds me. "If you are, then we've expanded our family. I mean, look at how well we're doing with the five we already have, so in all honesty, what's another one?" A huge smile is written across his face.

"You're actually happy about this?" He grins.

"Yeah, I kind of am." This surprises me. "I know we always said no kids, I mean, I already make a pretty awesome Mr. Mom."

"Can we do this? We have so much going on. I mean, it was never in our plans."

"Sometimes, the universe has other ideas." Picking up the pregnancy test, there's a big 'positive' across it.

"Shit. We're having a baby." I look at the test in shock.

"We're having a baby." He wraps his arms around me tightly.

"I'm a little shocked," I confess to him.

"Me too. We should get you to the doctor to confirm it all and get checked out."

"Holy shit. I've been drinking and stuff. What happens if I've done something already to the baby? I'm a bad mum already."

"Stace, breathe." He places his palms on my arms, holding me. "We've got this." How can he be so calm, so Zen about this?

"What about the kids? What happens if they don't like it?"

"They will come around to it," he reassures me.

"Shit. We're having a baby."

41

OSCAR

Stacey finding out she was pregnant was a huge unplanned surprise. I don't think we had discussed kids since she lost her family. I mean, we gained five overnight, and they were mostly fully-grown ones at that. Lockie was even toilet trained, so he was good to go. This little one, we're going to have to do midnight feeds, mucky diapers, vomit, not that I haven't done that for Easton or now little Mia. The only difference is this one is ours, and we can't give it back.

Tonight, we're telling the kids before we tell anyone else. Stacey is almost out of the danger zone, but we want them to know first. We ordered takeout, something that doesn't mess with Stacey's stomach or the smell, so pizza it is.

"Hunter." Lockie squeals, seeing his big brother walk through the door. Hunter picks him up and swings him around.

"Hey, little guy." Lockie giggles. Hunter kisses his aunt on the cheeks, shakes my hand, and greets his sisters.

"So, what's with the family meeting?" Hunter asks, sitting

down on the sofa. Stacey and I link hands and stand in front of the kids.

"Well, we're not sure how to tell you guys this," Stacey starts.

"You're breaking up?" Amelia shrieks.

"What, no," I quickly answer. I can see the panic on their faces now. "No. No. It's nothing bad," I say, trying to calm them down.

"I'm pregnant," Stacey blurts out. The room is silent. The kids' faces are pale with shock.

"Oh my God, congrats, guys." Hunter is the first to congratulate us.

"Can I babysit?" Becca squeals, realizing that a baby in the house means babysitting dollars.

"Of course, when you're older," Stacey tells her, making Becca pout.

"Can I be its stylist?" Amelia asks. "Cause this kid needs to be cool. I mean, it's going to be hanging out with Sienna's kids, and they are trendy." Oscar and I look at each other and smile.

"Is it a boy or a girl?" Emma asks.

"We don't know yet," Stacey tells them.

"Are you having a gender reveal party?" Amelia asks.

"Hadn't thought about it," Stacey answers.

"You need to have one. Like, you can't be basic," Amelia tells us. Basic? What the hell does basic mean?

"What do you think, little man? Stacey and I are going to have a baby." Picking up Lockie, he seems very confused by what's going on around him.

"Where's the baby?" he asks.

"In my tummy." Stacey points to her belly, which I can't wait to see full and blossoming with life.

"Does that mean you won't be my mommy and daddy anymore?" We all still, and the room falls silent. How the hell do we answer this? Lockie has never called us mom or dad, it's always Oscar or Stacey. Has he wanted to call us mom and dad? Is it okay if he wants to do that?

"Do you think Stacey and Oscar are you mummy and daddy?" Hunter asks Lockie. He looks over at his brother and shrugs, then nestles his face into my leg. Hunter gets up and kneels to Lockie's height. "Do you want to call Stacey and Oscar, mummy and daddy?" Lockie nods his head, and my heart breaks for the little guy. He was so young when his family passed away, and I guess the others were always old enough to understand. Hunter looks up at Stacey and me, gaging our reactions to Lockie's comments.

"I think we'd be fine if he wants to call you that," Amelia jumps in, and Emma and Becca nod in agreement.

"There you go, buddy, Stacey and Oscar would love for you to call them that," Hunter explains to his little brother. The smile on Lockie's face melts me. He opens his arms for me to pick him up, I do, and he wraps his little arms around my neck.

"Daddy," he whispers my new title into my ear, and it breaks me. My heart explodes with so much love that my eyes well up with tears. I look over at Stacey, and she, too, is crying. He pulls away and looks at me. "Can I have a brother?" he asks, making me chuckle.

"We'll try our best, little buddy." He nods at me and reaches out for Stacey, cuddling her before going back to his pizza.

"Well, that went good." Stacey snuggles into me as we lay in bed.

"Yeah, it did, once the shock wore off. What surprised me was Lockie."

"That was beautiful. He was so sweet. I wasn't expecting it at all. The poor little guy must have been thinking about it for ages and never knew how to mention it." Stacey's eyes are getting glassy again thinking about it.

"I guess he's going to be a big brother to this little one," I surmise, placing my hand on her stomach.

"Do you think we should bring them up like that instead of cousins?" Stacey asked, concerned.

"Technically, they are cousins. But in the family, if Lockie calls us Mom and Dad, then don't you think that would confuse the baby if we say you're cousins? I think it's something we can broach when they are older."

"I feel guilty, though. I feel like I'm taking Naomi and Simon's title from them."

"Oh, baby, no. Lockie is little, and he doesn't understand. Every night we tell him to say goodnight to his mom and dad, grandma and pop, and he does. If we keep that alive and explain to him the story of what happened, their memory will always live on." Stacey's arm tightens around me.

"Stupid hormones," she grumbles as tears fall down her cheeks.

"Little one." I look down at her.

"I know, I know. I want to do the right thing."

"Our family may not be conventional, it's no different to us being called uncle and aunty by the Dirty Texas kids." She nods in agreement. "We may not all be blood, but we're family."

"You're right. We are all one big dysfunctional Dirty Texas family."

"Exactly, so who cares what anyone else thinks? What works for us is what works for us. Our kids' happiness is the most important thing in the world."

"Fuck. I love you." Stacey grins, leaning over and kissing me. Something she hasn't done much of recently due to it making her feel sick.

42

STACEY

Today is the big reveal. We have invited everyone down to our place in Malibu for a party and told everyone it was to taste some new items on our menu, little do they all know we're going to hit them with a bombshell. I caved into Amelia's idea of a gender reveal party which, if I'm honest, is pretty cool. I mean, I'm totally dying to find out what we're having. We are both happy either way, Lockie said he wants a brother. So, fingers crossed—the poor little guy is outnumbered with girls.

Everyone is arriving, the kids have run off to play with the animals, and it's a beautiful spring night.

"I'm starving," Derrick moans, rubbing his belly. "Lucky I love you guys because there's no way in hell I'd be traveling to the ends of the earth for anyone else." We give him some champagne quickly. A beautiful selection of food has been laid out. We asked our chef to add in some new ideas to keep the rouse. Everyone is happy, drinking and eating, the kids are running around, and everyone is in a jovial mood. Oscar taps against his beer bottle.

"Hey, guys, can I have your attention, please." Everyone

slowly stops their conversations and turns their attention to Oscar. "Thank you all for coming down to Malibu. We know it's a long way." Oscar looks at Derrick. "So, thank you." I link my hand with his. "We hope that you like some of the new ideas for our summer menu." There's a murmur of agreement. "That isn't actually the reason we had you come down here." Everyone looks around confused, and there are whispers between each other as they try and work out what's going on. Then the kids walk out, each holding a white balloon with blue and pink tassels on them.

"You're pregnant," Derrick screams out as the kids stand by us.

"Yes. We're having a baby," Oscar tells everyone. There are screams and squeals, and everyone starts clapping. "And today we thought we'd find out what we're having," Oscar announced to our family and friends. "So, kids, in three, two, one, pop the balloons." There's a huge bang as the kids all pop their balloons and shower the crowd in bright blue confetti. "We're having a boy!" Oscar screams. He turns and picks me up, swinging me around in his arms. "We're having a boy."

"I'm going to be a big brother," Lockie tells the crowd, which makes everyone congratulate him.

"Your cheeky bitch. Hiding your little Viking baby from all of us." Derrick hugs and kisses me as I join the group sitting around.

"I know. I'm so sorry. We wanted to announce it all at once," I apologize, taking a sip of my mineral water.

"You're having a boy." Sienna squeals, bouncing Willow in her lap.

"Oscar is so excited. So is Lockie."

"That was the cutest thing, him saying he's going to be big brother," Isla adds, cradling a feeding Mia.

"I know. When we told the kids, he asked if the baby was going to be his brother. He's still too little to really understand, he knows he has two sets of parents… the ones who live in the stars and us." My friends give me sad smiles.

"I already feel sorry for your vagina, having to birth a mini Viking," Derrick adds, making me choke on my water.

"The Dirty Texas family is almost complete. We're waiting on Derrick now." Vanessa points to him.

"Fine. I wasn't going to say anything." He looks between all of us. "This is Stacey's moment." I wave him away. "Fine. I have started looking for a surrogate." Everyone gasps, and we all congratulate him. "You bitches, calm 'ya tits. I said I've started looking. You can celebrate me once I've knocked up the lucky lady." He grins.

"You're going to be the best dad." Sienna squeezes his hand.

"Thank you, babe. I'm kind of shitting myself," he confesses to us.

"Babe. If I can do it, you can do it." I give him some support.

"Yes, you all have hunky men beside you, helping you. I'm going to be doing it all alone." There's a deep sadness to his tone.

"You can borrow Axel any time you like," Olivia tells him. Derrick's eyes light up. "In a non-sexual way, that is," she quickly adds, which makes us all burst out laughing.

"You're such a spoiled sport, Liv," he jokes.

"So, this is going to be a big year," Vanessa muses. "Stacey is knocked up." She points to me. "My babies are turning two in a couple of weeks." She lets out a heavy sigh. "Then we have a heap of first birthdays with Poppy and Daisy." She points to Olivia. "Then Willow and Mia," she continues, looking over at Sienna and Issy. "And in there somewhere, Derrick is going to knock a lady up and meet the love of his life." Vanessa raises her glass to him.

"It's funny, in a few short years, Dirty Texas has gone from picking up groupies to changing diapers." Sienna giggles.

Things have changed so much in the five years since Sienna and Derrick jumped on a plane to fly halfway across the world to start over again. Who knew that decision would change all of our lives forever?

Fate had other ideas for me. I was so sure, so cocky that I thought I knew what I wanted in life and my ambition, goals, and plans would help me achieve where I wanted to be in life. Oscar wasn't in my plan—no man was—other than to be nothing more than a live sex toy. Would Oscar and I be where we are today if I hadn't taken the job? I don't think so. I know we'd have met because I'd have come over to see Ryder after he was born, would we have made the connection we did being around each other all the time? I doubt it. We probably would've had sex, that was a given, but we'd have been another notch on each other's bedposts.

It's funny how life has other plans for you when you're planning your life. I wouldn't change a thing about how mine has turned out. Well, besides one glaringly obvious one—my family. Everything else—the good, the bad—it's all brought me to this place of happiness, contentment, and peace. I'm excited about what the future will hold, and I am glad Oscar will be by my side on this crazy journey. There isn't anyone else I'd rather be doing it with.

43

OSCAR

"Oscar!" Stacey screams from the shower. Thankfully, I was in the bedroom putting the laundry away. I drop everything and run into the bathroom.

"What! What!" I skid to a stop in front of the glass.

"My water broke." Stacey's eyes widen, then a giggle escapes her mouth.

"Shit!" I run my hands through my hair. "Shit. Shit," I say over and over again.

"Hospital bag. And call your parents," Stacey tells me. I rush out of the bathroom then back in. "Do you need help out of the shower? Are you going to be okay?" I check on my heavily pregnant wife.

"Go. I'll be fine." Nodding at her calm reaction, I rush back into the bedroom and grab my phone. "Mom, it's go-time," I scream before she even has time to greet me.

"Oh. Okay, sweetie. Oh my God. This is exciting. Wow. Okay. See you soon, honey." She hangs up. I rush downstairs in a panic, the kids all look up at me, and they see it on my face straight away.

"It's go-time, team." The youngest girls scream and run around the living room crazily.

"I'll call Hunter. Go. We'll be fine," Amelia tells me. Okay, she's got this. She's fine. They're all fine. I rush back upstairs and see Stacey walking out of the bathroom naked, stopping me in my tracks. I take her all in—the swell of her breasts, the way her body has filled out, embracing its new journey into giving new life.

"Would you stop ogling me and help me get ready?" Stacey hisses as she grabs her stomach.

"Babe, are you okay?" She shakes her head.

"A contraction. They've started." Shit. This springs me into action, I grab her kaftan and throw it over her head, and she slowly dresses herself. I throw her ballet slippers at her feet. Grabbing the hospital bag on one shoulder, I wrap my arm around her and begin to navigate her toward the lower level.

"See 'ya, kiddos." Stacey smiles through gritted teeth. Lockie comes running toward her, and I stop him before he can headbutt her stomach.

"Is the baby coming?" Stacey nods.

"Yay, I want to see him."

"Later, sweetheart, he will be here later," Stacey tells him. Amelia picks him up in her arms, and he kisses Stacey on the cheek and then a kiss on her stomach.

"Okay. See you all soon." The girls wish her good luck, and I tentatively escort her to the car. Carefully, Stacey gets into the car, and I screech out of the driveway. Stacey's hand reaches out, and her fingers dig into my forearm. "Slow the fuck down," she screams at me. Right. Yes. I'm so stressed out, I didn't realize I was speeding. "It's going to be okay, babe. I'm not going to have the baby in the car." Cautiously, I look over at her and let out the breath I had been holding in.

"Congratulations, Mr. and Mrs. Eriksen. It's a boy." The doctor hands over the pink wriggly little thing, placing him on Stacey's chest. The little dude starts to suckle her breast straight away. My heart is bursting with pride at my warrior woman—she gave birth to a little human. A human that I love with all my heart before I even know him. He lets out a couple of cries before resuming his feed, and the doctor and nurses continue working around us. We're so blissfully in our little bubble, we barely notice them.

"What do you think we should call him?" I ask, looking down at my little family.

"Theo." Stacey grins. "Theo James Eriksen." Tears fall down her cheeks as she gives her father's name for our little man's middle name. I lean forward and kiss her forehead.

"It is perfect. He is perfect. You are perfect." I'm so overwhelmed with it all. "Welcome to the world, little TJ."

EPILOGUE
TWENTY YEARS LATER.

Where are they now?

Sienna and Evan Wyld

Sienna and Evan have retired to the white sandy beaches of the beautiful east coast of Australia in the beachside town of Byron Bay. Sienna and Derrick sold their popular boutiques ten years after starting them, having had shops in Los Angeles, New York, London, Saint Tropez, Hong Kong, Stockholm, Byron Bay, and Sydney at the time.

They moved full-time to Byron Bay to take over the health retreat Sienna and Vanessa's parents owned together when they all retired. Since taking over the retreat, they have expanded Tanderra, which means resting place in the local Aboriginal language, into many parts of the world. Their health and wellness retreats are the best in the world and can be found in some of the most exotic locations such as Bali, New Zealand, Iceland, Thailand, Mexico, India, Canada, South Africa, England, France, Italy, and United States, where they have several locations in The Hamptons, Malibu, and Napa Valley.

…

Dirty Texas Records was eventually bought out by a bigger company for over a billion dollars ten years ago. The guys had accumulated a large catalog of some of the best artists in the world with offices in Los Angles, New York, London, Sydney, and Stockholm. The boys celebrated their twenty-year anniversary as a band with a sold-out world tour, which they were able to bring their kids to, showing them all how they used to rock out back in the day. Evan is happy assisting Sienna in running Tanderra while semi-retired. He enjoys spending his days at the beach, golfing, or whale watching from his back deck.

Their fours kids are now all grown up. Ryder, age twenty-three, and Levi, age twenty-two, have followed in their father's footsteps and entered the music world. Evan takes pride in being heavily involved in Ryder and Levi's careers, helping propel *Wyld* to international stardom. The boys say that Evan interferes too much, especially when he joins them on tour. They think he's reliving his youth through them, and they find it utterly embarrassing. They complain to their mom all the time about it, asking her to give him something to do so he stops following them.

Willow, age twenty-one, graduated from university with a bachelor's degree in business, and she has worked in the family business since she was a teenager helping at the Byron Bay retreat. Willow has moved back to America to start management training at the Malibu retreat.

Matilda, age nineteen, also known as Tilly, has followed after her grandmother and is a yoga instructor. She used to teach the classes at the Byron Bay retreat, she wanted to join Willow in America and moved to the Malibu retreat with her sister.

Sienna is suffering badly from empty-nest syndrome, thankfully, she's extremely busy, keeping her from butting into her kids' lives. Evan enjoys having the house to themselves, so they can start enjoying naked date nights, something he started once the kids left.

EPILOGUE

Vanessa and Christian Taylor

Once Dirty Texas Records was sold, Vanessa and Christian took over the full-time running of the Tanderra health retreats with Sienna and Evan. Vanessa and Christian moved back to Byron Bay to help run the resort, once they started to expand globally, Vanessa and Christian moved back to Los Angles and settled near Malibu as they expanded into North America.

Ruby, age twenty-two, moved to London when she finished school to study fashion and started up a clothing brand with her cousin, Poppy, called Ruby P, which has become a viral trend online, catapulting them to international stardom.

Sadie, age twenty-two, followed a very different path than her sister, obtaining a teaching degree, hoping she could help educate people less fortunate than herself. While working abroad during the summers at the resorts, she met a lot of the staff, who could only work minimum-wage jobs because of their circumstances. Sadie came back from her first solo overseas journey a changed girl and started the Tanderra Foundation, which helps employees get an education so they can progress higher in the company.

The biggest surprise was Vanessa falling naturally pregnant a couple of years after the twins. Something she didn't think would happen.

Along came Max, age eighteen, a beautiful surprise for them. Christian was no longer outnumbered by the women in his life. Max is finishing his last year of high school, is the star quarterback on his high school team, and has his pick of colleges offering him full scholarships.

EPILOGUE

Olivia and Axel Taylor

Olivia and Axel split most of their time between Los Angeles and England until Dirty Texas Records sold. That's when they made the full-time move back to England, where Olivia could concentrate on preserving her family's estates. They joined Olivia's sister, Penelope, and her family, who have been living outside the village overseeing things while Olivia was commuting. They loved the fact that the cousins were able to grow up together as they were all similar in age.

Olivia's mother remarried a wealthy baron and moved full-time to Martinique to live in the sunshine all year round, and they visit her often.

Poppy, age twenty-one, studies fashion in London with her cousin, Ruby. They started a clothing line called 'Ruby P,' which took off when some celebrity friends were pictured in their clothes. They spend most of their time partying and designing.

Daisy, age twenty-one, has taken after her mother and is learning the ropes of the business that maybe one day the job might be passed down to her. She's finishing her history and business degree at a university in Edinburgh and commutes home on the weekends. Daisy likes a quieter lifestyle compared to her twin.

Leopold, age eighteen, Leo as he's now known, is finishing off his last year of high school. He's musical like his father and plays many instruments, his main love is rugby. He's been offered a scholarship to Oxford, as well as a couple of other well-known universities. His cousin and best friend, Max, who plays college football, wants him to change over and play football with him in the states instead of rugby. He played with Max's team one school holiday when he was visiting and was spotted by some recruiters who happened to be in the crowd during training. They are interested in his kicking ability, he's torn. He loves rugby, but the money he could make playing football is very tempting. Plus, Max is very persuasive.

EPILOGUE

Isla and Finn

Once Dirty Texas Records was sold, Finn and Isla decided they would retire. Finn wanted to move to Hawaii full-time, Isla wanted them to stay in Los Angeles to finish the kids' schooling. They moved down to Malibu to be closer to Oscar and Stacey, then Vanessa and Christian came back, and the old gang was back together again. And, it looks like Sienna and Evan will be joining the gang in Malibu now that their daughters are moving there.

Easton, age twenty-two, bucked the trend of his family and started working in the tech business, specifically cyber security and Artificial Intelligence. Growing up, he was fascinated with his Uncle Jackson, who owns his own security company. He loved working with him, but Jackson saw his love of technology and encouraged him to continue down that path—he's also a brilliant hacker. He graduated from MIT and now works with

Jackson full-time in Los Angeles, as well as working on some secret government projects.

Mia, age twenty-one, is a model and an accomplished artist. She's excited that Willow and Tilly are moving to Malibu, so they can hang out together. She spends a lot of time traveling around the world, enjoying life. Finn and Isla worry about her as she jumps from one thing to another, and her attention isn't held for long before moving on to another project or career. She isn't a trust-fund girl—all the money she spends is her own.

EPILOGUE

Stacey and Oscar

What a journey this couple has taken. Their restaurant, The Nordic Table, took off and turned into a hugely successful lifestyle brand, and they even had their own cooking show for a little bit, showing off their farm and produce. They expanded their restaurants worldwide, opening in New York, San Francisco, Miami, Toronto, London, Melbourne, Hong Kong, Mexico, and Stacey's hometown of Mudgee.

Oscar's love of farming from their time in Australia led them into a career they never thought was possible. They produced their own water from glaciers in Scandinavia, which every celebrity worth their salt endorsed everywhere. They thought they were securing a quieter pace of life, instead, they created an empire that they never realized they needed.

Hunter, age thirty-nine, is married with three little kids. Once The Nordic Table took off, Hunter became a very big part of the business. He was the project manager for each new build. When he was back home in Mudgee, creating the restaurant, he met and fell in love with an old school friend. They took over the family farm. His wife, Stephanie, comes from a farming family and started up the farm again, growing produce to supply the restaurant and other restaurants in the area.

Amelia, age thirty-six, is married with two kids, living in Los Angeles. She's head costume designer for one of the studios. She has won an Oscar for her work. She married a famous actor she met while on set, and they happily live in Beverly Hills.

Emma, age thirty-three, is engaged. She's an Olympic show jumper. She's engaged to an Argentinean polo player, and they live in Connecticut on a beautiful farm, teaching show jumping.

Becca, age thirty-one, is single. Growing up working at the farm, Becca fell in love with cooking. She studied to be a chef and worked her way up in the kitchens of The Nordic Table. She's now Head Chef of all the restaurants worldwide and works closely with the chefs in each area to make sure they are delivering the best food possible.

Lockie, age twenty-three, has followed in Oscar's footsteps and works in the company. He got his business degree, and now he's learning all about the business from the ground up, shadowing Oscar so that maybe one day he will take over the business. He's best friends with Easton and Sadie.

Theo, age twenty, also known as TJ, takes after his father's love of music, especially bass. His band is popular and has gone viral on mainstream music channels. His star is rising rapidly, especially as Ryder and Levi invited TJ's band to be their support band for their North American tour.

And last but certainly not least.

Freya, age seventeen, is a typical high schooler. She's part of the cheerleading squad and a straight-A student. She volunteers her time at the Tanderra Foundation, likes hanging out with her friends, and thinks her parents suck. She's close friends with Max, who is her school star quarterback.

EPILOGUE

And Uncle Derrick. What happened to him, you ask? All I can say is he's a retired stylist living in Beverly Hills.
He has kids.
He's married.
He most certainly gets his happily ever after.

THE END

ACKNOWLEDGMENTS

Thanks for finishing this book.
Really hope you enjoyed it.
Why not check out my other books.
Have a fantastic day !
Don't forget to leave a review.
Xoxo

ABOUT THE AUTHOR

JA Low lives in the Australian Outback. When she's not writing steamy scenes and admiring hot cowboy's, she's tending to her husband and two sons, and dreaming up the next epic romance.

Come follow her

Facebook: www.facebook.com/jalowbooks
TikTok: www.tiktok.com/@jalowbooks
Instagram: www.instagram.com/jalowbooks
Pinterest: www.pinterest.com/jalowbooks
Website: www.jalowbooks.com
Goodreads: https://www.goodreads.com/author/show/14918059.J_A_Low
BookBub: https://www.bookbub.com/authors/ja-low

ABOUT THE AUTHOR

Come join JA Low's Block
www.facebook.com/groups/1682783088643205/

www.jalowbooks.com
jalowbooks@gmail.com

ALSO BY JA LOW

The Paradise Club Series

Book 1 - Paradise

Spin off from the Dirty Texas Series

My name's Nate Lewis, owner of The Paradise Club.

I can bring every little dirty fantasy you have ever dreamed of to reality.

My business is your pleasure. I'm good at it.

So good it's made me a wealthy and powerful man.

I have one rule—never mix business and pleasure, and I've lived by it from day one.

Until her.

** **WARNING: If you do not like your books with a lot of heat then do not read this book.** **

INTERCONNECTING SERIES WITH DIRTY TEXAS

Reading order for interconnected characters.

Dirty Texas Series

Suddenly Dirty
Suddenly Together
Suddenly Bound
Suddenly Trouble
Suddenly Broken

Paradise Club Series
Paradise

International Bad Boys
The Hotshot Chef

Playboys of New York
Off Limits
Strictly Forbidden

The Merger
Without Warning

INTERCONNECTING SERIES WITH
PLAYBOYS OF NY

The Hartford Brothers
Tempting the Billionaire
Playing the Player
Seducing the Doctor

ALSO BY JA LOW

International Bad Boys Set

Standalone Books

Book 1 - The Sexy Stranger (Italian)

Book 2 - The Arrogant Artist (French)

Book 3 - The Hotshot Chef (Spanish)

INTERCONNECTING SERIES FOR BRATVA JEWELS

Reading order for Interconnecting Series

Bratva Jewels Series

The Sexy Stranger

ALSO BY JA LOW

Bratva Jewels Duet Box Set

SAPPHIRE - BOOK 1

An unconventional love is tested to its limits.

Mateo is used to being in the spotlight, he craves it in everything he does . . . except when it comes to his love life - that is firmly in the closet.

Tomas shuns the spotlight, the one he was born into, he wants nothing to do with it or his high-flying family who now reject him for his choices in love.

But Tomas' and Mateo's carefully constructed lives are turned inside out when they discover a beautiful, battered woman on their doorstep. The woman with the sapphire eyes has no memory of who she is or how she got there. She doesn't know about the Bratva Jewels - the Russian mafia's most desired escorts - or how her story intersects with theirs. Can Tomas and Mateo help her remember before the men who are after her find her first?

DIAMOND - BOOK 2

Round 2 with the Devil begins.

Grace thought she had left the nightmare of the Bratva Jewels behind her. Her days spent as one of the Russian Mafia's most desired escorts were some of the darkest of her life, but she was safe now. Or so she thought.

When Russian mobster Dmitri seeks revenge, he gets it, and Grace knows she must call on every ounce of inner strength she has to withstand what he has in store for her. What she didn't expect was to meet someone like Maxim . . .

Maxim is one of the Bratva's most skilled, and most feared, assassins. But his relationship to the Bratva is a complicated one. And when he meets Grace, suddenly everything becomes clear.

Manufactured by Amazon.ca
Bolton, ON